Pra‌

D1387438

"A captivating romp."

—*Entertainment Weekly*

"A stylish, funny combination of parable and moral tale . . . Imaginative, seductively written, and a pleasure to read, *Top Dog* is a first-rate entertainment."

—Richard North Patterson

"If Kafka and Tolkien shared an office on Wall Street, this is the novel they might have written . . . [Carroll's] tight, colorful prose proves zesty and absorbing. His characters ring oddly true. And his plot has touches of that Tolkienesque irresistibility, that thing that keeps you up past bedtime turning pages to learn what happens next."

—*San Francisco Chronicle*

"A witty, adult, and imaginative fable."

—Martin Cruz Smith

"The Shaggy Dog meets J.R.R. Tolkien in this entertaining debut effort. The premise is wildly silly and metaphorically transparent, and has absolutely no right to succeed on any level, but Carroll—through a combination of reasonably swift pacing and gruffly funny internal monologues—pulls it off."

—*Kirkus Reviews*

Ace Books by Jerry Jay Carroll

TOP DOG
DOG EAT DOG
INHUMAN BEINGS

JERRY JAY CARROLL

ACE BOOKS, NEW YORK

If you purchased this book without a cover, you should be aware that this book is stolen property. It was reported as "unsold and destroyed" to the publisher, and neither the author nor the publisher has received any payment for this "stripped book."

INHUMAN BEINGS

An Ace Book / published by arrangement with
the author

PRINTING HISTORY
Ace trade edition / July 1998
Ace mass-market edition / April 1999

All rights reserved.
Copyright © 1998 by Jerry Jay Carroll.
Cover art by Victor Stabin.
This book may not be reproduced in whole or in part,
by mimeograph or any other means, without permission.
For information address: The Berkley Publishing Group,
a member of Penguin Putnam Inc.,
375 Hudson Street, New York, New York 10014.

The Penguin Putnam Inc. World Wide Web site address is
http://www.penguinputnam.com

Check out the ACE Science Fiction & Fantasy newsletter
and much more at Club PPI!

ISBN: 0-441-00612-4

ACE®
Ace Books are published
by The Berkley Publishing Group,
a member of Penguin Putnam Inc.,
375 Hudson Street, New York, New York 10014.
Ace and the "A" design are trademarks
belonging to Charter Communications, Inc.

PRINTED IN THE UNITED STATES OF AMERICA

10 9 8 7 6 5 4 3 2 1

To the memory of my mother, Ruth.
And to my brother, Jim, a source of inspiration always.

The Hole: I don't know how long I've been here. I tried notching the table with a fingernail to keep track of time, but then I couldn't remember if I put the mark there five minutes ago or last week. Months could have passed. I don't feel anything. Not hope or dread. Just this blankness.

It must be the drug.

I think it is time-released. I slip into sleep without even a yawn to warn me.

My guess is I'm watched twenty-four hours a day. The video monitor is probably in the room where the radio is. The drug wipes out short-term memory. I'm walking around the room and then I am on the bed, unable to remember when I laid down. Then I wake from sleep. This must be what Alzheimer's is like.

Long-term memory is okay. I remember how I got every one of these. The knot on my head at first felt like the ones that pop up when a cartoon character gets bonked by a frying pan. It has gone down quite a bit. My left eye was a slit when I got here, but that swelling is better, too. They nearly dislocated my right shoulder when they wrestled me down and it still hurts. Ligament damage, I suppose. My bad back gives me grief.

I sit on a cot with sagging springs and a dirty mattress older than me. My knees are spread and my head is in my hands. A radio plays somewhere, an AM station with an oldies format and news on the half hour. Network feeds and a local roundup. Sports, weather, and traffic. This says a fair-sized media market. Traffic reports mean enough cars for traffic jams.

But I don't recognize the streets or highways the radio talks about. "There's a stall on Overhill. Right-hand lane," says the traffic reporter in Skyview One. This implies a fleet of Skyviews in the air. But that could just be hype. Take that out of radio and you would have twelve hours of silence every day. The Skyview One reporter alternates bulletins ("A two-car collision on Kennesaw by Haymarket is slowing things down.") with pitches for Soloman's Steakhouse. A T-bone with soup or salad is only twelve dollars on the Early Bird Special. Discount for seniors.

Overhill has a rural sound, and so does Haymarket. But they could have been named a hundred years ago. A road went over a hill so it was called Overhill. People spoke plainly then and didn't waste words. The name would stay even if the hill was bulldozed flat long ago. That twelve bucks for a T-bone has a heartland ring. Flyover land we call it on the coasts. You pay twice that where I live. My ear catches something about a serial killer, and the radio goes off. This always happens.

My guess is that's me they are talking about. Serial killer is wrong, as they will discover later. I have seen a couple in my time. Meek little bastards to look at them. That is how they fool their victims.

They jumped me in their ski masks and dark jumpsuits with "FBI" in yellow letters on the back. I'm pretty sure I broke one guy's nose with a wild haymaker before they swarmed me down. He was the one who gave me that shot in the ribs with a steel-toed boot when I laid flat on the sidewalk with handcuffs on. He would have clog-danced on me if they hadn't pulled him away. Maybe he got a letter in his personnel jacket, but I doubt it. I was a cop myself so I know how cover-ups work.

This room contains the cot, a blond table, and a fluorescent light overhead. A toilet and washbasin in a closet. There is a grate near the ceiling with recessed screws so I can't get at them. That is probably where the surveillance camera is. This is not paranoia. I know they are watching. Pale green walls, linoleum squares in a brownish-red pattern on the floor. A committee of bureaucrats must have voted on the color scheme. No window. One door, always locked. No television and no books, magazines, or newspaper. It is limbo except for the radio down the hall, and it's not on all the time.

Outside this place has the look of an old military base declared surplus and padlocked when the Evil Empire fell apart. I saw barracks when they rushed me in just as the light was going. When the sliding door of the panel truck slammed open, the view was rusted chain-link fences, tall weeds growing in cracks in the asphalt, weathered plywood nailed where windows used to be. I was half conscious, so "saw" is not quite right. "Impression" is closer. The whole thing has this dreamlike quality.

It must be the drug.

After I hit San Francisco and Atlanta, you didn't have to be a rocket scientist to figure Washington, D.C., was next on the list. That is where they nailed me. If they hadn't, I was going to go to *Larry King* or *60 Minutes* and tell my story. Whoever agreed beforehand to no censoring got it. They could check it out, but they had to let me tell the story my way. Take it or leave it. Media competition is so cutthroat somebody would have said yes. Afterward, I was going to give myself up. I would be so high-profile by then there would be no way they could strangle me on the quiet or put a bullet behind my ear. I'm thinking now I should have passed on Washington. But I wanted to make sure the message was loud and clear.

I would have to edit the story down for television. The networks wouldn't be interested in all the details. That is what I do mentally when my head is clear enough. But it is hard to know where to cut. One thing explains the next.

It goes back to when a new national company opened a kind of Private-Eyes-R-Us franchise three buildings down from my office in San Francisco's financial district. Bang, my business dropped 50 percent right off the bat, and then more as time went on.

You wouldn't think from watching television it would be possible. Private investigators look like they are in work that needs the personal touch. They crack cases the cops are too dumb to solve. Go back and you have the *noir* stereotypes. They squinted through cigarette smoke with eyes that had seen too much. They called women "dames" and took slugs of whiskey from the bottle in the drawer. They played fast and loose with the law. Otherwise, the bad guys got away with it.

There never was much truth to that image, and it's less today. The heavy lifting gets done by computers that comb databases on any subject you can name. You might get a surveillance case once every two years, and the only time you draw your gun is on the pistol range. That's if you bother. A lot of people coming into the business these days don't think carrying a weapon is worth the trouble. Private investigators used to be ex-cops but now run to accountant types and people with degrees in library and information science.

The old-timers cultivated sources to get what they wanted. They slipped somebody a bottle. Or cash always worked. You could get a sealed court record or arrest report or whatever else you wanted. That was business in the old days. Now everything is on a database somewhere. If you can't get it on your own, you hire a hacker. Silicon Valley is lousy with them. I use a whiz kid at Stanford so smart he reads CIA e-mail to unwind. He would do a job just for the thrill of cracking somebody's code, but I pay him. If there weren't databases to break into, he would be a thrill burglar or Peeping Tom.

When the new franchise opened its doors, I was back in court with Maureen. She wanted my visitation rights changed on grounds my neighborhood wasn't safe. It was what I could afford, thanks to the divorce. I would have been better off representing myself instead of hiring Martin Hanks of Tyler, Frontiere, Hanks, and Straud. Hanks had a brain tumor growing when I was going through the divorce. I thought his frowns were over the difficulties of my case, but I guess his mind was asking itself what was going wrong. He was later operated on successfully, but that didn't do me any good. He had missed court appearances and forgotten to file motions.

"You're lucky you got away with a change of underwear," my new lawyer said. He wanted me to sue for malpractice. But Hanks had also forgotten to renew his malpractice insurance, and medical bills had left him nearly as bad off as I was. "He's still got his house," my new lawyer pointed out.

Also a wife with bad arthritis and two kids in college. I told him to forget it. "I wouldn't want somebody to kick me when I'm down."

He had to laugh. "*When* you're down? There are people sleeping in cardboard boxes better off than you."

He was exaggerating only a little. I was already fifty thousand dollars behind in support. At ten thousand a month, it added up fast. Maureen's lawyer took the best month I ever had and convinced the judge they were all that good or better. I later found out that Hanks sat in court gazing off in the distance, as if quibbling over such paltry sums was beneath my notice and therefore his. When I asked how things were going, he always said super. I was spending a lot of time in Seattle at that point looking for a spoiled rich kid who had disappeared into the grunge scene. She was heavy into heroin and body piercing when I finally did find her. She ran away again after I brought her back and her parents said the hell with it, let her go.

"Do I send the bills to that fleabag on Ellis?" my new lawyer's secretary asked. She had red hair and blue eyes as cold as diamond chips. I guessed she was hired for the British accent that made her words stab like ice picks.

"For the time being," I answered.

Her look said she gathered that meant for good. Bad as that dump was, I wish I was back there counting the cockroaches and smelling the mildew.

Ellis Street runs through the Tenderloin, as cheap and gaudy as a seam of fool's gold. By day, cute Vietnamese kids dodge stumbling drunks and skip past drug users wired from crank or on the nod. If they are crackheads, they are usually yelling. By night, you got lots of purple neon over the sex shops and the dark dives with sticky floors and tables. Buy a dildo or see it used. The hookers are still up at dawn in short skirts that show bad legs blotchy from the cold. None looks like Julia Roberts in *Pretty Woman*, and forget about the heart-of-gold crap. I bought earplugs to keep out the sound of sirens. People get cut or shot nearly every night. The meat wagons haul them off while cops question people who amazingly didn't see a thing. Firemen use high-pressure hoses to wash the blood off the sidewalks.

It was amazing how fast my business disappeared. The name of the newcomer was Security Concerns, based in Atlanta. Nobody local had even heard of them before. One Monday morning they had salesmen making office calls and hustling accounts in the courthouses. They offered unbelievable service at unbeatable prices. Lawyers I'd known for years, people I had drinks with and considered friends, turned cold. "These guys charge half what you do," one told me on the phone. I could tell he thought I had been screwing him for years.

It was classic cutthroat capitalism. Come into town, slash prices to the bone, and knock out the competition. Afterward, jack prices back up where you want them. I tried to explain this to my clients as they bailed, but nobody wanted to listen.

"You charge a hundred ten bucks an hour and these guys charge fifty-five," Abe Kallenbach told me. He's the best personal-injury lawyer in the Bay Area, bar none. "What's to decide?"

I let go my assistant and my secretary and moved my office in with Barney Mulhenny, a private investigator with an office on the wrong side of Market Street. He was a beefy guy with broad shoulders and a gut that put a serious strain on shirt buttons. When they popped, he got down on hands and knees to look for them. This gave you a good look at the high polish his pants had from the stools at the Elks Club bar. Barney left the police department eight years before I did and had made a decent living in insurance investigations and assignments for the public defender's office.

"Those bastards at Security Concerns are murdering me," he said bitterly. "Allstate in San Mateo just canceled on me. Norv Gillman, the district manager who I thought was my friend? I showed him where to fish for sturgeon. The bastard won't even return my calls. I been doing business with them for fifteen years."

I walked the three blocks to check out Security Concerns. It was in offices that sported the sterile, high-tech look. Looking past the counter, I saw maybe sixty people talking on phones or working computers. A group came back from lunch while I waited for the receptionist to get off the phone. They had the devoted look of people who couldn't wait to get back to work. Or maybe the ones who pass out tracts promising salvation if you follow their way.

"May I help you?" the receptionist asked.

"Goodwin Armstrong," I said, handing her a card. It showed a big bicep with my name below. The arm belonged to a guy at Gold's Gym, but I didn't discourage people from thinking it was mine. "Who's the boss?"

"Mr. Logan is tied up right now." She was the plain-Jane type with mouse-colored hair in a bun. Somebody had given her bad advice about eyeglass frames.

"Could you ask him to call me?"

There was a stack of promotional literature about the company on the counter. I studied one of the glossy pamphlets in the car. It said the information explosion was too great for the old-fashioned detective agencies. A drawing showed a medieval craftsman pounding a forge with a hammer. This was to illustrate how obsolete we were now.

I showed it to Mulhenny when I got back. He breathed through his busted nose as he read it. He twirled a little finger in one ear when he was finished. He glared at me.

"What a load of bullshit. Do you really think people are going to buy that?"

"We wouldn't be sharing an office and a secretary who does crossword puzzles all day if they didn't." This wasn't the full truth. She also talked on the telephone to friends. She had a nose ring and a couple more in her eyebrows. She changed hair color every couple of days. That day it was green. My share of the secretary overhead was four bucks an hour.

"There's more to this business than 'information extraction,' for crissake."

"Tell it to Allstate."

"Those assholes? Screw them." He scowled out the window at the lot where you stuffed five bucks into a slot for twenty-four hours of parking. "Gimme a fucking break."

The following day, Mr. Logan called. He asked how he could help me. I complimented him on his setup.

He guessed that as I was a private investigator, I wanted to work for them. "We're happy to send an employment application, but I should warn you we have quite a number on file already. We have no openings and don't expect any in the foreseeable future."

His voice was as flat as a dead man's brainwave. I try to put a smile in mine when I'm dealing with the public.

"You're getting a lot of applications?"

"We expected it. What we offer in the way of service, frankly speaking, is so much better than what was previously available in this market. We are already exceeding our most optimistic business forecasts."

"What's the big secret?"

"We call it DataPower. It's a copyrighted term, like Kleenex. It refers to the array of information extraction services we bring to bear on a problem. You, for example. Would you like to hear what Security Concerns was able to learn about you in a relatively small time frame, Mr. Armstrong?"

"Sure."

He told me all about myself. "Forty-four years old. Six feet, one inch, a hundred and ninety pounds. Blue eyes, blond hair beginning to thin. Born in Palo Alto. Parents deceased. An older brother, a surgeon in Milwaukee. Younger sister a social worker in Tucson. She is the mother of two and expecting again. You went to public schools, graduating from Gunn High School. Quite a good athlete. A hurdler,

All-League quarterback and third-team All-State. Good enough that you were recruited by Annapolis, where you flunked out in your junior year."

"Electrical engineering. It tripped up a lot of people. I also banged up my knee against Air Force. That finished my football career." They would have found a way to keep me on as a midshipman if it wasn't for that. Dumber guys graduated.

"Surgery on that knee, I see. It made you 4-F. A period of rambling around Europe when you left the academy. Your knee was rehabilitated and you joined the navy and volunteered for the SEALS. Service in Granada. I won't read you the citation for bravery. Discharged with NCO rank. Inactive reserve. Joined the San Francisco Police Department. Made patrol sergeant in five years. Passed the exam for inspector and lieutenant with excellent scores."

"Everything's easy after electrical engineering."

"Sex crimes detail, then robbery. Early disability retirement for a back injury received in the line of duty. A fall from a fire escape."

"Somebody was shooting at me."

He mentioned the detective agency I founded seven years ago. The divorce was in his file. "I see there is an application before the court for a change in visitation rights." My financial free fall. "You're at the credit limit with Visa and MasterCard and close with Discover." Even my new address. "You live at the Ajax Arms, 311 Ellis Street, Apartment 3."

I was blown away.

It would take me a month to dig up all that stuff, and I doubt that I would find out I was a hurdler in high school or come up with the name of the physical therapist for the back injury. Security Concerns did it overnight. I called my sister Sally in Tucson to congratulate her. She gasped. "How did you find out? I just learned myself this morning."

The Hole: When the radio is turned off down the hall, the silence is almost total. This room must be in the middle of the building. I did hear an airplane's drone a minute ago, maybe Skyview One looking for traffic jams.

I see why prisoners make pets of bugs and rats. At least you get a break from thinking about yourself. You think about the mistakes you made, how you went wrong. All your character flaws: Nature or nurture? How you wound up where you're at. One small change at any time and you end up with a different result. Pretty soon you are thinking about fate. If you could step back far enough, would you be able to see a pattern, or does chaos theory explain everything? Did I really have choices, or were they just illusions?

"He had everything right except the thinning hair," I said to Mulhenny when I told him about Mr. Logan.

"He had that right. I've been meaning to point it out myself." Mulhenny was in that unhappy time of life when a man combs side hair over the top to fool the world. The world knows better.

I scoffed.

"I'm serious. You're getting thin the same place I began to and look at me now. You don't know if somebody doesn't say something. A barber told me they don't mention it unless the customer brings it up first. Emily gave me the news when it started happening. She doesn't hold back." They were one of those devoted childless couples married a long time who go everywhere and do everything together. She put in a couple hours after work as a volunteer secretary at her church, while he shook dice for drinks at the Elks Club. Otherwise they were always together. He was a heavy smoker and wheezed from emphysema. He limped from a trick knee he claimed he got from a fall running after a shoplifter. The retirement board had denied him a disability pension, however. It was politics, Mulhenny said. He talked about it boringly.

I reached back with my hand and felt my hair. "Feels the same."

"You can see scalp, I kid you not. There some way this Logan guy could have known you were going to come in and got a head start digging that stuff up?"

"Not unless he reads minds."

Mulhenny twirled his finger in an ear. I had figured out this aided thought. "Oregon's looking better and better. We got a lot of equity in the house."

When I got back from lunch the next day, a heavy woman sat in one of the two chairs in the reception area. She watched critically as Mitzi the secretary did her crossword puzzle.

"This is Princess Dulay," Mitzi said. "She doesn't have an appointment."

"That won't be a problem this one time. Come right this way, Ms. Dulay."

"Princess Dulay," she said. She heaved herself up from the chair. It made a grateful sound.

"I beg your pardon, Princess." I led her into my office and closed the door. She settled into another chair. She had chins to spare and wore a flowing neck-to-ankle dress in a pattern that made you think of Willem de Kooning. Plump feet with violet toenails were stuffed into mules that slapped when she walked. The bold scarf tied under her chin represented a rival theory of art. Sausagelike fingers covered with rings had long nails, also violet. A large pendant on a thick gold chain around her thick neck and jangly bracelets on both wrists. Her eyes were wide and staring, as if she found something about me surprising. She undid the scarf and showed strawberry blond hair. You could have bounced a rock off it.

"How can I help you?" I said.

"You ought to give that girl something to do. She's been working on that puzzle since I walked in."

"Things are a little slow right now." I was brisk, as if this could change any minute.

She was silent for a moment, as if she were collecting herself, then her eyes welled. "Something terrible's going to happen."

I waited for her to explain.

"Have you heard of me?" she asked.

"The name rings a bell." Not even a tinkle. But I frowned as if trying to remember.

"I've been on all the local talk shows. I was nearly on Oprah once. I'm the psychic and clairvoyant."

"Another minute and I would have had it."

She seemed to relax. "I was afraid to come."

"I don't bite. It's bad for business." I smiled reassuringly.

"A lot of people don't believe in psychic powers. They're scornful. It can be very hurtful."

I put on a sympathetic look that said the world can sometimes be cruel.

"I'm not taken seriously by some."

I added a nod to the look. It takes some clients a while to get to the point.

"Do you dream, Mr. Armstrong?"

"Doesn't everyone?" Mine hadn't been pleasant lately.

"But do you remember them?"

"Hardly ever."

"Then you're average."

"That's not the worst thing I've been called."

"It's not a criticism. Most people don't remember dreams. Mine are different. They're the source of my powers. I see things."

Powers. I began to have a bad feeling. "Terrible things?" I asked.

"Yes." She looked out the window at the parking lot. Then her words came in a rush. "Aliens are on our planet. They've traveled a long time, longer than humans have been on Earth. They were moving through the terrible darkness they believed was without end. Then they found Earth, a jewel in the void. They were ravished by its beauty. They want our planet." She stopped. "You have a look on your face, Mr. Armstrong."

I stood. "I actually just came in for messages. I have a busy day. Things to do, places to go."

She took a piece of paper from a bejeweled snap purse like the flappers carried. "This is a certified check for twenty-three thousand dollars made out to the bearer. You can phone the bank to confirm it."

I sat down. As with the gallows, money concentrates the mind.

"I cashed in a CD. That's why it's an odd amount." She passed it over to me.

"I don't have a problem with odd." I batted my eyes like William F. Buckley, Jr.

"I have many wealthy clients, Mr. Armstrong. They rely

on my guidance in making life choices. I have helped them, and they have been generous in return. Many wasted money and had sad experiences with people who claim psychic powers but are frauds. These, unfortunately, are the majority. They read palms or deal tarot cards or other such silliness. They prey on people, and it puts the few of us who are legitimate in a bad light. It ends up we're all mistrusted."

It doesn't matter what the business is, people bad-mouth the competition. I do it myself. I told lawyers Mulhenny couldn't find his ass even if he grew an extra hand back there. He said worse about me.

"What is it you want me to do?" I wouldn't kill for the money, but otherwise I was open to possibilities.

"That's for you to decide. People must be told, the president and so forth."

I slipped the check into a drawer. "These aliens came to you in a dream?"

"No, no." She shook her head. "I know about them from dreams. I can sometimes direct them."

"The aliens?"

"My dreams. Most people have no control over theirs. They're swept along like corks in a river. Images or scenes have no connection. Most can't make sense of them afterward, if they remember at all. Dreams can be silly and ridiculous or have deep meaning."

"So you interpret dreams?"

"No, I tell what my dreams say, what messages are encoded in them."

"How did these aliens get here? Spaceship?" When I was a beat cop, I usually asked these questions in an emergency room. You would find someone in bad shape on the street, or people would call. A head case stops taking his medicine and ends up with a bad case of the heebie-jeebies. Doctors dose them with Thorazine and they are locked up for seventy-two hours. They're let go and the same thing happens. Cops get to know all the crazies, as well as what the demons chasing them are called. Quite a few complain aliens are messing with their minds.

"They are the spaceship," Princess Dulay said. "It's hard to describe. They traveled joined together and became individuals when they reached here. I know I'm not doing a very good job explaining."

"So they're machines?"

"No, living things. But very small. When they're all joined up for travel, they're sort of like a bowling ball. She paused. "Is something funny, Mr. Armstrong? I was told you'd take this seriously."

"Sorry. It was the bowling ball."

"I don't know any other way to describe it. It was round and dark. Maybe I should say cannonball."

I got out a legal pad and pencil and asked her to tell me about herself. Her real name was Ronda Rabin. She used Princess Dulay professionally and thought of it as just as much her name as the one her parents gave her. She owed her psychic gifts to a fall on the head in childhood.

"I was in a coma for three days. Before, I was just another kid. Afterward, I had what the world calls extrasensory perception. I saw events before they happened. It was terrifying. I would pass someone on the street, and before I knew it, I foresaw their deaths months or years later. Some in accidents, but most of diseases like cancer. I would see them old and wasted in their deathbeds and burst into tears. My parents are teachers. They were worried about my mental stability. They took me to see many psychiatrists and psychologists. Some weren't very nice. They thought I was making it up. If they made me mad enough, I would close my eyes and my gift would say how they would die. I'd open my eyes and tell them. It made them pretty uncomfortable, I can tell you."

She began having dreams where she could test various scenarios. "Should I go out with Michael rather than Albert? Simple stuff like that. What I should say on a date. What I should wear. If I said or did something one way, it led to a different outcome than if I said or did it another way. I could pick which one. Most of the time what happened in real life followed pretty close to the scenario. The dreams were like rehearsals."

She was a widow with two grown children. Her late husband was head of an accounting firm, and it was through him that she met her wealthy clients. He drowned in a cruise ship swimming pool off Bermuda. Although she had dreamed she would marry him, she did not foresee his odd end. "It came as a total shock."

Her technique was to have long conversations with clients to understand what bothered them. Then she dreamed to see if Plan A was better at solving the problem than Plan B, or if a Plan C was better than either.

I doodled on the legal pad. "Do you do this dreaming at night?"

"Sometimes. Mostly, I fall into a light doze at the time or right after. Do you mind if I smoke?"

"Let me open a window." I got up and turned the crank. I gave her an ashtray.

"It's such a nasty habit, I know."

"I used to smoke."

She fired up a Marlboro with a Bic lighter. "Why'd you stop?"

"My son was born. I wanted to be around later."

"How old is he?"

"Ten years."

"You haven't had a cigarette all that time? You're strong. I wish I could quit."

"The dream scenarios don't help?"

"They offer possible alternatives, not certainties. I'm not infallible, Mr. Armstrong. Only God is."

At least she didn't think she was God. Some a cop meets do. They point a finger and yell in a language learned from the cone of light that appeared to them. They're amazed when you don't go up in a puff of blue smoke.

I asked more questions and made notes. She became aware of the aliens one night as she meditated before sleep. A consciousness she had never experienced before burst in on her thoughts.

"You know how they say a teaspoon of the stuff in black holes weighs as much as Earth? It was that huge, only it was mental. I felt their elation after the endless journey. No, that's not right. At that point it was 'it,' not 'they.' It only later became 'them.' What came to me was an explosion of pure feeling after a long time when nothing had been felt. It was like an awakening."

She never had the feeling so strongly again. "They're very disciplined." She crushed out the cigarette, waving away the smoke. "I might try one of those nicotine patches. Some people have luck with them." She probably wasn't bad-looking when young. She had let herself go the way some women do when they figure landing another man isn't worth the bother.

Nothing much had happened for a long time. Now and then she got a sense that the alien life form was up to something, but she didn't know what. The clients she dreamed about paused in midsentence and looked as if they listened to something far off. "In the beginning, I thought they might be good. Why does something have to be bad just because it's from space?"

I looked out the window. A jet contrail was high overhead

in the blue sky. Your job isn't safe even up there behind the controls. One airline buys another and pilots get the sack.

"What changed your mind?" I asked tiredly.

"People in my dreams stopped talking altogether. 'What's the use?' they'd say. 'They're coming.' This in the middle of a scenario. They'd just stop talking and stare off. They looked so unhappy, as if what they saw left no hope. Of course, I can't solve any problems for my clients if they don't talk in my dreams."

People in her dreams stopped talking, therefore the aliens were after us. Logic is a beautiful thing.

"Have you talked to anybody else about this?"

"Yes, of course."

"Who?"

"The FBI, for one. The CIA, for another. The National Security Agency."

"You talked to *all* of them?"

"One of my clients is Harriet Cox, wife of the congressman. He's very influential in Washington. She's very influential with him. Another person might have been ignored, but they sent agents to talk to me."

"And?"

"The FBI man grinned all through the interview. Funniest thing he ever heard." She sniffed. "The rudeness is hard to take."

"They didn't believe you?"

"It didn't take a genius to see. They sent letters afterward thanking me for being a good citizen and saying the government was vigilant against any threats to the nation, blah, blah. I could tell they thought I was crazy. As maybe you do." Her eyes narrowed.

I thought of the check in the drawer. "I always keep an open mind, Princess Dulay."

She softened. "Sorry. So many people are cynical. You're

a detective, Mr. Armstrong. Dig up facts. Make our leaders see the danger. I can tell you Harriet is as upset as me by the way I was treated. She'll see we get a hearing."

"She agrees with you?"

"She trusts my gift."

"Who did you say told you I'd take you seriously? I like to know where my referrals come from. It's a professional courtesy I appreciate."

"Mr. Mulhenny. I called him first. He said this was right down your alley."

I got the names of the agents she had talked to and showed her out to the reception room. Mulhenny turned his back to us. His shoulders shook from silent laughter.

"Haw, haw!" he burst out when the princess left. "Sorry, Goodwin. It was too good to pass up. If anyone can find these little green men, it's you. Hee, hee." He was still rubbing tears from his eyes when I came back from my office and showed him the certified check. That wiped the smile off his face.

I went back into my office. He followed a minute later. "I should get a cut for referring her."

"In your dreams," I said. I felt it was fairly witty under the circumstances.

He glared at me as if I had stepped on his diachondria. People didn't love their kids more than Mulhenny did his lawn. I bet he was wishing he hadn't made me sign a sublease so he could kick me out on the street. He yelled at Mitzi to get busy on something besides the fucking crossword puzzle.

I tried telephoning the agents whose names Princess Dulay gave me, but everyone was gone for the day. I left my name and number on voice mail and drove to the bank with the check. I turned it into cash and stuck all but a thousand bucks in my safety deposit box. If I put it in checking, there was a chance Maureen and her lawyer would get their hooks into it.

I drove over to Millard School as usual, parking on a cul-de-sac where I watched the kids pass on their way home. It always upset us when we saw each other, so I always parked out of sight. After a minute, I saw Brady pedal past on his mountain bike. He's big for his age and stood up to pedal. He looked, I don't know, intrepid. I see the man in the boy and it makes me proud I did something right. The kinds of words I think of when I see him are "spirited," "dauntless," "kind." I love him so much it is like a physical pain. I leaned my head on the steering wheel.

The Hole: They left me a clean new sweat suit, and about time. It lay on the blond table when I woke up. Gray and the labels gone, like the one I'm wearing. I have had this one on day and night as long as I've been here, and it has a bad case of the droops. My beard is pretty long. There's no mirror, but I feel it with my fingers.

The Hole: A couple days ago, they left a sandwich that smelled a little off. Meat loaf on rye, black olives in the meat loaf. The sandwiches come wrapped in white butcher paper from a deli. If I had been really hungry, I might have taken a chance. I wasn't and don't need an excuse not to eat meat loaf anyhow, so I flushed it down the toilet. This qualifies as a major event in my life here, all the more remarkable because I remembered doing it. It made me realize food is how they give me the drug. Whoever watches the video monitor probably didn't see me flush it down. His monotony has got to be worse than mine, even with the radio to listen to. Dull as my days and nights are, how infinitely more boring to watch me go through them. I get up from bed, walk around (the room is thirty feet by twenty feet, measured heel to toe), listen at the door, sit on the bed, lie down again. Then I do it all over again. You would go crazy watching. Of course, it wouldn't just be one person. They would have shifts and breaks to stretch and go to the bathroom.

Time passes with amazing slowness. I feel like I've been here long enough for continents to form. If I were interested in figuring out the meaning of life, this would be the perfect spot to do it. No interruptions, nothing to distract a man. Unfortunately, it is not a subject with much appeal for me. What happens when you figure it all out? Do you sit cross-legged and hand out advice? People wouldn't pay any attention. I suppose this means I'm shallow.

I can live with that. I was always one to live for the day. I took things as they came, the good with the bad. But these days are the same one repeated over and over. Why not leave me something to read? Even a bus schedule would be a gift from the gods. I could memorize routes and times and test myself. It would be something to do. I suppose they are afraid I will eat the paper and cause an intestinal blockage. They would have to bring in a doctor or take me to the hospital. They don't want to take the chance. No pencil or pen for fear I will stab myself.

Mr. Patel owned the ratty residential hotel on Ellis where I laid my head at night after the divorce. Various Mr. Patels, all small, dark men with silent wives in bright saris, run most of the hotels in the Tenderloin.

Like the others, the Mr. Patel at the Ajax Arms came from India. Theirs must be the innkeeping caste. They have rented rooms to strangers for so many centuries that suspicion is bred into Patel bone. The Mr. Patel at the Ajax Arms had a room by the entrance to keep an eye on comings and goings. He sat with the door open. Exotic smells came from the kitchen. No visitors after ten o'clock, and rent a week in advance. No cleaning deposit was required. It wasn't hard to see why.

Mr. Patel couldn't understand why I lived there. It was one step up from a flophouse. I wasn't old and didn't have any of the disabilities that qualified the other Ajax residents for rent subsidy. I was clean and well dressed and seemed to have a job. He didn't ask what, in the certainty I'd lie. Possibly I was an undercover investigator sent by the city housing agency. But more likely I practiced some unspeakable vice that made me an outcast.

The Ajax residents made up a roster of losers, people thumbed out of the game of life. They didn't quite live in the street yet, but that was the next stage. They couldn't work because they were old or too sick. They had heart problems or lungs blackened by cigarette smoke. They had withered limbs or brains soaked in alcohol. They lived alone because they couldn't get along with other people, particularly the invisible ones who dogged their footsteps and criticized every move they made. They didn't take this criticism lying down, but argued back endlessly. You heard them bickering with themselves in their rooms and when they passed in the hallways.

"You said I did."

In another voice: "No, I didn't."

Sometimes a kibitzer in a third voice would get into the act and the first two voices would turn on him.

"They haven't cheated on the heat since you got here," Jen Thorwaldson told me the week after I moved in. He was a retired longshoreman in room four whose hands shook so bad that most days he didn't shave. He nipped from a bottle of vodka from the corner liquor store, where he cashed his disability checks. He ate lunch at the Protestant free dining room and dinner at the one Catholics ran. But not much at either place, judging from his bony frame. He told me that before I moved in, people wore all their clothing to keep from freezing.

My room on the second floor had a window that looked down on the street. The sunlight seemed thin and defeated in the Tenderloin. Even the sidewalks looked more kicked around than in other parts of the city. Decades of filth had been ground in, giving them a bruised look. When the buildings blocked the sun, it looked as if dark blood pooled just below the surface. You would never get the sidewalks clean again. You'd have to jackhammer them up and start fresh.

I lived at the Ajax as penance. I would have worn a hair shirt if I could have found one. Losing just about everything wasn't a big enough price. My kind of stupidness deserved more. One stereotype about my trade is true. There are lots of wronged women looking for a shoulder to cry on. Mine got damp from all the tears. Maureen found out it didn't stop there.

She hired a private eye. Being in the business, you would have thought I'd notice. But I never did, not once. Bob Crabtree was his name. He called to apologize afterward, and I complimented him on his work. It was textbook stuff. A log with dates, times and addresses, stills, video footage—the works. The hot tub stuff of me with Heidi was brutal. There was no wiggle room for Hanks to work with, even if he'd been playing with a full deck. Crabtree was a real pro, a credit to the profession.

"I could see why you did it," he said jokingly, one man to another. "She was something."

Not really. The world is full of unhappy people, and it seems most are women. Men don't like to admit it when they are unhappy. It makes them feel like losers. Women do and work at getting over it. One way is proving they can still attract a man. No problem in my case, I was a roundheels, a pushover. Maureen was raising Brady and getting her doctorate in anthropology, busy every minute. It was so easy to cheat I got careless.

She had a friend who was a lawyer, a man-hater named Gloria Rodell-Heifitz. She looked like those stone gargoyles on gothic cathedrals. No cause is too far out for Gloria. She has marched in support of the free-speech rights of Nazis and tenure for Jew-hating black nationalists. She had death camp numbers tattooed on her shoulder to show her firm beliefs about genocide. We disliked each other on sight and things went down from there. My background damned me in her eyes as a tool of the oppressor state. I admit I played to that. When she brought one of her reedy boyfriends in beard and sandals to dinner at our place, I found opportunities to praise the NRA or quote Howard Stern.

"I don't see why you dislike her," Maureen said. "She doesn't mean half of what she says."

"Then she should shut up half the time. Silence is golden."

"Gloria likes the clash of ideas. Thesis, antithesis, and synthesis." She admired how Gloria had overcome her looks to make something of herself. Women find this inspirational. I think she was entertained by the dustups Gloria and I got into. I admit I didn't win many of these. In addition to her legal mind, Gloria had a tongue rough enough to sand floors. The agreement Maureen and I had was that if she had to put up with my boring cop buddies, Gloria was the price.

When she confided her suspicions about my infidelity, Gloria talked her into hiring Crabtree. They acted on the evidence he collected when I went to Cleveland on a case for two months. A sheriff's deputy I knew served me the court order when I got back. "Sorry to do this," he said. He looked away from what he saw in my face.

People who knew me began to cross the street when they saw me coming. They didn't want the *mea culpa* scenes I became expert in. I told them how wrong I'd been and how life without my family wasn't worth living. I even opened up to total strangers. It's embarrassing to look back on.

I cornered Mulhenny in a bar at the time. "I thought you had went nuts," he told me later. "I wasn't the only one either. People avoided you, in case you're interested."

"It was temporary insanity, I guess."

He scoffed. "Nobody buys that crap no more, not even the courts."

I had lost everything. A wonderful wife, a great kid, a nice home, and a dog who whirled in ecstasy when I came home. We were too busy, like everybody these days, but we were happy. Maybe we would have gone down the tubes economically because of Security Concerns, but we would still have each other.

It all happened because I got into the habit of letting my dick lead me around. Maureen herself gave me the rationale. She said biologists have a theory that it is male nature to mate with as many females as possible. This maximizes the survival chances for his genes, supposedly the point of existence. Women, on the other hand, look for males they think will stick around to protect them and the offspring. It's behavior programmed so deeply we're not aware of it. This is a subject that comes up often at the feminist discussion groups Gloria leads.

"But don't get any ideas," Maureen warned me. Then she laughed. She trusted me.

She's ten years younger and lots smarter. Short brown hair and small features, except for big cornflower blue eyes. A skinny athlete's body that she keeps that way running 10K races in masters competitions. We met at one to benefit the Police Athletic League. I worked in Chief Mo Sontag's office at the time. He sent me to events not important enough to warrant his own personal appearance. As the chief had a high opinion of his importance, I was kept busy.

I was way out of shape, but it was understood I had to at least jog the course and wave at the crowd. But I got locked in a silly duel with a fat guy at the back of the pack. Everybody was pulling for him as we thudded crimson-faced toward the finish line. From pity, I guess. He sounded like a steam engine. You could hear him even over my own sob-

bing gasps for air. He nipped me at the wire as the crowd cel-
ebrated. Chief Sontag would have been mortified. He liked
winners around him.

As I bent over sucking wind and worrying about a coro-
nary, Maureen sympathized. "I always cheer for the underdog," she explained. The fat guy by then was tossing up his
last two or three meals. I had looked like the underdog?

"You sure know how to make a guy feel good." She
brought Gatorade in a paper cup. Two months later we
moved in together.

The first thing I did was to check out Princess Dulay. She
had no criminal record, unless you count a citation for failing
to yield. She owned a home on the best side of Pacific
Heights, high enough for a nice view of Alcatraz. Credit card
records showed she bought heavily from the shopping channels and dined at trendy restaurants. She drove a two-year-
old Mercedes, which had been broken into eight months
before. She put in an insurance claim for a knife slash in the
leather upholstery. She was lucky they didn't shit in the driver's seat, which is pretty common.

She took medication for blood pressure and had had a
hysterectomy, but was otherwise healthy except for the forty
pounds of excess baggage she carried. She owned property in
Scottsdale and the Bitterroot Valley in Montana and had a
time share in Maui. Her name had appeared in the society
columns four times in the previous year. The picture that
emerged was an affluent, well-connected woman. Not what I
would have expected. When you think of fortune-tellers, the
image you get is turbans and beaded curtains in the carnival
booth next to the cotton candy.

I drove to Berkeley and the university to talk to Professor
Whitman of the physics department. If there was any dirt on
her, he would know. Professor Whitman had a desk piled

with ungraded papers and walls full of books. He enjoyed a second career debunking paranormal claims and was often on TV and in the papers. He was a man in his sixties with thick, snowy hair, ironic tufted eyebrows, and a red bow tie. I had read that he learned magic tricks to better expose healers who yanked cancers from the sick with their bare hands. He found a coin behind my ear as we shook hands.

"A strange place to keep your money," he said with a twinkle.

"I'm glad you missed the rabbits."

He looked at my business card and made it disappear. "A private investigator. Well, well. I guess we're in the same game, finding the truth behind appearances."

We talked about how things sometimes aren't what they seem. "Except in science," he corrected. "If you don't understand what you see, it's because theory or data are faulty. What can I do for you?"

"Do you know a woman named Princess Dulay?"

He grinned. "Ronda Rabin is her real name. A preposterous fraud. Claims to be clairvoyant and possess ESP powers. There are some pretty important people who buy it." He gave me an eager look. "Is she in trouble? She's a slippery one."

"How so?"

"Nobody's been able to get the goods on her."

"What goods?"

"She says she can see the future, Mr. Armstrong. That makes her either a liar or in the grip of delusion. Which it is hasn't been established yet. Is she being sued?"

"This is just a preliminary inquiry," I said with professional evasion.

"I don't wonder if she is. Sooner or later they go too far."

"What can you tell me about her?"

He gazed at the ceiling, as if that was where he kept the

stuff on charlatans. "She's the scenario lady. People have a problem and she explores ways to solve it in dreamland. Patently ridiculous, but many people swear by her, including, I'm told, a certain someone mentioned often as a candidate for high office." His smile was malicious. "If and when he throws his hat in the ring, we will inform the media."

"It might help. Look at Reagan."

The smile left his face. "Nancy's traffic with astrology leaked out only in the second term. By then it was too late to put his feet to the fire."

"You say she's slippery."

"Her fraudulence is hard to expose. The people who consult her profess satisfaction. But how do you measure that objectively? Who's to say that if they followed another course they wouldn't be equally satisfied? It's the swamp of the subjective."

"She never steers them wrong?"

Professor Whitman spread his hands. "Again, who's to say? Just as doctors bury mistakes, nobody hears about Princess Dulay's. People don't like to admit it when they are gulled." The ace of spades appeared in his hand. "Now, where did that come from?"

"What's her reputation with others in her field?"

He laughed. "With her fellow con artists? Very high. That's why the Society to Expose Occult Quackery would like to bring her down. Did you know she was on *Ricki Lake?*"

"I missed it."

"The cultural mainstream, God help us, you should excuse the expression. A lifetime of teaching and I've touched barely a tiny fraction of Lake's audience. We asked for rebuttal time, but they turned us down flat. Sober science isn't sexy enough. We've done a *Nova* segment, but you're preaching to the choir there."

"I missed that, too."

I had missed a lot of things. That happens when you're growing a business. You always figure you will slow down at some point and smell the roses. But your feet never move fast enough on the treadmill. Maureen went to all of Brady's teacher conferences. I usually wasn't available on the weekends for soccer or Little League. Too busy. I got home late most nights and was asleep when Brady went to school. I had plenty of time to think about this at the Ajax Arms and the cheap restaurants where I ate by myself.

"I'm available as an expert witness if this ever reaches the trial stage," Professor Whitman promised. "We have a panel of scholars to select from. Experts on precognition, psychokinesis, palmistry, and all the other hokum. We see it as part of our scientific mission."

I said good-bye and drove back to the office. Mitzi looked up from her nails. "A Special Agent Danforth from the FBI called from Washington."

I went into my office and shut the door. Danforth was in a meeting but called back a few minutes later. Cops don't like the FBI, especially in the big cities, where we see more of them. If you work a case with them, they're the prima donnas and everybody else carries spears in the chorus. They are also experts at taking bows for work somebody else does. Chief Sontag could go on quite a while on the subject. "I've been burned by those overrated bastards more than a few times," he said.

I explained to Danforth that I was a private investigator and Princess Dulay was my client.

"I guess everybody has to make a buck," he said.

"You can save me some time."

"That's not exactly what we're in business for." It was the attitude you expected. I pictured him sitting at his gray steel desk. Shoes shined, creases sharp, white shirt, and a quiet tie. It's their uniform. Short hair, a class ring. Smiling as he looked out the window at another government hive across the street. Glad for this comic interlude.

"You did look into what she said?" I asked.

"I'm not in the habit of discussing FBI business over the telephone with someone I don't know." That put me in my place.

"I guess I could take it up with Congressman Cox. He sits on that committee that approves the Justice Department budget, doesn't he? What's it called, Ways and Means?"

I bet he sat up straight and lost the smile. "You know the congressman?"

"You want to call him, or should I have him get back to you?"

"We looked into her story."

"What'd you find out?"

"Find out?" Danforth couldn't hide his disgust. "What do you think we found out?"

"So you wrote her off as a screwball? Not that I'm saying she's not."

"Can I call you back?"

I said sure and hung up. He would run a background check to find out if I was somebody he should worry about. Cox was a bigfoot in Washington and you didn't want to be on his bad side. Don't kid yourself that the FBI is any more above politics than city hall. No greater horror awaits an agent than getting a call from the director's office asking what happened to upset a bigfoot. Visions dance of reassignment to Fargo or another gulag.

When Danforth called back I had Mitzi keep him on hold a couple of minutes to establish my importance. "Armstrong here," I said briskly.

There was a quiz show host's smile in his voice. "I checked with our San Francisco office. They say you're a good guy."

"So are they," I lied.

"So how's life in the private sector? They say you were a good cop until the accident."

"It was no accident. The guy was shooting at me."

"I've thought about going into business for myself."

"Don't be in any big rush. It's dog-eat-dog out here." It was nice we were sharing confidences.

His voice turned official. "We did what we could to check out Princess Dulay's story, as per the request from the congressman's office. She said she got this communication or whatever it was July seventeenth. NASA developed a few thousand satellite photos for us early, but there was nothing unusual that date. On the other hand, they wouldn't pick up anything as small"—he paused—"as a bowling ball. No sunspot activity or unusual electromagnetic surge. There were a couple hundred small earthquakes out where you are that night, but that's not unusual." I heard him leaf through pages. "No unusual radio traffic, according to the airport tower. That's south of you, right, toward San Jose?"

"Correct."

"Her neighbors didn't hear or feel anything out of the ordinary. The Russians have a consulate near her house that we monitor pretty close. Nothing there. Nothing anywhere. I can overnight the summary if you want."

"Great." It was something to show Princess Dulay. The FBI had gone through the motions fairly thoroughly, it seemed. All you could expect under the circumstances.

"What if she was right?"

"About what?"

"Aliens."

He laughed.

"No, I'm serious." I wasn't, but I was curious.

"Aliens? What's in the water out there?"

"Stranger things have happened," I said.

"Like what?"

"Maybe 'stranger' is the wrong word."

"I'll say."

"So the government doesn't have any plans in case aliens come?"

"The government's got plans for everything, tons of plans, and more being put on paper as we speak. They go into file drawers and nobody ever looks at them again. But, no I don't know of any specific plans for handling aliens."

The Hole: So my choice is starve to death with a clear mind, or eat and exist in a fog where the present comes and goes like a fever dream. This dawned on me after a couple of days of covertly flushing the food down the toilet. I can think straight again, but maybe I was better off before.

When you haven't eaten for a while, lethargy supposedly sets in and hunger pains are not so bad. I can hardly wait. In the meantime, I'm jittery and food images dominate my thought. Steaks, burgers, mashed potatoes and gravy, slabs of fruit pie with whipped cream. They are so clear my mouth waters and my hands reach out for them. I sit down to gargantuan feasts in dreams. Crisp drumsticks battered and fried in oil, leg of lamb with mint sauce and garlicky red potatoes, buttered corn on the cob, great slices of prime rib marbled with fat, crab washed down with a fruity chardonnay, French-fried onion rings, eggs over easy, cottage fries, rashers of crisp bacon, pigs-in-a-blanket, chicken-fried steaks. Big Macs, Whoppers. Milkshakes so thick they clog the straw.

Princess Dulay's house was on Pacific just off Divisadero. Farther west, toward the Presidio, the homes become mansions

built to overawe. Hers was narrow and elegant. It was red
brick with ivy climbing artfully and a porch with white
columns. You would see the bay from the third-floor windows. A postage-stamp lawn that looked like a barber shaved
it, and a lacquered black door with a fan window above it. A
brass knocker that thudded importantly. A small gray woman
who looked like she spent her days pressing flowers or doing
needlepoint answered the knock.

"My name's Armstrong. The princess is expecting me."

She had called, sounding very upset. The message was on
my answering machine when I got back to the office from
the library. I had been there to read up on UFOs. One thing
was clear. People who don't believe in UFOs don't write
about them. That is not the case with believers. There must
have been six feet of books on UFOs, some with pictures of
blurry objects in the sky that looked like pie plates or Fris-
bees. The authors agreed that the government would never
admit it knew UFOs were real.

The gray woman said she would see if Princess Dulay was
available and closed the door. The wind blew. I watched the
fog being torn to rags above the roofs on the other side of the
street. My trouser legs snapped like sails. They used to think
Mark Twain said the coldest winter he ever spent was a summer in San Francisco. But now it appears the credit goes to
that even greater wit, Anon.

Maureen and I used to keep a sailboat in Sausalito. Win-
ters were becalmed and summers windy. The best part was
the hot buttered rums at the Pemberton after a day of being
blown around the white-capped bay. We sat in our foul-
weather gear and warmed frozen hands on the mugs.

I sold the boat when my business took off and I couldn't
spare the time anymore. I used to think about sailing at the
Ajax Arms when the nights dug in their heels against dawn

and the streetlight shining through the tear in the shade made a pale diamond on the floor.

I had walked to Pacific Heights from the Tenderloin. Forty-five minutes from direst poverty to amazing opulence. I had plenty of time for strolling. Those few accounts left were for background checks on job applicants. But none of the companies I had contracts with was hiring. Two said when the economy picked up they would accept the very attractive package Security Concerns offered. The way I added up the numbers, I might keep them if I threw in free janitorial service and blow jobs. I wondered how I would scratch out a living until I could collect my pension. Maybe I would try the post office. Hope to luck out when somebody came in with an assault weapon to even scores.

There was not all that much time left before they started sending me *Modern Maturity* magazine. Mulhenny said you get it without asking. Becoming a member of AARP is a big milestone. Another click of the odometer and you get senior discounts. The next click is when they are playing organ music over you in a room with too many flowers. I didn't think about this sort of thing before.

The gray woman opened the door. "Please come in," she said. "That awful wind."

The home had the kind of simple taste that costs plenty. Polished floors, dark wood, flowers massed in vases, paintings that looked like they were by artists who mattered. I was shown to a cozy little study where Princess Dulay sat in a chair with a gay yellow and orange pattern. She wore a dark, floor-length brocaded housecoat. The door closed behind the gray woman with a quiet click. The princess poured tea and handed me a cup and saucer. They rattled in her shaking hand and the tea sloshed over. A laurel tree flung itself back and forth on the other side of the window.

"They're here." Her enormous eyes were full of fear. I guessed she meant the aliens.

"I see," I said. I was paid to take her delusion seriously. I wondered if I should offer to search the house with gun drawn. Some clients are disappointed if they don't see a firearm. It is conditioning from TV.

"They were far away before, watching us. But now they're here. They aren't cloaked anymore. I feel danger."

I took a sip of tea. " 'Cloaked'?"

"It's hard to explain." She got up and went to the window and stared out. The wind beat at the house. I waited for her to say more.

When she didn't, I said, "Explain what you mean by 'danger.' "

She turned from the window. A hand rose and fell. "It's a feeling."

"Do you have a security system here?"

"I don't think you understand."

"I'm trying to."

"A security system," she said with scorn. "What good would that do?"

"Can't hurt, might help."

"Everyone on the block has Semper Systems."

I got out my notebook and wrote it down. "They have a good reputation." I tried to sound upbeat, but my heart wasn't in it.

"Did you read the newspaper today?" she asked.

"I gave it my fast skim."

"The little article about Madame Everett?"

"Who's she?"

"A medium. Famous for her work on financial markets. She told investors when stocks would go up and down. She lived in Palo Alto. I knew her slightly. She had a gift."

"Did something happen to her?"

"It was an obituary. I think you should see about it." She returned to her chair. "I have a bad feeling." It was the second time she said that.

Feelings are important. Mister Rogers says so. But facts are what count. If a cop tells the court he had a feeling, the defense eats him alive.

"I'll check it out," I said. "By the way, I'm getting the FBI report they did on you."

Princess Dulay took a sip of tea. Her face said she wasn't impressed.

"You know how hard it is to get these things? Sometimes they won't even let a police department see them."

"What does it say?"

"A lot of science stuff that adds up to zip. You don't have a history of mental illness, as far as they can tell."

She smiled mockingly. "How do they know?"

"You mean you do?"

"No, but how could they know?"

"Medical records."

"They are private."

"Pick somebody at random. I bet the FBI could say whether he's got piles. Nothing's private anymore."

"I have a terrible feeling they killed her."

"I'll look into it."

"Thank you, Mr. Armstrong."

I said "Don't mention it," and left. I was thinking maybe I should see an employment counselor. I could read meters or install telephones. Heavy lifting was out because of my back. I felt guilty taking her money. A lot of guys in the trade wouldn't—Mulhenny, to name one. He bragged about the people he screwed. Maybe there was a place for me at the Golden Arch.

I drove down to San Jose to the county building and rode the elevator to the coroner's office. I asked at the counter for

Ray Fellows. He was a deputy coroner in San Francisco until his wife nagged him into moving to the suburbs. I used to see him when I was a cop and he drove the meat wagon picking up bodies. People die every night in a big city, most of natural causes. So cops and coroner's deputies see a lot of each other. He was a peculiar guy, like a lot of people who work with corpses. I don't know whether they are drawn to the work because they're strange, or the job makes them that way. One time Ray came up with the idea of sending stiffs to Africa to relieve the famines.

"Only the healthy ones," he emphasized. "Dehydrate them or freeze them and ship 'em down. What they've got in Africa is a protein shortage. These bodies just go to waste. They could feed the hungry. I'm talking about the ones that aren't claimed or ones relatives would give up for famine relief. It could be like the organ transplant program. Look at this letter I wrote."

It was to go to the president, with copies to senators and members of the Congress. It was on coroner's office stationery.

"You didn't mail this, did you?" I asked.

"Not yet."

"Kiss your job good-bye if you do."

Ray hadn't considered the cannibalism aspect. He got bogged down in the details of dehydration and freezing and the bigger picture didn't register. A lot of people in narrow specialties have that problem. Ray saw all that protein going to waste and didn't look beyond. A couple of days later he told me he had burned the letter. "I asked some other people," he said. "Real upset. Wanted to know how I could think of such a thing. You know the saying about too close to the forest? That's me."

We went down to the employee cafeteria for a cup of coffee from a machine and chewed the fat about the old days.

They didn't seem so great at the time, but you know how that is. Time rubs a mellow glow into the past.

"I'm interested in Madame Everett. She died a couple days ago," I said.

"A mind reader or something, right?"

"Did they do the autopsy yet? Anything unusual about her death?"

He shook his head. Ray had chin whiskers, which made him look like a folk singer who had left-wing politics. He scratched them. "I didn't hear anything. Want me to check?"

"I'll have another cup of coffee while I wait."

He got up and ambled off in the unhurried way of government employees. He was back in five minutes with a computer printout. "Nothing unusual that I can see. Read it yourself, though." We shook hands and said good-bye.

Paramedics had been called at 11:30 P.M. to the home of Donald and Margaret Allyson Everett at 1132 Dante Place, near Stanford University. Police were interviewing Mr. Everett when M. Watson of the coroner's department arrived to collect the body. Mr. Everett had heard the subject cry out in her bedroom and fall to the floor. It appeared the subject had left her bed and was attempting to vacate the room. She was found face down. Attempts at resuscitation were unsuccessful. The autopsy showed the subject, aged forty-eight, suffered from obesity but appeared in good health. Cause of death was an apparent heart attack. Mild arteriosclerosis was found by the pathologist. Results from other tissue samples sent to the lab for analysis wouldn't be available for a couple of weeks.

I got a newspaper from a rack and looked up the death notice. A memorial service was scheduled that night. To kill time, I decided to go over to Stanford to see Mike Deutsch, the computer phenom I use. He slept all day and spent nights in the computer lab. He lived with five or six other wireheads in undergraduate squalor in an apartment off-campus.

I climbed the stairs past a tangle of bikes chained to the railing and knocked. A kid I had met before named Izzy came to the door and said he'd see if Mike was up yet. I wondered if there was furniture under the pizza boxes. Mike appeared scratching and yawning in jeans, a ripped T-shirt, and bare feet.

"Is pizza all you guys eat?" I asked.

"Huh?" He looked around as if he'd never seen the place before. "These guys are such slobs. Somebody should clean this place up."

"There might be something growing at the bottom of these piles." That was where alien life forms would be found.

"Really." He yawned.

Mike Deutsch had an IQ off the charts. All the guys he hung around with had stellar minds, but even among them he stood out. He was doing something in computer design. He tried to explain a couple of times, but I couldn't follow. There was a reason I flunked electrical engineering.

"You haven't given me a job for a long time," he said. "I could use the bread."

"Things are slow."

Mike was a skinny kid with frizzy finger-in-the-socket hair who wore wire-rim glasses and looked like your standard nerd. But beneath that appearance beat the heart of an outlaw. In the Old West he would have been a gun for hire. He didn't think the people who made rules meant to include him.

"Any torrid romances at the CIA these days?" I asked.

"A couple. One's between the number-four guy and somebody who works at the embassy in Cairo. That somebody's also a guy. Want to see their e-mail?"

"I was just kidding. Don't you have anything better to do?"

Mike showed his toothy sociopath's smile. "What's better

than finding out what spies want kept secret? You know how much trouble those clowns got us into over the past fifty years?"

"You'll get caught one of these days. They'll throw away the key."

He stretched. "That's part of the thrill."

"There is something you could do for me."

"What's it pay?"

"Five thousand."

"You must want it bad."

"It'll be hard to get." I wanted to know if the government put out any kind of alert July 17. Maybe Danforth was holding back or maybe he hadn't been told. Government agencies keep secrets from each other.

"What am I looking for?"

I explained what I was after.

"It's not easy breaking into the DDN. It'll cost you seventy-five hundred."

"What's DDN?"

"Defense Data Network. Unbelievable security. Crackers chip away for years and never get nowhere."

His eyes lit up at the chance for another notch on his gun. This would make him a celebrity in his circles. "Can you pay something up front? I'm a little short."

I told him I knew enough about that subject to teach it. A Little Short 101. I pulled out the cash I hadn't put in the safety box and peeled off eight Benjamin Franklins. "I'll FedEx the rest. Send me a receipt for my client."

Mike stuffed the bills into a pants pocket. Steak instead of pizza for a while. I always paid him cash so it would be his word against mine.

"There's another thing," I said. "Check out a new private detective agency based in Atlanta called Security Concerns. They're taking everybody's business."

"Another twenty-five hundred. Same question. What am I looking for?"

"They underbid everybody. Get me evidence they keep prices artificially low to kill off competition."

I would have a lawsuit in that case. I could bring in private eyes who had already gone under for a class action antitrust suit. I personally knew four who collected unemployment and hung around the house and drove their wives crazy. "Security Concerns might be part of a corporation whose other companies cover its losses. I want evidence a lawyer can run with." I knew a couple of litigators who took cases like that on contingency if there were deep pockets on the other side.

Mike ran fingers through his electric hair. For him, this was like chess. All things equal, the superior intellect prevails. He had no doubt whose that was. "I'll start tonight."

I asked how long it would take.

"No way of knowing. I need a lot of computer power to outfox DDN's defenses. A friend at Ann Arbor knows encryption. The National Security Agency wants him when he gets out of school, but they don't pay shit."

I had dinner and got to the memorial service for Madame Everett just before it started. It was a well-dressed older crowd. A tall silver-haired man in a dark suit shook hands as people entered. Although it was warm, he had on a heavy sweater under his coat. Despite that, his hand was cold.

"Princess Dulay couldn't be here," I told him. "She asked me to say how sorry she is."

"Thank you," he said blankly. "I'm Donald Everett, her husband." There was something about his eyes. Grief, I supposed. He turned to the person behind me.

I found a seat and sat down as New Age music began. People studied hands folded in laps or looked off into space. The music went on so long I got sleepy. Then it faded and a man in a sort of lavender military tunic and shoulder-length blond hair stood and faced the audience.

"It's a sad but a glorious time," he said. He spread his arms in blessing. "Most of you know me. I'm Zorwanda. Our friend has departed to another dimension. Sad for us left behind, but glorious for her as she begins a new stage of the journey."

He asked us to stand and join hands. Holding hands with strangers isn't my favorite thing. A bony woman in sequins and a tall headdress was on my right. A short bald man in a dark cape stuck out his hand on my left. Hers was dry and cold. His was soft as putty and damp. Zorwanda continued, his voice lifting like an evangelist talking about redemption.

"She led a full and happy life in this sphere and used her gift for humanity. Madame Everett was personally very helpful to me when I began my profession as a medium. You might say she took me under her wing." He smiled in memory. "It was she who advised me to accept credit cards for readings. Some of you know the problem with checks." Rueful insider chuckles around me. "But even more, she helped me understand the gift and the divine purpose given to me vis-à-vis helping humanity."

He sketched Madame Everett's life and career. A pillar of the psychic community, always there for you in time of need. A founder of their association, elected chair of the convention three times running. A good wife and mother to her children.

"Some of us know her final days were not as happy as they might be. We shared her fear, some of us. Now I'd like to invite those who knew her to share their memories of our friend." We let go hands and sat down. Many people shared many memories. My jaw hurt from clinching it so I didn't yawn.

We were well into the second hour of remembrance when Zorwanda said, "Anyboy else?" Silence. "No?" A further pause while memories were vainly combed. "Many of us recall how Madame Everett saw food as a celebration of life. We'll now adjourn for a light buffet."

Madame Everett's photograph stood on a table lit by candles next to the buffet. She hadn't held back any in the celebration of life. Princess Dulay was svelte in comparison. Zorwanda was spreading mustard on a ham sandwich. I introduced myself.

"I'm a friend of Princess Dulay."

"Oh, yes! How's she doing? I just love her."

"She's doing fine," I said. "She wanted to be here."

He looked around the room. "I'm surprised so many showed up, considering." He took a bite.

"Considering what?"

Zorwanda held up a finger while he chewed. He wore pancake makeup. Maybe he had hoped TV would be there. He got the bite down. "Princess Dulay hasn't shared? Everyone here feels it." He glanced around and dropped his voice. "At least those whose gifts are genuine. Madame Everett was a kind soul and did not judge, though I'm sure she knew."

"Shared what?" I asked.

"Princess Dulay hasn't mentioned being afraid?"

"Afraid of what?"

"If you're scared, your gift is real. If not, you're just faking it. Some people are even afraid to leave their homes. Madame Everett was one." He licked his fingers.

"Princess Dulay can't quite put her finger on it," I said casually.

"Nameless dread is what I call it," he said tiredly. "I know it well. It began in July."

I nodded. "The seventeenth."

"She marked the calendar, too? It was about eleven-fifteen at night. It was like a power surge." His eyes searched mine.

"Everybody's got theories. Mine is the Earth is getting ready to shift polarity. What does the princess think?"

"Aliens."

"That's funny."

"What's funny?"

He took another bite. "That's what Madame Everett thought." He looked at the widower standing by himself and looking at the crowd. "Poor Douglas. I guess he's just numbed by grief. She was retiring, and he was always the life of the party. That's what made them such a good couple."

I walked past Mulhenny's dirty look and shut the door to my office. I had slept lousy. I couldn't stop beating myself up over Maureen and Brady. I made a couple of attempts in the beginning to try to talk things out, but she wasn't buying.

"Get away from me!" she had shrieked when I poked my head into her office at the natural history museum in Berkeley. I had hoped enough time had passed for her to cool off. Instead, she got red and her eyes seemed to shoot off sparks. She hated to lose in anything, and what could be worse than losing a man to another woman? Not that I was really lost. I had just pursued my male nature—unwisely, as I was now prepared to admit. In fact, I was ready to surrender without conditions if she would just take me back.

Maureen was an expert on the Pomo Indians, a boring tribe she had studied for years. They wove baskets and made arrowheads. That pretty much sums up their civilization before the Spanish. Or so it was commonly thought. Maureen hoped to prove they had beliefs similar to a fish-eating tribe in Alaska lucky enough to live beyond the reach of the Spanish. These beliefs proved there was communication between the two tribes. So what? I thought. But I was smart enough to keep that to myself. From what I picked up from Maureen's friends, many devoted scholarly lives to even duller subjects.

A security guard had escorted me from the museum premises, and later I nearly got nailed with contempt for violating the court's no-harassment order. "All I want to do is talk, for crissake," I told my new lawyer, Hal Trump.

"Let me do the talking," he answered. "This judge used to be a lawyer for NOW. She's death on stalking."

"Stalking? I'm just trying to talk to my wife."

"Ex-wife. She's got the papers to prove it. Once more and you go to the cooler. I got that off the record, my friend."

Because I couldn't sleep when I got home from Palo Alto, I thought about the case. If you ever need the services of a private detective, hire one who is unhappy. He will do just about anything to get his mind off personal problems, even put in hours he doesn't bill for.

That other psychics were afraid put a different light on matters. At least I wasn't investigating a lone woman's sad delusion. The case had risen to the dignity of mass hysteria. In the interest of balance, I supposed I had to give weight to the possibility aliens had arrived and were up to no good. Maybe I could write a paper with footnotes and impress Maureen.

Why did only psychics detect their presence? It must have to do with intuitive ability. Maybe they could be compared to the canaries coal miners took below to warn of poison gas. By the time the rest of us were onto the aliens, it would be too late. The analogy was so neat I almost wanted it to be true.

Princess Dulay telephoned the next day. "There's been another death," she said in a voice that shook. I said I'd be right over. It was sunny and the bay already had sailboats on it. I wished I was on one of them with a picnic lunch and beer on ice. I used the door knocker.

The gray woman answered right away. "The princess is very upset," she whispered. I followed her into the study. Princess Dulay looked like she hadn't slept any better than I. She grabbed me by the hands and led me to a sofa and pulled me down beside her. Her chin quivered. "It was on the news." A small TV set had the sound muted. "Iola was found on the street with her throat cut. People heard her scream as she ran from her house."

"She was a friend of yours?"

"We had our differences. There's so much backbiting among sensitives. That's why I keep clear of the others."

"It happened last night?"

"They showed her body being wheeled to the ambulance on *Good Morning*."

"Did they say if there are suspects?"

"Just that it was being investigated." Her enormous eyes seemed to bulge, as if she was so emotional she could barely keep it in. "I'm so afraid."

"I know a couple of guys in Homicide. I'll find out what's up." She nodded and asked in a faint voice about Madame Everett.

"There didn't seem to be anything out of the ordinary. I got a copy of the autopsy report if you want to see it."

"It would mean nothing to me. She was murdered, I know it. Just like Iola. They said she was nearly decapitated." That word did it. Princess Dulay hid her face in her hands and cried. I patted her shoulder. After a long time, her sobs stopped.

"I'm sorry," she said in a contrite voice. "I'm usually stronger." She blew her nose.

"You don't have much to do with other psychics?"

"There's so much jealousy. Madame Everett was the exception."

"Some feel the same way you do, scared. I got that from Zorwanda. You know him?"

Princess Dulay was stern. "He has tried to approach me," she said. "I haven't encouraged him." Hers was the disdain of aristocrat for *arriviste*. "He's just a vulgar entertainer."

"He's frightened."

She softened. "Perhaps I misjudged him."

"He told me Madame Everett was scared of aliens, too."

Princess Dulay clasped her hands to her bosom. "There's the proof. The government has to listen."

"I wouldn't count on it."

There was a tap on the door. "Yes, Alice."

The gray lady stuck her head in. "There's a car that has gone up and down the street twice. I've never seen it before."

"Alice is watching from the window for anything suspicious," Princess Dulay explained.

"It's blue with two men in it. Four doors. I don't know what kind. They all look alike to me." She led us up narrow stairs to the third floor and a small bedroom. A tall, narrow dormer window looked down on the tops of trees and the street beneath. Beyond the rooftops of the houses across the street, you could see Alcatraz.

"It was driving really slow. Look, here it comes again," Alice said. She stepped back from the window so we could look. Two men in a pale blue Ford Taurus drove slowly up the street. It continued past us and turned right on Divisadero. A California license plate, but I couldn't make out the numbers. We waited ten minutes, but it didn't return. They could be anyone, including tourists seeing how the rich lived.

"Mr. Armstrong," Princess Dulay said, "I'm going to ask an enormous favor."

"The worst that happens is I say no."

"I don't know what your personal situation is. A wife, I suppose? Children?"

I nodded but said nothing. I didn't want to get into that.

"Would it be terribly upsetting to your family life if you moved in with me for a time?" Her words came more quickly. "I could speak to your wife. I'll pay extra, of course. It's just that I'm"—her voice had begun to quaver and she stopped to take a deep breath—"so afraid. I'd feel better if you were here to protect me."

From the Tenderloin to Pacific Heights, the difference between the outhouse and the penthouse. Hal Trump had already advised me my visitation rights would be cut if I didn't move. It was anyhow clear that Maureen had not been budged by my penitence. But I hesitated, as if weighing the question.

"Money's not a question," Princess Dulay said again.

Other than "The sky's the limit," are there any sweeter words? "Okay," I said with a show of reluctance. "It's your bank account."

"What good is money if you're dead?" Deeper thinkers than I tackle that and come up blank, so I let it pass.

"There's room in the garage for your car," Princess Dulay said. "Maybe you could move in today? Shall I call your wife and explain?"

I told her that wouldn't be necessary. I said I'd be back with some things and went down to my car. I drove around the block and double-parked for a few minutes, then drove back past her house. No sign of the blue Taurus.

I was sticking the key into my door at the Ajax Arms when Jen popped his head out of his room. It was one of his shaky days, and he hadn't shaved. "You had a couple of visitors."

"Did they say who they were?"

"Not hardly. They were trying your door when I opened

mine. Kind of scary the way they looked at me. I yelled at them to clear out or I'd call the cops."

"What did they say?"

"I didn't give them time to say nothing. I slammed the door and pretended I was talking to the police on the phone. I heard them leave."

"What'd they look like?"

"Average-looking." You would be surprised how many people think this is a good description. "I figured them for bill collectors."

"Thanks for looking out for me." I gave him fifty bucks.

"No need for that," he said gruffly, making a halfhearted effort to wave the money away. I told him I was moving out. I went to the closet and began piling clothes on the bed.

"Because of them?"

"I got another place."

"I bet they turn the heat off again."

I threw my stuff in the backseat and drove to the Hall of Justice. The corridors were filled with the usual cast of criminals, victims, cops, and lawyers. It never changes much. I rode the elevator to Homicide and asked for Bryce Bergen.

"Goodie Armstrong," he yelled when he saw me. We shook hands.

"I told you not to call me that."

Bergen was a clown, the guy you counted on for a gag to lighten people up when the tension got too tight. "Yeah, I know. Where you been keeping yourself?" He was a little guy who wore bow ties and looked like Dick Cavett. A bulldog when investigating a murder that grabbed him.

"Just trying to scratch out a living," I said. "Got time for lunch?"

"Christ, no. The chief's been wearing the rag all week."

A different chief had been appointed since I left. His name

was Phil Blas. I had heard he was popular with the rank and file.

"What's his problem?"

"Nobody's sure. The best guess is he came back from a seminar with a head stuffed full of some new management philosophy. He's calling all the department heads in and grilling them. I mean, beginning with basic stuff, like how many men are under them and what they do. People who've been through it say it's like Police Science I all over again."

"I wanted to ask you about the murder last night."

"Which one? There were six. I haven't been to bed."

"Gang war?"

He shook his head. "I wish it was. It's easy to track down those scumbags. This was six different ones, all but one high-profile. This place has been swarming with media all day. What one are you interested in?"

"A medium by the name of Iola."

"She's the only one who isn't somebody. You mean to tell me she is?"

"I've got a client in the same business who knew her."

"Iola's head was nearly lopped off. Whoever it was had to have the strength of Samson. Or maybe he was on angel dust."

"Any idea who did it?"

"Somebody heard her running down the sidewalk and screaming they were after her. Who 'they' were is unknown at this point. Probably a boyfriend. Your client have any ideas?"

"Nope. Who else got whacked?"

"Matt Styles, the news anchor. Some navy big shot. The guy who bossed the Lawrence Livermore Laboratory. He got nailed in a hit-and-run, so that might not qualify as murder. Then again it might. The wife of Dutch Werner, the CEO of

Germand Corporation, and Abigail Forsythe, the newspaper publisher."

"What a haul."

"The media assholes keep asking if there's some tie-in. I tell them my theory is sunspots." He smiled tiredly. "Maybe you can think of a better one?"

"Sunspots sound good to me." It sounded sane compared to aliens knocking off psychics. "Any witnesses or physical evidence in Iola's case?"

"I don't know. Carlson's handling the case. He would find a way to lose it if there was. Burglary sent him over on loan. They're glad to get rid of him. We were down to the bottom of the barrel by the time she was killed. Busiest night I ever saw."

"The mayor must be raising hell."

"The biggest mystery of all," Bergen said. "Not a peep. Everybody thought he'd grandstand for the cameras, promising arrests within forty-eight hours as usual. It must be shell shock. He supposedly knew all the victims but Iola. Hell, maybe he knows her, too." He rubbed his face. He needed a shave.

"You better go home and get some sleep," I said.

"Wish I could." He said he would call if Carlson somehow turned up something about Iola's murder, which he seriously doubted. I felt sorry for him and the rest of the poor bastards in Homicide. The mayor would be on their backs as soon as someone revived him with smelling salts.

The car radio was full of the murders as I drove back to Princess Dulay's home. That and some big snafu involving the telephone company. I kept changing the station to see what they knew about what one deep voice called the worst night of murder in city history. The talk show hosts were going wild. One threw out Bergen's sunspot theory for serious discussion. I carried my clothes from the car.

"You didn't tell me about the others who got killed," I told the princess.

"I just saw the tail end of *Good Morning* when I called. It's so horrible. So many important people. Is your gun with you?"

"It's in the car. I'll bring it up as soon as you tell me where to put this stuff." I decided against telling her about my visitors. She was spooked enough as it was, and maybe they were just bill collectors. If so, their look around the Ajax would say to write off the debt.

She led me upstairs to the second floor and opened the door to a bedroom with wallpaper that had yellow sunflowers on a green background. "My bedroom is across the hall. The bathroom is down there. A phone's on the nightstand if you need it. I'll let you get settled." She closed the door and I hung my clothes in the closet. When I was finished, I tested the bed. Firm, the way I liked it. I called Agent Danforth in Washington.

"Things must be back to normal," he said.

"It depends on what you call normal."

His voice was buried by static for a few seconds, then came back. "I guess they still haven't got it fixed."

I asked what he was talking about.

"Communications. You people have been cut off from the rest of the world for—what is it?—fourteen hours. Some kind of virus freezing the computers that run long distance. It screwed up the satellites, too. Nothing coming in or coming out, not even network feeds. You been on the moon or something you don't know this?"

"Sometimes there's just too much news," I said. "You ever get that feeling?"

"Every day but Sunday. I play golf then. What's on your mind?"

I told him about Madame Everett and Iola. There was silence on the other end as if he waited for more. I thought it was enough for him to at least comment.

"Is that it?" Danforth said finally. "One psychic dead of possible natural causes and a second who is victim of homicide. Do I leave something out?"

"The rest are scared, at least the ones who are legitimate."

" 'Legitimate' isn't a word I'd use in this context."

I told him Princess Dulay's number would reach me if we had to talk.

"You moved in with the lady?"

"I'm her bodyguard for a while."

I hung up on his smirk and lay on the bed and stared at the ceiling. I was thinking about what Bergen said about Iola's killer. I might need something with more knockdown power. When I was a rookie cop, a .38 with six shots was all you needed. Nowadays that's pathetic. I went downstairs and told Princess Dulay I'd be back. She gave me keys to the house.

I drove to my storage locker in Daly City and got the shotgun and a box of shells and more clothes. My new closet was lots bigger than the cupboard at the Ajax Arms.

Alice showed me through the house when I got back, beginning with the big basement and ending in an attic crowded with furniture covered by sheets. The security console was in a little room off the kitchen, where an Asian chef chopped vegetables. It featured motion detectors outside that turned on floodlights and an alarm system that dialed 911.

"A big house for two people," I said to Alice.

"It was Mr. Dulay's. He inherited it from his mother. When he was alive and the children were still home, it didn't seem so big." She was a faded woman, but maybe the colors had never been bright. She was the sort who melted into the background with a little smile that said, "Excuse me for living."

"Anybody else have access?" I asked.

"The cook and the cleaning people. A gardener comes once a week." They had been with the princess for years, but I took their names anyhow to run a check.

"Dinner is at seven," Alice said. When I hesitated, she said, "Or perhaps you have other plans. The princess thought—"

"No, I don't have other plans." Somebody else could have

my seat at the counter at Ruby's Café. You got three courses for six bucks. People sat eating in cones of silence. Even the waiters were depressed.

We ate lamb chops, red potatoes, and brussels sprouts. It beat Ruby's by a mile. The princess and I sat across from each other. I guessed Alice ate in the kitchen when there were guests.

"I checked out your security system. It's good enough."

She paused with knife and fork. "I got threats once. It was a long time ago."

"What was the problem?"

"People say they want to know what the future holds, but sometimes they don't like what they hear. They blame the messenger."

"I should have their names."

Princess Dulay returned to her chop. "You don't need them. Their fate was realized."

"Meaning?"

"They died as I said they would, Mr. Armstrong."

"Your dream scenarios didn't let them dodge the bullet?"

"They revealed it was impossible to do so."

We chewed in silence. "Why not peek into the future about yourself?" I asked. "You could save yourself a lot of worry."

"Or maybe I wouldn't," she said with a level look. "Would you like to know the time of your death?"

"I guess not."

"I don't either."

They say people who have near-death experiences don't fear dying anymore. That isn't exactly what I had when I fell from the fire escape, but it was as close as I wanted to get until the final curtain. A man was going to teach his wife a lesson by killing their little kid in Hunters Point. Normally you wait for the hostage negotiator to get there and wear the individual down with talk. But I could tell by the look in his eyes there wasn't time. He was going to blow away the little girl and kill himself. He was a bodybuilder and they said afterward it was a case of steroid rage. The trade-off for building muscle mass with anabolic steroids is a hair-trigger temper. I got his attention, and my partner snatched the kid and ran out the door. That left me the job of wrestling Mr. America. He was cracking my ribs in a bear hug when I banged both his ears with cupped hands. I brought them together the way the cymbal player does in the 1812 *Overture*. Do it right and you rupture the eardrums. The pain is hellish. I did it right. He screamed and tossed me aside like a candy wrapper. Unfortunately, it was through a window. I dangled by one hand on the fire escape three stories up as the glass tinkled on the alley below. I might have worked my way around to the ladder except that he appeared at the window with my gun, which had fallen from the holster.

He began firing but kept missing. I couldn't count on that to continue, so I let go. My back was broken when I landed. As I lay in the trash-filled alley, I worried at first that I was paralyzed and the rats would get me. Then I realized I felt too much pain in too many places. When the ambulance came, they strapped me to a board and hauled me off to the hospital. The suspect found Jesus in prison and sent me nice letters during my recuperation. He's doing fine now, working as a mechanic.

After dinner, the princess retired to her study and I went upstairs and watched television. There was nothing on the news except the murders and the big blackout. One station had an essayist who sat on the edge of a desk and wondered whether we could be said to exist for the rest of the global village when communication links were down. I love it when these guys go deep. It's like watching someone try to play Mozart on a kazoo. He quoted an expert who said the odds against that kind of breakdown were so great as to be impossible.

The essayist turned from him and the camera moved in tight. "And yet," he said, "the impossible happened." There was a lot of yakking by other talking heads about the murders, but nothing new had come to light, and wasn't the mayor's silence puzzling?

I dozed off in my chair and was awakened after midnight by fire trucks roaring out of the station down the hill. I put my shoes back on and patrolled the house from top to bottom. After the sirens faded, the night was still. The fog was back, and it looked like the streetlights had been sanctified and given halos. I went back to my room and lay on the bed. I tried to stay awake but fell asleep again.

I showered and shaved and got dressed the next morning and was on my way out when I heard the TV on in the princess's study. I knocked, and she said to come in.

"A quiet night," I said. "The best kind."

She was watching the screen. A woman was interviewing a psychologist about the murders. The princess had a troubled look.

"That's Kathy," she said. "She's one of my clients."

"The newsperson or the psychologist?" I asked.

"Kathy's host of the show." She had the kind of standard good looks TV recruits from Blond Land. "There's something about her."

I waited for her to tell me.

"She's different."

"You mean her hair?" That's what women usually mean by different.

"No, not that," she said slowly. "It's not appearance. It's something else." The psychologist was explaining that people are upset by murder. A lot of obvious things get said on TV.

I spoke. "Did you get any vibes or whatever you call it from the aliens last night?"

She looked at me, still puzzled. "What? Oh, no. Nothing."

"I'll be back later."

She didn't answer, and I closed the door. I drove to the office and walked in. Mitzi looked up from the newspaper, shock on her face.

"You're not dead," she said with a gasp.

"Try saying 'good morning.' It sounds better."

"Your hotel burned down. There were no survivors."

The front page had a picture and article about the Ajax Arms. A fire of unexplained origin had raced through the building, trapping residents "in a fiery inferno." That was where the fire trucks had been going. It would be days before it was known how many had died. The building had been notorious for building code violations, a possible clue to the cause of the tragedy.

"There sure has been a lot of bad news lately," Mitzi fretted. She had recovered from the shock of me still being alive. I wondered how many people she had told. She would have to call them back. Her hair was magenta today. The ring in her nose gleamed.

I went into my office and closed the door. When you're young and stupid, you think you will live forever. Most of that gets knocked out of you as the years pass, but enough sticks so most people don't believe it when the Grim Reaper comes to call. *Me?* There must be a mistake. Check the list again.

I telephoned Maureen, and Brady answered.

"Why aren't you in school?"

"Hi, Dad. I've got a cold. Mom said I could stay home."

"No cold ever kept me home when I was your age."

"I know. You walked to school over broken glass with no shoes." One of our jokes.

"I just wanted to check in. You watching cartoons?"

"Mom said it was okay. She's still in bed. She was up real late working."

"Tell her I called. You ready for the 'Niners game?"

"You better believe it."

I told him to stay warm and hung up. I hoped Maureen would understand I called not to harass her but so that she wouldn't think I had died in the fire. She and Gloria would congratulate themselves at having their belief confirmed that I lived in a dangerous neighborhood.

I called Bergen at the Hall of Justice. "Tell me about that fire last night."

"I don't have enough to do I should stick my nose into fucking Fire Department business?" he snapped.

"I just wondered if it was arson."

"How the hell would I know? Ask them. Look, I gotta go. The mayor's coming."

"He's going to make an announcement?" I liked to needle him, too.

"What's he gonna say? That we don't know anything? He hates 'Police Are Baffled' headlines."

"Do you suppose those murders and the fire are connected?" One night under the princess's roof and intuition was kicking in.

"What's the connection?"

"Aliens."

"Not funny, asshole." He hung up.

Mulhenny blustered through the doorway. "Still among the living, I see. Congratulations. Here's the gas and electric bill. You got your half so I can send a check?"

I looked at the bill. "Is cash okay?"

"Christ, it's always cash with you. It's like doing business with a drug dealer."

"Are you still mad?"

"Life's too short. I'd of done the same thing as you probably, though I'm a lot nicer guy. How'd you escape being
burned up like the rest of those poor bastards?"

"I spent the night at the princess's house."

He winked. "A little tubby for my taste. But any port for
you single guys."

I ignored that. "I'm doing bodyguard work. I might ask
you to pull some shifts if it goes on."

"What are you charging her?"

"My standard rates."

"What are they?"

"That's between me and the IRS."

He laughed and the heaving of his stomach popped a button. "Seeing as how I'm not so busy right now, I could probably work it in."

I drove toward Ellis Street. I parked in the Union Square
garage because the fire lines blocked traffic in four directions.
I showed the badge they let me keep when I retired to get
past the lines. A charred smell hung heavy in the air, and firemen played hoses on the smoking rubble. I spotted a lieutenant I knew, Dave Winstedt.

"Know the cause yet?"

He shook his head. "It's still too hot to get in there and
look around. Might be a day before we know."

"Has anybody talked to the people across the street yet?"

He shrugged. "There's a couple guys from Arson scratching their asses around here somewhere."

I picked my way through the hoses and puddles to the Re-
gency Hotel across the street. It was an armpit like the Ajax.
I climbed a stairwell as dark as a mole's tunnel and knocked
at one of the rooms that faced the street. It was opened by a
tall gay guy in a black cowboy outfit. I told him I was an investigator and showed the badge. I asked if he saw anything
unusual the night before at the Ajax.

"Christ, yes. I wondered if somebody would ask. There were flashes of blue light at that place before it burned down. I was standing at the window watching for Steve—he's my friend—when I saw them."

"How many flashes did you see?"

"One in every window at the same time. It lit up the whole street really bright. Next second, the place was in flames and people were screaming. It happened unbelievably fast. They never had a chance. It was the worst thing I ever saw in my life."

I knocked on more doors. A couple of other people told me they also saw the blue flashes. I told this to Winstedt when I went below, and he said he'd let the Arson guys know.

I walked to John's Grill and sat at the bar and ordered a gibson. They were just seating the first customers for lunch, and two men slammed liar's dice for drinks. I felt like one of those lawyers in Latin America who start defending guerrillas in court and end up in the hills themselves fighting the government. I didn't like the feeling. I'll take professional detachment, thanks.

The cowboy said the flashes of blue light were simultaneous in every room. You might be able to get into a few rooms to rig an incendiary device, but not all. Somebody was bound to hear his room being entered and wake everybody with his yells. They didn't like or even know each other at the Ajax, but they saw the need for a common defense against the dangers outside. Plus, the invisible people kept many on their toes.

I admit I was slow connecting the dots. It was the old story of all those trees blocking the forest. The blue flashes made me think of power, and power led to the big communications foul-up. The expert had said on TV it was supposedly impossible. But it would be easy for aliens capable of space travel to figure how to pull the plug.

I asked the waiter for a menu. Aliens were pictured in books as having small bodies and big heads with almond-shaped eyes. This would be noticed, even in San Francisco.

I only saw them from a distance, but the men in the blue Taurus looked human, and poor Jen would have mentioned it if there was something otherworldly about my visitors. Was it possible the aliens looked like us? Or maybe they could transform themselves. Once you admitted their possibility in the first place, anything was plausible. After lunch I got my car from the garage and drove to Princess Dulay's house.

Alice must have been watching because she opened the door right away.

"Is everything all right?" I asked.

"Yes. No sign of those men in the car."

I went into the princess's study and closed the door. She looked up from the desk where she was writing in longhand with several open books around her.

"You're not interrupting," she said in answer to my question. "I'm doing an astrological chart. I had to put my mind to work."

"I thought your line of work was dream scenarios."

"I also do charts. They give insights. Have a seat. You remember Kathy?" Her voice was unsteady again.

"The lady on TV?"

"Yes. She's not Kathy."

I started to say we had bigger fish to fry, but stopped. "What do you mean?"

"I told you she's one of my clients. Our minds are attuned, which is why I've been able to give her such good career direction. When her program was over, I closed my eyes and went to her on the astral plane."

"You went into a trance?"

"That's such a dated term, Mr. Armstrong."

"Sorry. So you're on the astral plane."

"Something else occupies her mind and body. Something cold and hostile, something infinitely intelligent and aware." She gave a little sob. "Kathy's gone. She was such a beautiful person. A husband and two sweet children."

I sat in silence, longing for the golden days when I investigated insurance fraud.

"I know it's one of them," she said. "One of the aliens."

"How do you know?"

"Kathy and I had a deep psychic closeness. She's a generous and loving person. That was why she did so well on television. The camera saw those qualities. Just between us, she was going to ABC in the spring to host a newsmagazine program in New York." Her hands rose and fell. "I guess it doesn't have to be secret anymore. She won't be going."

"You noticed a difference just watching on TV?"

"Only someone who knew her very well could tell. Whatever controls her now is a skillful mimic."

"Maybe you're wrong?"

She seized the point. "Oh, how I wish I was! I've been so upset. Maybe I'm just not reaching clarity."

"I'll check her out."

She gave me Kathy Birkshire's address in Belvedere, and I drove across the Golden Gate Bridge and east across the Tiburon Peninsula. Belvedere is an island where people tear down homes costing three million dollars and replace them with ones costing six million. Saudi princes have homes they visit only a week or two out of the year, and there are the megarich from Europe and Asia as well. It has a knockout view of San Francisco on the south side, which is where Kathy lived with her husband. Princess Dulay told me he was a major player in Silicon Valley. I pulled my car to a gate and waited for someone to say something on the speaker box.

"Who is it, please?" a man's voice asked.

"Goodwin Armstrong. Is Ms. Birkshire available? Princess Dulay sent me."

There was silence, as he wasn't sure this warranted opening up. Then there was a click, and the gate silently rolled open. I drove into a compound with a Tudor mansion at the end of the drive. A tall, trim man in a jogging outfit came out the front door and was waiting when I reached the entrance.

"Kathy's with her personal trainer." He looked at his watch. "It'll be another fifteen minutes." He opened the car door and I got out. "How's the princess?"

"Never better," I said.

"Come on in. I'm Jeb Birkshire, better known as Mr. Kathy Birkshire." I had the feeling he had used the line a few times. He led the way to a solarium with a killer view of Angel Island and San Francisco. With a strong enough telescope you would be able to pick out the princess's house way across the water. He motioned me into a chair and sat down himself. We looked at one another.

"She couldn't come herself?"

"She's really busy," I said. "There was some stuff on Kathy's chart she wanted her to see. I got it here." I showed him a manila envelope. Princess Dulay had written some mumbo jumbo she said Kathy would understand. "She was going to send it FedEx, but as long as I was coming over, I might be able to answer any questions." If she had any, I would scratch my head and say that was a little beyond me and she should talk to the princess personally.

Birkshire had the gaunt look you often see in Marin people. They are such diet and fitness fanatics they look like plane crash survivors who walked out of the wilderness living on seeds and berries.

He smiled tightly. "No offense, but I don't believe in your kind of stuff. Kathy and I agreed to disagree when we first started going together."

"There are many paths to the truth."

"You want something to drink?"

"A beer would be great."

He went off and came back a couple of minutes later with a beer and a bottle of designer water to show he made better choices. We each poured our own. I studied Birkshire over my glass. He looked like something was eating him.

"Princess Dulay wanted me to ask about Kathy."

He shot me a look. "What about her?"

"Kathy's chart shows her moving under the influence of Saturn." If he didn't know astrology, that wouldn't mean anything to him either.

"So?"

"She'll seem somehow different to loved ones," I said casually. "More distant, possibly."

"They sure got that right." He studied me. "How long does it take before she gets back to normal?"

"Princess Dulay might be able to say."

"Like most marriages, ours has its ups and downs. But she's always been a wonderful mother. The kids don't understand it."

"Understand . . ." I prompted.

He hesitated and then finished. "Understand why she pushes them away. It's like she doesn't love them anymore." He looked at me like a man ready to grasp at a straw. "So you say astrology explains this?"

"Explains what, darling?" Kathy stood at the door in a heavy sweat suit. The TV cameras hadn't flattered her a bit. She had Grace Kelly looks. The woman who was her personal trainer squeezed past her, dripping with sweat and pulling on a windbreaker.

"That was a good workout," the trainer said, panting. "I gotta run. See you tomorrow." She went out the front door.

"Don't you think you should introduce me, Jeb?" Kathy said. A real ice queen. Too much of a lady to sweat.

"Sorry, thought you knew each other. Armstrong, wasn't it? He's a friend of Princess Dulay."

"Goodwin Armstrong," I said to Kathy. Her hand was as cold as her eyes. They made me think of Madame Everett's husband.

"The princess wanted you to have this." I handed her the manila envelope. "She says it's self-explanatory, but to ask me if you have any questions."

"I'll look at it later," she said without interest. She turned to her husband. "Explains what?"

"It's not important." There was an edge in his voice. "Excuse me," he said to me. "I have to get back to work." He left the room. An ancient Irish setter asleep by a potted plant awoke as he passed. The dog got to its feet and limped stiffly in Kathy's direction. Cataracts had blinded it. The dog stopped just short of her and showed its teeth in a senile snarl.

"Jeb," Kathy called. He came back into the room.

"What do you want?" he said in a flat voice.

"I want that dog put down."

"You couldn't bear the thought of it last week." He looked at me. "She's had her eighteen years."

"I don't care what I said. Get rid of her."

"What about the children?"

"The children will have to deal with it."

"I better be on my way," I said. "I can find the way."

"Warm and generous?" I said to Princess Dulay when I got back to the city. "The woman's a bitch on wheels."

"It's not Kathy." She twisted a handkerchief in her hands. "I know it's not. She's the kindest person."

The Hole: I've got a new respect for people who go on hunger strikes. It takes guts to deny your body what it needs. Cut off food and it gets right in your face. Those dreams about food are just the start. After that, it is hammering headaches, joint pain, weakness, irritability, insomnia. Nightmares when you do manage to drop off. The body pulls out a whole menu of torture to force you to feed it.

What pushes me over the edge is they stop giving me drinks in a can I open myself. The camera must have spotted me sneaking food to the john. My drinks now show up already poured in a glass. If I don't swallow the drug in food form, I'll have to in liquid. I go without both for three days before giving up. You can last a lot longer without food than water. When the body is craving water at the cell level, the strongest will is conquered. Starvation is a day at the beach in comparison.

I go berserk. It is like a hot poker suddenly pierces my head temple to temple. I break the table apart and hammer holes in the wallboard, exposing the brick on the other side. I knock the light from the ceiling and pound at the door with the table legs until they fall apart in my hands. You bastards, you lousy, stinking cowards. I call them every name I can think of before I pass out. The next thing I know I'm on the floor. The place has been cleaned up. I barely have the strength to crawl to the glass on the table. I reach for it with a shaking hand. Warm cranberry juice is in my mouth, then down my throat. My body rejoices.

The Hole: They can't keep me locked up here forever. So they either kill me or let me go at some point. There must be traffic in and out of this place and lights that show at night. The world is full of nosy people. No one knows better than a cop. Walk down any block and at least a third of the residents are checking things out from behind curtains. Getting them to admit having seen a crime is the problem. Word will leak out that the old military base is in use again. Building and zoning inspectors or other paid snoops will pay calls.

The drug is either in the food or the drink, but not both. It only takes about fifteen minutes for me to become a semi-vegetable. Maybe a double dose would be risky, and they're not ready yet to put me away for keeps. If they split the dose between food and drink, it wouldn't be enough if I boycotted one. So it's a question of which shell the pea is under. Some days I don't drink and some I don't eat. I had three days of being clear-minded, then two of being drugged. I think it was two, but naturally I can't know for sure. Like playing red or black in roulette, the odds seem equal. But a quirk of statistics is that while they average out over the long haul, in the short run they can come down heavily in favor of one color.

I tell myself it's better to have a clear mind even though the days creep by with agonizing slowness. Somebody might forget sometime and leave the door ajar. I wake and make a break for it. But if I'm drugged, the open door might not register. Or if it does, I forget when I turn my head and blow my chance.

I took Brady to see the 49ers play on Sunday. It was a close one and we had good seats, but my mind wandered. We had settled into a routine at Princess Dulay's. At dusk I went through the house and unplugged everything, even telephones. We made do with candles and battery-powered lamps. Some monster power surge had zapped the Ajax like a prisoner in the electric chair. I didn't want it happening to us if I could help it.

The women played hearts by lamplight until they went to bed. Princess Dulay hadn't blinked when I recommended turning off the juice and unplugging everything. "If you think it's necessary," she said timidly. I didn't explain why because I didn't want her nerves stretched any tighter. She seemed always on the edge of a scream as it was. Alice gave pleading looks that said please do something to help her friend. But other than returning to the candlelight era and looking firm, I didn't know what to do. I did ask Princess Dulay to set up a meeting with Congressman Cox, who was due in on Monday for a visit to the home district. If I could get him on the case, maybe the FBI could be squeezed into doing more.

I catnapped at night between patrols of the house with a flashlight and my .38. Princess Dulay had a strong feeling the house was watched. After a couple of nights I began to think she was right. Maybe it was only the power of suggestion, but sometimes as I looked out windows on my night watchman's rounds I had the feeling something lurked in the darkness. I'm as modern as the next man and know that "evil" is a word that has pretty much lost its meaning, but I couldn't think of a better one to describe what I felt. I saw and heard nothing, yet the hairs on the back of my neck rose. That response is a holdover from knuckle-dragging ancestors, I guess. They didn't see anything at the water hole, but a sixth sense told them something lay in wait, and their hackles stood up and saluted. Maureen would have an opinion. She liked to talk theory. Maybe hackles warned whoever walked behind that danger was ahead.

What did I mean by evil? What I felt was a sense of something aware and watchful that meant me harm. But maybe I'm intellectualizing after the fact.

Mulhenny spelled me for the football game. He came through the door wheezing and took a slow look around. "You got yourself a gold mine, buddy." I stepped back from the crude cologne he wore. He must have bought it by the gallon. His sense of smell probably went when he busted his nose, but what was Emily's excuse?

"Did you bring a weapon?"

He patted under an arm. "Right here."

I took him in to meet the princess, and we walked back to the front parlor.

"What am I looking for?" he asked, switching on the television with the remote. "They got anything to eat here?"

"You're looking for anything unusual."

He flipped through the channels. "And what do I do if I see anything unusual?"

"Shoot it, I suppose."

"Riiight." He winked. Getting paid to sit on his butt and watch TV put him in a good mood.

Maureen was digging in her Adidas bag for her car keys by the front door when I came to pick up Brady. He jumped into my arms with a glad face. "Dad!"

She didn't look up from her bag. "You'll give him dinner

and have him back by six?" She had adopted a brittle way of speaking to me. Finding her keys, she glanced up and her face softened. "You look tired."

My bitterness leaped out like flame from a stoked furnace. "Sure, I'm tired. I work day and night, otherwise I can't pay spousal support. How about calling off your dogs?"

I think she thought I said "dog" and meant her lawyer, Gloria.

"She's also a friend. I'd appreciate it if you didn't talk about her that way."

Brady pulled worriedly at my arm. "C'mon, Dad, let's go to the game."

"She's a vicious shark. You hated that type of lawyer before. What's different now?"

Maureen stuck out her chin. "Not you. You're the same jerk you always were." She stopped herself. "Gloria says I'm not supposed to have these conversations with you."

Brady tugged more. "C'mon, Dad. Let's go now." Guilt stabbed me. He was too young for the pain in his eyes.

"Yeah, sure. Off we go," I cried dizzily. I turned toward the car.

"Six o'clock," she snapped.

Brady told me about school as I drove to 3Com Park and I asked about his teacher and friends. I never had many of these conversations. Too fucking busy. I thought of telling him about the case. It would be just our secret. But he might accidentally let something slip. I could see Maureen's lawyer going before the judge to say I was concerned about an alien presence on Earth.

Brady's going to be a big kid, maybe bigger than I when he gets his full growth. He ate hot dogs, Eskimo pies, and popcorn. The prices they charge you at ballparks are robbery. I kept wiping mustard and other stuff from his face.

"Come on," I joked, "don't you care what you look like?"

"Nope."

Kids don't at that age. In a couple of years, looks would be all he thought about. I wanted to be there to tell him not to sweat the little things. Bad as things may seem at the time, they always get better. Sometimes you get through to them.

The third quarter was half gone when I got a feeling we were being watched. It didn't just creep up. It was as if heads turned to openly stare with malevolent intent. It was the same feeling I got after dark at Princess Dulay's, only stronger. I had left my gun in the car because sometimes they search you for liquor. The 49ers were driving for a score, and everybody's attention was on the field below. I looked for eyes turned to us, but only saw vendors scanning the crowd for sales. In the middle of a huge crowd I suddenly felt naked and alone.

"C'mon, let's go."

Brady's face was full of surprise. "They're just about to score."

"I want to beat the crowd to the parking lot."

"It's only the third quarter."

"Let's go."

"What's wrong, Dad? You look scared."

I grabbed him by the arm and we crawled over fans angry their view was blocked. Brady kept asking what was wrong as I pulled him down the horseshoe concourse to the parking lot. "Is somebody after us?" he asked when I kept looking behind.

"I remembered I have to be somewhere."

"Jeez, Dad, this isn't fair." He was trotting to keep up. "Why are we walking so fast?"

"We can listen to the game in the car."

He was overwhelmed by the injustice. Who could blame him? We reached my car and got in. Brady tuned in the game as I drove through the parking lot. The 49ers put six points on the scoreboard, and the stadium went wild.

"And *we* missed it," he said. He switched off the radio.

"Look, I'm really sorry." I was looking in the rearview mirror. "It's just that I forgot this meeting."

"A meeting's more important," he said accusingly. I couldn't meet his stare.

"You know that's not true."

"I don't either know it."

I drove aimlessly, looking for a tail. I got on the freeway to Daly City and then went north up the coast past the Clift House, still watching the rearview mirror. Brady turned the game back on. "I told all the guys I'd be there."

"I'll make it up to you."

"You can't! There's no way you can."

The rest of the day went badly. We had a silent dinner at a drive-in, and he didn't say anything when I let him off. He trudged to the house, head down. Maureen had been watching for us and opened the door before he got there. I could tell she was asking what was wrong.

I drove back to Princess Dulay's and let myself in. Mulhenny turned off the TV. "Great game, huh? Wish I coulda been there." He got up and tucked his shirt in. "Nothin' happening here. That'll be five hundred bucks."

I gave him two hundred and fifty and he had the sense not to complain. He said give him a call anytime. "Oh. There's some old broad talking to your client. I thought of shooting her when she came to the door, but I decided she wasn't unusual enough." He wheezed out a laugh and left.

I went to the princess's study and knocked. She was with a tall, well-dressed woman with silver hair and refined looks in her sixties. She looked like the kind who chair alumni committees and sit on museum boards.

"This is Harriet Cox, Mr. Armstrong," the princess said. "The congressman is her husband."

I said, "Pleased to meet you."

"I came home a day early," she said. "The princess tells me this is serious."

"Did she tell you I want to talk to your husband?"

Mrs. Congressman looked uneasy. "Well, yes, she did."

"Is there a problem?"

"Harriet's not sure how he'll take it," Princess Dulay said.

"How he'll take it?" I said tiredly. "I'll tell you how he'll take it. He won't believe it." I almost added, "Unless he's nuts like you and me."

"I'm not sure what more my husband can do," Harriet said carefully. "I mean, can you actually prove this newsperson has been taken over by"—she had trouble getting it out—"an alien?"

"I can't prove it." I wondered how you could. Hope Kathy Birkshire came clean when you asked?

"Princess Dulay and I talked most of the afternoon about this. Because of our past together, I believe something must be badly wrong." Harriet looked at the princess. "She's told me things that were unbelievable at the time but turned out to be one hundred percent true. I mean really unbelievable things. My husband and I were married to different people, but she said we would divorce and marry each other. My mouth dropped open and I almost walked out on her. I didn't even know Paul then. *Had not even met him.* That kind of unbelievable. But this is so . . ." She groped again.

"Yeah, I know," I said.

"My husband has a great deal of confidence in my judgment. He says I have good instincts." She looked pained. "Put yourself in his place. A political person's greatest fear is ridicule. Given a choice, I think most would rather be seen as corrupt than ridiculous."

"The FBI thinks it's a joke," I admitted.

"The agent named Danforth," the princess put in. "I told you about him, Harriet. Rude."

Alice came in with two lit candles. "Should I unplug this lamp? Everything else is."

"We do this every night," Princess Dulay explained.

"Oh, dear," Harriet said.

"Mr. Armstrong says it's safer," Alice said.

The congressman's wife shot me a look. "You sit in the dark?"

"Oh, no," Alice said. "We have the candles." It was beginning to sound like a drawing-room comedy. The actor playing the absent-minded uncle would walk in any minute in a smoking jacket to ask if anyone had seen his pipe.

"I didn't want to tell you," I said to Princess Dulay. I looked at Harriet Cox. "You heard about the big hotel fire we had?"

"A terrible tragedy."

"It was the Ajax Arms. I lived there."

"I don't follow."

"I think they burned the place down to get me."

The princess gasped and put a hand to her bosom.

"People across the street said they saw blue flashes in every room at the same second and then the place went up like a torch."

"Arson?" Harriet asked. "What does the Fire Department say?"

"It's still under investigation."

Alice unplugged the lamp and left the room. We stared at the candles in silence. Princess Dulay looked like she would benefit from a long scream.

Finally, Harriet Cox spoke. "I will make sure my husband sees you at eleven o'clock tomorrow morning. I'll tell his chief of staff to clear as much time as you need."

I thanked her, and she rose to go. Princess Dulay showed her to the door. They hugged one another.

After she was gone, Princess Dulay said, "I think she believes us."

"At least she didn't laugh out loud. That's a plus."

"You sound discouraged, Mr. Armstrong."

That night it felt like the house was watched again. Princess Dulay opened the door in her robe as I passed her bedroom on one of my rounds. "It's out there," she said quietly. She looked at the shotgun I cradled. "I'm not sure that would help."

"Ever seen what one of these rounds can do?"

"I'm opposed to guns."

"So is anyone on the wrong end of this." My bravado seemed to reassure her and she closed the door.

I arrived in plenty of time for my appointment with Congressman Cox. He was at his office in the huge brutal slab the federal government built on Golden Gate Avenue that looks like an homage to Stalin. I felt as pessimistic as a salesman hoping to talk Nordstrom's into a line of plastic shoes. "No, really. Lots better than leather."

An aide escorted me into a large paneled office hung with photographs of Cox shaking hands with various big shots and left us alone. The congressman got up from behind his desk.

"What are you trying to pull?" He was tall and wore a baggy man-of-the-people suit for us rubes in the home district. It didn't go with the hundred-dollar haircut. He smiled unpleasantly. "What bill of goods did you sell my wife?"

"Excuse me?"

"She said it was urgent I talk to you, but I couldn't get from her exactly what the subject was."

"She didn't tell you?"

"She said you would make everything clear. I had to cancel a meeting with Senator Paxton." He sat down and folded his hands across his stomach. "Go ahead."

When I was finished, Cox fiddled with a letter opener. He laid it down and walked to a window with a view of the windswept plaza far below. "To sum up, a bunch of psychics get a feeling late one night that something arrived from who knows where. Princess Dulay hires you when one dies of undetermined causes. Another is murdered in the street, screaming that someone is after her. Who it is is unclear, although you and the princess have this theory it's aliens. She's among several prominent people who die mysteriously the same night. I knew three of them, by the way. Your hotel burns down when you're not there. Witnesses report seeing blue flashes of light." He paused to peer at me. "Why were you living in a shithole like that?"

"Divorce," I said.

He looked sympathetic. "It's murder what they do to men these days. But back to business. Two men in a blue car are seen driving up and down the street by the princess's home. Throw the big communication blackout into the mix. A television personality behaves queerly. Her family can't figure it out. Her dog growls at her. The FBI thinks the princess is nutty as a fruitcake. Stir well and what do you get?"

Danforth couldn't have summed it up better. The difference was, Cox wasn't laughing. He frowned, waiting to see if I had anything to add.

"She thinks her home is being watched." I hesitated. "So do I. It's a feeling you get."

"Ordinarily," Cox said in a steely way, "I'd have you thrown out on your ear. But Princess Dulay is an amazing person. Did Harriet tell you she predicted we'd be married?"

"Yes."

"Hadn't even met yet. How's that for calling a shot?" He

walked back to his desk. "That's not the only time, either. I could tell stories about her predictions that would blow you away. I wouldn't be standing in this office without her. She told me once—well, never mind what. She's the real goods. But that's off the record. You don't want voters to believe you think there's anything to the occult." He left the window and settled into his chair with a sigh. Cox gazed off in space for a minute. "I owe the princess a lot. If it makes her feel better, I'll talk to the director. I'll say privately I'm disappointed the agency is kissing this off. I'll tell him I might have to go back into his budget and squeeze a little more fat out." His smile was malicious. "That turns a burner on under their butts."

I went over to the Hall of Justice afterward to look up Bryce Bergen. He was drinking coffee and reading the sports page. He looked up. "Look who's back. You see that game on TV yesterday? Fantastic."

"I was there."

"You lucky bastard. What a comeback. The papers call it the best game in years. The problem with TV is you don't get the whole experience. You've got to be part of the crowd to get it all."

"I had to leave in the third quarter."

Bergen couldn't believe it. "You missed the best part. They couldn't have got me out of there with dynamite."

I changed the subject. "You have time to read the paper and drink coffee? What about all the pressure from the mayor?"

He smiled over his paper cup. "As we speak, a network of informants provides leads as highly trained investigators explore them under my direction."

"I'm serious. What happened to the mayor and his announcement?"

"Search me. Maybe the chief talked him into being reasonable for a change."

"So are you guys getting anywhere?"

"We found the car that ran down the laboratory boss. That's about it."

"It's nice the mayor's being so patient. Is the chief still asking about the ABC's of running his own department?"

"Find a captain to ask. I'm staying out of that."

I thought of Kathy Birkshire. "Funny how the mayor's being reasonable all of a sudden. Six high-profile murders."

"Five. You're counting the medium. It turned out the mayor didn't know her after all." He let out a sigh. "It won't last." He had the veteran cop's fatalism. Things might get better now and then, but the long-term trend is down the crapper.

I remembered reading a story about Chief Blas getting a seventy-foot schooner ready for his retirement. "Are he and the wife still planning to sail off into the sunset in a couple of years?"

"I think so," Bergen said. "But he doesn't really confide his hopes and dreams to me. I think I make him shy."

"Did the Fire Department figure out the cause of the Ajax fire?"

He shrugged. "Arson's what I heard. I mentioned your theory about aliens but it didn't fly."

"You did?"

"Cross my heart."

I said to stick it where the sun don't shine. He went back to the paper and I left.

I drove to the Marina, parked my car, and asked the harbormaster which berth was Chief Blas's. "Who wants to know?" he asked. He was an old salt with a fringe of white hair and a pink face. I showed him my badge.

"You're supposed to show me, without I ask. The chief

doesn't want every nut case who shows up knowing where he lives. Berth seventy-two." He turned back to watching sailboats through the window. It didn't look like he had much else to do. The civil service can be great.

"Are he and his wife still living on the boat while they get it ready?"

"Yup. Haven't seen much of her lately, though."

"Did she go somewhere?" I asked casually.

"Must have. You see her most days when the weather's good, painting or varnishing topside. Works below when it's not. Might be she's visiting family."

The floating dock jerked underfoot as I walked to where the schooner rode in its berth. A dozen gulls sat on a railing at the deep turning basin opposite. The water heaved glassily, as if something huge had blundered into the harbor and circled below looking for the way out. The dock rose and fell a couple of inches at a time. Those gulls not grooming themselves stared at me with lidless eyes. Their heads turned to keep a bead on me as I walked. They reminded me of spectators at a sports event that had lost its interest for them.

Blas and his wife had done a lot of work to restore their schooner, but they still had plenty to do. Buckets and tools lay around. I stepped onto their teak deck to look around. The hatch was closed and locked. I knocked a couple of times but there was silence.

The first gull hit me on the back of the head as I stepped back to the dock. Its bill felt like a stiletto. The air whistled through pinions as wings beat at my shoulders. Then they were all around me, a blizzard of white, hovering and shrieking. I struck at them but they drove me backward on the bucking dock toward the water's edge. Something was rising to the surface.

I bent beneath the swirl of gulls and lunged forward. Whatever was in the water exploded into the air behind me and half landed on the dock with a splintering sound. The dock leaped and reeled underfoot. I nearly went down as the birds screamed and hammered me with their wings. I was like a crust being fought over. I broke into a stumbling run toward the harbormaster's office, the birds all around. They rose and dove to attack again and again. One hooked claws to my shoulder and tried to stab out my nearest eye before I knocked him off.

"Jesus, hang on!" a voice yelled. The harbormaster ran with a broom. He swung it like a bat, hitting a couple of the gulls and making them squawk. The rest rose and circled, as if calculating angles for the next dive. The old man followed me into the office and slammed the door.

"What the hell," he said with a gasp. "Are you hurt?"

"Am I bleeding anywhere?" I panted.

He looked me over. "Your coat's torn a couple of places, but I don't see blood. Damn, I never saw anything like that. Thirty years watching gulls and I never saw them go after a man. What happened?"

"There was no warning." I sat down.

"Look at them up there." I followed his gaze up to the skylight. "Damned if they don't look like they want more. Think I ought to call 911?" He reached for the telephone.

The skylight blew in and a white blur shot down with the falling glass. The gull's beak drove into the harbormaster's shoulder like a bayonet. He yelled. "Yaw!"

I grabbed the bird by its neck and yanked the beak out. I gave it a spin, breaking the neck. I threw it against the wall.

The harbormaster sank to the floor. "Help me. It hurts bad."

I remembered I was armed. I pulled the .38 from the shoulder holster and fired through the wreckage of the skylight, knocking a gull from the sky with an explosion of feathers. The rest wheeled higher. I stooped alongside the harbormaster. He had a hand clamped on his shoulder to stop the welling blood. His previously pink face was white as chalk.

I dialed 911. "There's been a shooting at the harbormaster's office in the Marina," I said. "Robbery." I hung up before the operator could ask questions. I didn't want to waste time explaining about birds. I ran toward the parking lot. A man and a woman with a picnic hamper shrank together when they saw the gun.

"There's a man hurt back there!" I yelled. "He needs help!" The gulls were spiraling upward in lazy circles.

By the time I turned the car out of the parking lot onto Marina Boulevard, I heard a siren's wail. I pulled onto Doyle Drive leading to the Golden Gate Bridge and put the pedal to the floor. I got off at the Park Presidio and headed south toward the avenues. When I ran my hand through my hair, I felt tiny bits of glass. I turned at Geary and pulled over. I couldn't get the shaking to stop for a long time.

If the aliens could take over humans, why not animals? That explained the Hitchcock scene at the Marina. The gull that came through the skylight was after me. Coming through the glass had thrown its aim off and the harbormaster got nailed instead. I wondered what that thing was in the turning basin. Great white sharks bred off the Farallon Islands outside the Golden Gate and sometimes attacked surfers along the coast. But I never heard of any inside the Gate, much less a yacht basin.

I thought of Queenie, the cat that the princess and Alice spoiled. I started the car and drove until I spotted a pay phone. I telephoned Princess Dulay. "Put the cat outside," I said. "I'll explain later."

"But . . ."

"I gotta go." I hung up. Fear sometimes gives off a physical stink and I smelled it on me now. I didn't want her psychic antenna picking up how scared shitless I was. Only a thread kept her from falling apart as it was.

A tavern across the street was lit inside by beer signs. People sat by themselves studying the bottles on the other side of the bar, as if waiting for them to speak. A jukebox played sad country-western ballads about two-timing lovers and waking up on the floor. I ordered a scotch. Men die of heart attacks from lesser shocks than I just had. I knocked back half my drink and asked where the phone was. There were three messages on the answering machine at the office. Danforth was on his way to San Francisco and didn't sound too happy. Jeb Birkshire wanted me to call. He wasn't happy either. The last was from Mike Deutsch at Stanford. It seemed ten years had passed since I saw him. Whatever he had dug up didn't interest me much anymore.

I felt like a drowning man. Each flail of an arm seemed to take me into deeper water instead of toward shore. As far as I knew, I was the only person with evidence of an alien invasion. The odds against that were roughly six billion to one, six billion being the number of people on Earth.

"Evidence" was the wrong word. All I had was a crazy theory and a string of odd occurrences, any one of which could be laughed off or explained away. I wouldn't get a hearing on even *Oprah* or *Sally Jessy* unless I showed up the day they featured people in the grip of strange delusions.

My guess was Danforth wouldn't land in a very good mood. His ears were probably still red from the blistering his boss gave him about the need to stay on Congressman Cox's good side. Telling him about the gulls and that monster of the deep would not be a good idea. There are limits to what people will put up with. But maybe there was one worry I could do something about. I telephoned Maureen.

"I need to see you."

"What about?" She was wary.

"I can't go into it over the telephone."

"We're not supposed to meet."

"Pick a place. It won't take long."

"Tell me what it's about." Somebody fired the jukebox up again. "What's that music? Are you in a bar?"

"I stopped to use the phone. Look, it's important. Really important. I wouldn't call if it wasn't."

She was silent.

"Maureen, I'm begging."

She knew me well enough to tell I wasn't faking. "Okay, when do you want to meet?"

"A half hour from now."

"That soon?"

"That soon," I said.

"Well," she said cautiously, "all right. I'll meet you at Bistrot M on Fifth Street."

I went to the bank and got the rest of the cash from the safety deposit box. I stuck it in an envelope and put it in my inside coat pocket. I parked in the public garage at Fifth and Mission opposite the newspaper and walked in Bistrot M. I ordered a Pelligrino. She walked in a few minutes later and slid onto the next stool, wearing jeans and a North Beach leather jacket. She looked great.

"This better be good." She also wore her don't-shit-me look. She glanced at the fizzy water in my glass. "You shouldn't drink that stuff. You know it gives you gas."

"Never mind that. I want you to take the boy and go to Hawaii for a couple of weeks. On me."

Her total surprise would have seemed comic under other circumstances.

"You know that place on the Big Island we love?" I said. "Why not go there?"

"With you?" she said freezingly.

"Just you and Brady. Take your mother if you want." I put the envelope on the bar in front of her. "There's the money."

She looked inside and saw the thick stack of hundred-dollar bills. "Where did you get that?"

"A client. My printing press was destroyed in the fire."

Sarcasm is almost always a mistake. Maureen swung from the heels at that one.

"I never understood why you lived there in the first place. All those derelicts. I'm not surprised it burned down. It was as if you wanted to debase yourself."

I knew what was coming next. "The way I debased you," I said tiredly. The bartender was a young guy in a starched white uniform jacket and black bow tie. He stopped polishing glasses and moved down the bar out of earshot.

"All right," she blazed. "Yes, the way you debased me with your sordid love affairs."

"I was showing how sorry I was by living there. Okay, it was stupid."

"Sorry for fucking those sluts? I still can't understand how you could do that to me. I had the doctor check me for sexually transmitted disease. I don't suppose you bothered to use condoms?"

This was ground plowed so many times we were down to bedrock. "I've said I was sorry a thousand times, and I'll make it a million before I'm through. But there's no time to go into that now."

"Why do you hate marriage?"

"I don't. I want to be married. To you."

"You told a different story when you came out of surgery."

"What? When I broke my back?"

"In the recovery room. You said awful things. How you'd like to be free."

This was new ground. "I don't remember that."

"You were still groggy. I didn't say anything at the time, but I was hurt by it."

"You can't hold that against me, for God's sake. People say anything when they're out of their head."

Maureen ignored that. "Even when you were home, you

weren't really home. You were on the phone or you were too tired to talk. You just watched TV. Typical male behavior."

"Why bring this up again?"

"I was talking to my therapist. She said it was one of my unresolved issues."

"Can we deal with it some other time?"

"Why do you want us to go to Hawaii?" She sounded like a prosecutor trying to trap a witness in a lie.

"I'm working on a case."

"You're always working on something. That was a big part of the problem."

"The case has some people who could be dangerous. I'd just feel better if you and Brady went away for a while to be on the safe side."

"Who are they?"

"The Mafia. You never know with them."

"But we're divorced."

"I know. The odds are overwhelming nothing will happen. Still, I'd feel better, and Hawaii's great this time of year." I wished somebody was trying to talk me into going to the sun-kissed tropics. I'd be gone like a shot.

She read my face, looking for an ulterior motive. I smiled back as innocent as the washed lamb. "All right," Maureen said suddenly. "Mom's had a cold for weeks. Maybe she can shake it with sun. I'll have to get lesson plans from school for Brady." Maureen got out a notepad and pen. She was a great one for lists. "I need someone to watch the dog. How long do we stay?"

"I'll let you know." I tried a little humor. "It's not as if you have to go to Bakersfield." She struggled against a smile.

"A couple weeks out of school and on the beach should make up for the Forty-niner game," I said. "Or however long."

"I'll tell the school it's a family emergency."

I kissed her on the cheek. She didn't pull back, as I feared.

Maybe I had taken the first step on the long comeback road. Maureen never doubted I loved her. It sounds sexist, but in my opinion most women will forgive just about anything if a third party isn't stirring things up. "I gotta run," I said. "Maybe you could leave tomorrow?"

"That soon?"

"Just throw some bathing suits into a suitcase. Buy what you need there."

Doubt clouded her face. "This isn't some trick? You seem jumpy."

"How can it be a trick? Don't even tell me where you're staying if you like. Call when you feel like it."

I left her to her list before any more misgivings came up. I drove to Pacific Heights and parked one street over from Princess Dulay's house. I walked to the house that backed up to hers and strolled up the driveway as if I owned it. I climbed a gate, passed through the backyard, and scaled the wall beyond. I reached the back door and knocked. Alice looked through the window and unlocked the door.

"Mr. Armstrong, how did you—"

"I climbed the wall."

"Oh."

Princess Dulay was on the telephone in her study. The TV was on as usual and she reached to shut it off.

"No, leave it on," I said. A woman gave the news. No progress on the chain of murders and still no explanation for the communication blackout. An astronomer who was interviewed said the sunspot theory was "total nonsense." A city employee had been stabbed in the harbormaster's office in an apparent robbery and was at San Francisco General Hospital. He was in a coma and not expected to live. In an odd twist, Chief Blas himself happened to be in the neighborhood when the call came and was first on the scene. The chief had taken personal charge of the initial investigation. *Action News* had learned a lone gunman was being sought.

I've seen a lot of wounds. No way the harbormaster's was life-threatening.

"The poor man," Princess Dulay said. She had hung up the receiver.

"I was there when it happened."

Her hand went to her mouth. "You were?"

I nodded. "Did you put Queenie outside, like I said?"

"It made Alice very upset."

"If aliens can take over people, why not animals?"

Understanding dawned. "There's no reason why not."

"I was attacked by birds at the yacht harbor and something came up out of the water after me. A shark, I think."

Princess Dulay couldn't hold it in anymore. She screamed and kept screaming. Alice threw open the door and ran to her side. Princess Dulay finally stopped. "Queenie might be one of them," she said, sobbing.

"Oh, that's taking things too far," Alice said sharply. She shot me a resentful look. "I've known that cat ten years. She's no different than she ever was."

"That could change," I said.

"That poor, innocent cat," Alice said. People watch war's carnage on TV or see masses dying of starvation and don't bat an eye. But if an animal is involved, they get emotional. "Why does Queenie have to be dragged into this?" It was the first time I saw Alice have an opinion.

"Luck, I guess," I answered, "same as the rest of us."

"There are limits."

"What are they? I'd feel a lot better if I knew."

She left the room without answering. Her back was stiff.

"I don't know how much more I can take," the princess said exhaustedly. She put a hand to her forehead.

"I got a call from Birkshire," I said. "He wants to meet." He had sounded guarded when I returned his call.

"Are you going to tell him that thing is not his wife?"

"Maybe he'll tell me." We could use some company. A man like Birkshire would have connections. When I called, Birkshire asked if we could have lunch tomorrow. "Green's?" I said "sure."

"Poor man, and those dear children. What will happen to them?" She dabbed at her eyes with a handkerchief.

I went upstairs to my room to call Deutsch. He asked how I was. I said I'd been better.

"I got something to tell you."

"Go ahead."

"I'd rather it was in person."

"You want to drive up now?"

"No, I gotta crash. I've been up thirty-six hours." His yawn into the receiver made the point.

"I'm having lunch at Green's tomorrow. Want to meet me there afterward?"

"That vegetarian place run by the Zen guys?"

I said that was the one and he promised to be there. "It's pretty weird, what I'm gonna tell you."

More weirdness was something to look forward to. I went down to the kitchen and made myself a sandwich. I was eating it when Princess Dulay walked in. "I don't understand it," she said. I put the sandwich down.

"I saw a crystal cat on the shopping channel. I thought it would be nice for Alice. Help make up for Queenie having to stay outside. I called to order it."

"And?"

"They said my Visa account was canceled."

"They do that when you don't pay the bill."

She was huffy. "I pay my accounts promptly. I gave the

operator my American Express card number. That was canceled, too. Same with my MasterCard."

I thought for a minute. "Where do you bank?"

"Wells Fargo. The Union Street branch."

"Call and get the status of your account." I followed her to her study. She dialed the bank and asked for her checking account balance. She frowned. "What about savings?" She put the receiver down and looked at me. "Both are empty. I had seven hundred and fifty thousand in CDs and thirteen thousand in checking."

"Do you have any money around the house?"

"A few hundred dollars, that's all. I do have some bearer bonds. They're like cash."

"How much?"

"I don't know. Twenty thousand, probably."

"Get them. We're going to your bank."

So they had figured out a person was just about helpless without money. I wondered if they were amused by how primitive that was. Or probably they had advanced beyond being amused. Princess Dulay led me to a safe hidden in a paneled wall in another room. She punched in some numbers and its door swung open. She removed the bonds and got on her coat.

"We'll go in your car. Mine's parked the next block over."

"What is the matter?" she asked. "What has happened to my money and my credit? It's the last straw, as God is my witness."

She told Alice we were going out. She gave me the keys and we walked downstairs to the door to the garage. I pulled out my gun before turning the doorknob. There was a sound like a rat scurrying, but I didn't see anything. We got in her Mercedes and I hit the door opener on her sun visor. The garage door rose to a street empty except for parked cars.

The branch manager spotted Princess Dulay when we

walked through the doorway and made a beeline, a smile on his face. They shook hands, I was introduced, and he escorted us to his office.

"What can we do for you today?" he said brightly when we were seated. He was an elfin man in a sober banker's suit. A little sign on his desk said he was Arthur Hartley.

"Two things. I need to cash these." She handed over the bonds.

"Yes, indeed," he said, examining them.

"And I want to know why there's no money in my CD or savings accounts."

Hartley looked like he had been hit. "That's not possible." He sat at a computer terminal, and his fingers tapped the keys. "I don't understand." He beckoned another man into his office and pointed at the computer screen. "What do you make of this?"

"Everything's in order," he said. "A standard wire transfer. All the authorizations are there. Password, codes, and the rest of it."

"I didn't authorize anything," Princess Dulay said firmly.

The man didn't seem to hear. "Currency speculation is my guess. They say that bank is often used for that purpose."

"Princess Dulay does not speculate in currency," Hartley said.

"I most certainly do not."

"You would have something in writing with her signature authorizing wire transfers, right?" I put in.

"Yes, of course. I'll get it." We watched him go to a bank of file drawers and rummage around. He came back looking puzzled. "There's nothing on file."

"The bank is embarrassed," Hartley said. "I promise we'll get to the bottom of this."

"In the meantime," I said, "what about the money she had here?"

Hartley flushed. "Our hands are tied until we get the answers." He looked at the princess. "I'm deeply sorry."

Princess Dulay rose with her jaw set. "Then perhaps you'll be good enough to cash my bonds."

"Yes," Hartley said humbly. He set off in a dog trot to the walk-in safe at the rear of the bank. He came back a moment later with a stack of currency. Princess Dulay watched grimly as he counted the money out, then she stuck it in her purse. She turned on her heel and left the bank like a stately liner leaving a hellish Third World port behind. If she'd had stacks, smoke would be coming out.

"Her lawyer will be in touch," I told Hartley.

"Nothing like this has ever happened at this branch." He looked around the bank as if already trying to guess who the embezzler was.

I caught up to Princess Dulay outside. She was walking fast. "I'll sue," she said.

"Maybe it's not the bank."

She gave me a scared look. "You think it's the aliens?"

"The bank doesn't have anything to do with your credit cards, right?"

"No. But what's the point of stealing my money?"

"Maybe you're an experiment."

"What kind of experiment?"

"To see what makes us tick. They're still feeling their way around. They've figured out money talks. Maybe they want to find out just how loud. Maybe they want to see what happens to you when yours is gone. They've got to be pleasantly surprised nobody's pushed the panic button yet. Maybe they think we're so stupid they've got time to play mind games to study how we react."

"You're just guessing," she burst out. "That's all you're doing is guessing."

There was no point in denying that, so we walked to her

car in silence. We passed two men wearing parkas in a parked blue Taurus three cars down from her Mercedes. The princess didn't notice and I didn't say anything. I unlocked the door for her, then went around to the driver's side and let myself in. I started the car. We sat with the engine idling.

"What are you waiting for?" she asked impatiently.

"For the bus behind to pass."

She looked back. "It's a block away. You've got plenty of time."

"Trust me."

When the graffiti-smeared side of the bus passed, I stomped on the gas and yanked the Mercedes out of the parking spot. We squealed to the opposite side of the two-lane street. I threw the car into reverse and finished the full turn with smoking tires. The driver of a Coca-Cola truck following the bus stood on his brakes and blasted the air horn. I looked in the rearview mirror as we fishtailed west on Union Street. The Taurus was pinned to its parking spot as the bus let off passengers.

I hung a right down Divisadero toward Lombard. I shot a quick look at the princess. She was white-faced. I sped downhill two blocks, then did a controlled skid into another right turn.

"Why are you doing this?" she screeched.

"Standard security measure," I yelled.

"You could kill someone."

I slid my gun out of its holster as we approached her garage and hit the door opener so we didn't have to wait on the street. I drove in, and the door closed behind. "Stay inside," I said. "Let me check around." The garage was silent and empty. "Okay, c'mon."

She unlocked the connecting door with a key and we closed it behind us. When we were upstairs, she sank into a chair. "Send Alice."

I looked through the house but didn't find her. On the third floor, I looked out the window down onto the backyard. Alice sat in a chair under a tree with Queenie in her lap. I raised the window and shouted for her. She put the cat down.

There is something about stress that doesn't get mentioned much. That is how it drains you. This is why in combat you see soldiers sleeping every chance they get, even standing up. It is as if they have narcolepsy. I had been stressed out and not getting enough sleep for days, and that Indy 500 sprint from the bank pushed me over the edge. I was suddenly totally wiped out. My head buzzed and I felt as if my feet moved in molasses. I was no good to anybody in this shape. Alice could take care of her boss without me. I went to my room, locked the door, and fell face flat on the bed.

It was nearly dark when I snapped awake, instantly alert. The house was too quiet. I stood at my door, listening. My shotgun leaned against the wall near the bed. I got the gun and silently unlocked the door. It was past the time Alice went through the house with candles. I checked across the hall in the princess's room, but it was empty. I stood at the top of the stairs. Silence.

I went downstairs and opened the door to her study. Princess Dulay sat in a chair in the darkness, light from the window showing her wide eyes. There was reason for surprise this time. Her mouth was open, and a second was agape just below, two black circles of astonishment. Her dress front was covered with blood from the huge slash. There couldn't be much that held head to body. My feet stepped in something sticky.

"Yiiiiiiiiiiiiiiiiiiiii!"

If Alice hadn't screamed as she lunged, I think she would have gotten me with the knife. I jumped and my trigger finger jerked. The blue muzzle flash showed the uplifted knife and her face twisted with insane rage. The blast knocked her back. The knife pinged as it hit the floor. I groped in the blackness until I found a flashlight on the princess's desk and shined it on Alice. There was no more need to take her pulse than Princess Dulay's. She lay flat on her back with her arms spread out.

I might have stood there frozen in shock quite a while if the smell of gas hadn't reached me. I stuck my head out the door and it was stronger. Alice had probably tried my door and decided it would be safer to blow up the place and me with it. Another ten or fifteen minutes and the buildup of gas would have been enough. I found Princess Dulay's purse. The money was still there. I stuck it in my pocket. Holding my breath, I went downstairs and through the kitchen, where gas hissed from every burner and the open oven and out the back door. I cranked another shell into the chamber when I got outside. I climbed the back wall and went through the neighbor's yard and driveway to the next street. I was sticking the key into the car door when lights came on up the street. The blue Taurus gunned down the street toward me. By the time I got the shotgun raised, it had covered half the distance.

Deep breath, steady the sight.

Squeeze the trigger. KA-BLAM.

I put the first round in the windshield on the driver's side. The car veered to the left, ramming a parked Jaguar and richocheting back to the middle of the street.

Still holding that breath. KA-BLAM.

The second went into the windshield on the passenger's side. The Taurus rammed a car on the opposite side of the street and fishtailed around so it faced the opposite direction. I got into my car and started it. When I pulled away, porch lights were coming on all over the neighborhood.

ulhenny kept a bottle of scotch in a glassed-in book-case filled with books he had bought by the yard in the hope clients would think he was deep. He smoked a pipe for the same reason. I found a glass that wasn't too dirty and poured a stiff one, just like Sam Spade.

I felt rotten about Princess Dulay. I had kept her alive for a few days, but she still got it in the end. Tired as I was, the alarm bells should have gone off when I saw Alice with the cat.

I had thought about calling the fire department to say the house was full of gas and about to blow, but decided against it. Explaining away two dead women is tough under the best of circumstances, and "best" didn't describe mine. The explosion would buy a little time. The bodies wouldn't be found until firemen went through the rubble.

Maybe Queenie wasn't how Alice got taken over. Maybe they had another way of taking possession and there was no way I could have known. The red light was blinking on the answering machine. I hit the playback button and heard Danforth say he was staying at the downtown Hilton and could we meet for breakfast tomorrow.

The Hilton was an island of light in the menacing darkness of the Tenderloin. A ghostly fog was coming in, making the streets look even more scary. I called Danforth on the house phone and said I was in the lobby.

"I'm just about to sack out."

"It's only eight fucking o'clock."

"It's eleven o'clock East Coast time. Like I said, let's have breakfast."

"I might not be around tomorrow."

Bed versus duty. He gave out an impatient sigh. "All right, come on up."

Danforth wore striped pajamas, slippers, and the kind of maroon silk robe a man gets for Father's Day. He was strapping and had strong, square features that looked like they had been chiseled from good stone. We shook hands and he motioned me to a chair.

"Sorry to drop by so late," I said.

"No problem. You want something? The room's got one of those little bars. A beer?"

I said no thanks. "Glad you could make it out here."

"This is one of my favorite cities." He had a confident manner. It said even crazy people didn't faze him. He squared a yellow pad and three sharp pencils on the table. "So fill me in."

"It's hard to know where to start." A golf bag with clubs stood in a corner. It looked like he didn't expect to work too hard.

"You know how we say the beginning's a good place?" he said. We smiled, one cop to another.

"You're going to think this is nuts."

"I've heard a lot of strange things in my time." He chuckled tolerantly.

"Nothing like this."

"We'd deny it, but the bureau has worked with psychics in

kidnapping cases. So we're not exactly virgins. Congressman Cox mentioned Princess Dulay to the director. She's afraid someone is after her?" An eyebrow lifted. "Aliens?"

"She's not afraid anymore. She's dead."

The eyebrow went down. "What?"

"Her companion slit her throat. It happened tonight."

His brow furrowed officially. "Some sort of domestic problem?"

"It would be nice if it was that easy."

"Meaning?"

"Aliens killed her."

His eyes flickered toward the nightstand, where his service revolver lay in its holster, and came back to me. I could tell he kicked himself for not sticking it in his robe pocket.

"You saw this happen?"

"No."

"Then how do you know?"

"The companion was possessed by the aliens, like others here. The chief of police and probably the mayor. A television anchorwoman. There've got to be others I don't know about."

Danforth nodded as if he heard this sort of thing every day before noon. "Like some coffee? It might wake me up. I'll call room service." The phone was next to his gun.

I pulled mine from the shoulder holster. "I know what you're thinking."

Danforth turned pale. "Now, wait a minute."

"I don't want you going for your gun."

"Why would I do that?"

"You think I'm psycho. I would, too, if I were listening to this."

"I have a wife and family."

"You won't get hurt unless you try something stupid. I just want you to listen."

"That's what I'm here for." His smile was sickly.

"I found Princess Dulay dead. Alice nearly took her head off with a knife. I was sleeping upstairs. Some bodyguard, right?"

"Alice?"

"The companion. She came at me and I had to blow her away."

"So she's dead, too?"

"As dead as the princess. Maybe more so. She turned the gas on to blow up the house to get me."

Keep him talking, he was thinking. "The house didn't blow?"

"I don't know. I got out of there. Some guys in a blue Taurus have been following me. They were waiting when I got to my car. I put a couple of rounds through their windshield with a shotgun. They stopped, but I don't know if I got them."

"This all happened tonight?"

"Just a little while ago."

"And the police know?"

"I don't know what they know. Not as much as you at this point."

"I see."

I decided to give him the rest. "That's not all. I was attacked by seagulls and a shark today at the marina."

His eyes went yearningly to his gun. "Okay," he said, licking his lips, "you were attacked."

"Sounding crazier by the minute, right?" I was almost starting to enjoy it.

"Yeah, well," he said hopelessly.

"I want you to check some things out."

Hope flickered. Maybe I wouldn't shoot him down like a dog when I was finished with my raving. "I'm eager to do what I can."

"Find out how many people in the psychic community are missing." Danforth made a note on the yellow pad.

"Check," he said.

"Find out what's killing the harbormaster, if he's not dead already."

"The harbormaster?" he asked timidly.

"One of the gulls came through the skylight and stuck him with its beak. He's at San Francisco General. I saw the wound. It wasn't enough to kill him. Something else is wrong."

"I'll sure look into it."

"Find out who the two guys in the Taurus are. It would be interesting to know who they work for."

He wrote that down.

"Check out this TV anchor, Kathy Birkshire. Talk to her husband. He'll tell you she's changed. Check out the mayor and police chief and find out where their wives are. Both these guys are acting different and are probably possessed. My bet is their wives are dead." Danforth wrote furiously. "There were a bunch of murders of prominent people. There's got to be a connection there."

"Right." Danforth pretended he was beginning to be fired with enthusiasm.

"Princess Dulay's bank account was looted and her credit cards canceled. If we can find out who did that, we'll have another piece of the puzzle."

When he finished writing, he looked up expectantly.

"That should keep you busy for a while," I said. "Somebody's got to help me. One man can't carry the whole load. Are you going to stay here?" He nodded.

"I'll call. You'll try to trace it, so it will be short and sweet and from a pay phone." Danforth looked about to deny he was capable of such treachery, but thought better of it.

"Anything else?" he asked.

I went to the nightstand, took his gun out of the holster,

and put it in my pocket. "The government will buy you another."

"You're leaving?" Danforth couldn't hide his relief.

"Stay in your room five minutes." I smiled thinly. "Consider me armed and dangerous."

I went out into the hall. An elderly couple waited at the elevator with backs to me. As I joined them, the woman turned and smiled.

"You might be better off using the stairs," she said. "This darned thing's taking forever."

Just then the elevator doors opened. "Finally," her husband said. They stepped in and I was following when some instinct stopped me. I stepped back just as the doors slammed like a trap snapping shut.

I didn't want to wait for the next one in case Danforth had another gun stashed somewhere, so I headed for the stairs and took them two at a time. In the lobby, the hotel staff ran back and forth shouting. "What's wrong?" I asked a woman behind the registration counter. She was crying.

"An elevator fell to the basement," she said. "There were people in it. Someone heard them screaming as it went past."

I went to the lobby phone. Danforth's line was busy. That was no surprise. He was probably talking to the cops or the FBI's field office. I dialed the operator and told her it was an emergency and to break in.

"This is Danforth."

"I've got another little mystery for you."

"What do you mean?"

"When I left your room, I started to get on the elevator."

"Yeah?"

"I stopped just in time. There was a man and a woman in it."

"Go on," he said impatiently.

"It dropped to the basement. The two nice old people riding it are history, just like I would've been. Coincidence?

Check it out." I hung up. Danforth wasn't going to have much time for those golf clubs.

I walked quickly through the wet fog to where I parked. How did they know I would be at the Hilton? The lightbulb went on as I was unlocking my car door. Of course. My phone line was tapped. As soon as they heard Danforth's message, they knew I'd pay him a visit and were waiting. But how could they monkey with the elevator that way?

That was easy, too. Our technology had to be a cinch, no more sophisticated to them than rubbing two sticks together to make fire. I got on the freeway and headed south. I had dodged a lot of bullets so far, but I didn't feel any survivor's elation. All it meant was the odds had shortened in favor of the next one scoring a bull's-eye. You are born with only so much luck. When it's gone, generally you are, too.

I pulled off the freeway when I saw a Denny's and got something to eat. It was nine-thirty when I left, sucking a toothpick. I found a Thrifty's and bought toilet articles, underwear, and a change of clothing. It looked like I would be on the run for a while. Then I continued south to Palo Alto. I checked into a motel on El Camino Real, paying cash and giving a phony name and license number. I drove to Mike Deutsch's communal apartment and rang the bell. While I waited for someone to answer, I looked through the window. The pizza cartons were gone. It looked like they had switched to Chinese take-out.

After a minute, Deutsch came to the door frizzy-headed and yawning. He wore a sweat suit. "Oh, hi. I thought we were going to meet tomorrow."

"I was in the vicinity." I moved some junk off a chair and sat down. "What have you got for me?"

He wanted to brag first. Experts like you to know how smart they are. "You know how hard it was cracking into the military's database? They've got security management systems up the wazoo. I had to keep moving around while I figured them out. I was using a computer in Frankfurt when I finally broke through."

"Frankfurt, Germany?"

"Yeah, a research institute there." He saw my puzzled look. "You cover your tracks. Move from country to country, computer to computer. You do that so the FBI doesn't come knocking on the door."

"A German computer can break into our military's database?"

"No, no," he said, running a hand through his hair. "I did the code cracking on parallel Crays at Ann Arbor. I bounced the solution by satellite to the computers I was using to gain access. Ecuador, Iceland, UCLA, University of Kentucky, Trinity College in Dublin. I've got a bunch I use."

"Save the details for later. I've got a lot on my mind."

"What I found out wasn't all that interesting."

"You were going to drive all the way to San Francisco to say that?"

"There was no military alert or whatever you call it on July 17. There was nothing unusual in the archives except about a robot radio-telescope run by the University of North Carolina for the Defense Department."

"What about it?"

"It was listening to radio waves from some galaxy to see how fast it's moving away from the solar system. I don't see why the Defense Department is interested in that, but anyway. All of a sudden, it goes silent. When they get up there a couple days later, they find all the circuits have been totally fried. The thing's a complete loss. Nobody can figure out what went wrong. It's totally strange." Deutsch looked at me hopefully. "Is that what you wanted?"

"I don't know." Danforth could add that to his list. I got up. "Well, thanks for your help."

"Wait a minute, that's not the weird thing."

I sat down again.

"This company that's giving you such a hard time? Security Concerns?"

"What about it?"

"I figured it would be simple to crack into its database. It wasn't. In fact, it looks impossible." He shook his head. "Wild, isn't it? The government with all its money and resources can't keep me out, but some crummy little company nobody ever heard of stops me cold."

"Maybe you burned yourself out."

"No way." He had a far-off look. "And there's something else."

"What is it?"

"When I was logged on today still trying to figure a way, I suddenly had the feeling the screen looked back." He gave a nervous little laugh. "Crazy, isn't it?"

"Looked back?"

"I had the creepy feeling Security Concerns had come through the phone lines to my screen to see who was probing its defenses. It was like there were eyes watching me. I couldn't see them, but they were still there. It was like a . . . presence."

I didn't say anything.

"I knew I shouldn't tell you. You think I've gone funny on you, but swear to God."

"It so happens I'm familiar with the feeling of being watched. When did this happen?"

"Just before I called you. I was about to throw in the towel when it happened. I told myself it was sleep deprivation."

I looked at him. "What if I told you it was aliens?"

"Go ahead, laugh. I shouldn't have told you."

"I'm serious."

He laughed uncertainly.

"Where were you when this happened?"

"At Stanford. The computer center."

"Is there any way to track you back to here?"

"I always sign on as somebody else. It's what you do."

"Who did you sign on as that time?"

"A gnarly guy named Forbes. A real geek. Pimples and plastic pocket protector. Looking like he does, you'd think he'd write better code."

"I'm serious about the aliens." I told him the whole story. He kept shooting me looks that said he was waiting for me to begin laughing. If the memory of that computer screen experience hadn't been so fresh, he probably would have kissed me off as a wacko. The dead people made it real for him.

"Whew," he said after a moment of silence. "I'd be totally freaked out if I were you."

"I'm getting there."

He got up and walked around the room and sat down again. "You'd think the FBI would be more cooperative. I mean, this is what we pay them for, isn't it?"

"They deal with screwballs with insane theories all the time. I'm just one more. But all these dead bodies will make them take things more seriously."

"So, like, are you a fugitive or whatever?"

"They are going to want to talk to me in a major way, if that's what you mean."

"What's it like to kill somebody?"

"You feel better about it when they're trying to kill you."

"So can they pin all this stuff on you and make it stick?"

"A smart lawyer could probably get me off."

"Maybe you ought to hire one."

"He'd tell me to let him do the talking. Then he would want to surrender me to custody. I'm trying to warn people, and you can't do that from a jail cell. The government would keep me silent so I didn't cause a panic."

He nodded. "I can see that. People would be running around scared shitless if they heard there were aliens. But even if they put you in jail, the story would come out sooner or later, wouldn't it?"

"Who knows how much time we've got? These whatever-they-are aren't just fucking around. They've got a plan."

"How do you know?"

"It stands to reason. It's like this whole thing is an experiment."

"What do you mean?"

"A lot of things. Why'd they pick on the psychics first, and why just this area? The credit cards and bank accounts. They're learning how we tick as a society."

"How do you know it's just this area?"

"That big communication blackout. It only hit the San Francisco region. Our visitors wanted to see how easy it is. Taking out the psychics gets rid of the only people able to sense their presence. If they can possess the mayor and the police chief and the people who run the local media, they can do the same to the president, the generals and Congress. All of a sudden they're running the whole show. You refine your technique on a small scale until you're ready for the whole thing. Does this make sense?"

"Sort of," Deutsch said. "But if they're all this advanced, why not just take over without all the messing around?"

"Maybe they're cautious. Going step by step. They've been looking for someplace that looks promising. Maybe they're not sure this is it. In case it isn't, they don't want to get into a situation they can't get out of. It could be they're blown away by how many of us there are. Our sheer numbers might spook them. Or our primitive nature. We might be like savages with bones in our noses to them. If they scare us too much, we hit the nuclear button and make the place unlivable."

"But if they've got the know-how you say, they could stop us from doing that," Deutsch said.

"I'm just thinking aloud off the top of my head."

He nodded. "So if they pick off the elites, they manipulate the outcome they want? We lay down and they can take over, or whatever?"

"Or whatever."

"That might explain Security Concerns," he said.

I had forgotten them. "What do you mean?"

"Private investigators find out things that don't want to be found out. The aliens could control what government checks out with cops and others by taking over the people at the top. But you guys don't answer to a central authority."

"So?"

"They eliminate your threat by pricing you out of business. Maybe they've read Adam Smith and know how capitalism works. All that stuff is on CD-ROM now. Any university library has it."

"That sounds pretty far-fetched."

"Far-fetched? *You're* telling me something's far-fetched?"

I saw what he meant.

Actually, it didn't seem like a bad theory. Security Concerns had come out of the blue like the aliens. I had been right in thinking nobody could be that efficient in digging up stuff. Or so cheap, either. Nobody human, anyhow.

"I knew you were brainy, but I wasn't sure you were smart," I told Deutsch.

"Thanks, I guess."

I got up to go. "What happens now?" Deutsch asked.

"You tell me. I'm making this up as I go."

"Anything else I can do?"

"I'll let you know." A thought occurred to me. "Maybe you better get out of town."

"Huh? Why?"

"Just to be on the safe side."

"I've got midterms coming up. I can't just blow them off. My parents would have a fit."

The Hole: I wake up sobbing, the deep kind that tears at your throat. It could be afternoon or six in the morning. They say confusion about time happens in extreme isolation. The body adopts its own cycle. I haven't heard the radio and Skywatch One for some time now. They want to drive me crazy.

Or maybe that is why I'm here—I'm a mental case and was locked up. Did any of the awful things I remember really happen, or did I make them up? I hold my head and rock back and forth.

Maybe the cycles of clear-mindedness and mental fog are really from treatment. I read somewhere that electroshock therapy causes amnesia. There are demonstrations against it in places like Berkeley. It went out of style but made a comeback. Maybe attendants come in and pump the juice through me a couple of times a week. Electroshock wipes memory clean and even changes personality. I'm not a weeper. Or at least I wasn't before. It could be I'm so loony the doctors can't help. Maybe my subconscious has finally owned up to it and that is the reason for this crying jag.

The food tray is by the door. It wasn't there a minute ago, but I've had my face in the pillow. It is damp from tears. Maybe it was more than a minute ago. A sandwich, drink, and salad, as usual. And something new. A blue pill that says multivitamin in tiny red letters. I toss it down the toilet. I may be crazy but I'm not stupid.

I peel back the bread from habit to see what is in the sandwich. A tiny piece of paper is under the ham. "Hang in there," it says. It is signed "Danforth."

I drove back to San Francisco the morning after I talked to Deutsch and checked into one of the motels off Lombard that cater to budget travelers. The room had a stove and refrigerator for a break from fast food. I called Maureen but got the answering machine. Her voice said she and Brady would be gone for a while but she would be checking messages. *"Aloha,"* she said.

I disguised my voice. "This is Mike at Quality Dry Cleaning. Your clothes are ready."

I had stopped at the storage place and picked up my old uniform and the rest of my police harness and changed at the motel. I drove downtown and parked in a financial district garage. I walked to the security office on the first floor where two guards slumped in chairs staring at monitors that showed people walking in and out of doorways. Their job was keeping out bums. Their eyes had the glaze of the terminally bored.

"Who's in charge this morning?" I asked briskly. They straightened up when they saw my uniform.

"Lieutenant Macaffey," one answered. He pointed to a door. Rank has its privilege, and in this case it was sitting with feet up reading the sports section. Macaffey looked at me in blank surprise and then put his shoes down on the floor. The others wore nylon jackets with fur collars, but he rated a blue blazer with a patch on the breast pocket that said First-Rate Security.

"Yes, sir," he said. He was a balding, tubby guy in his fifties, old enough to have had a career in something else, maybe the defense industry before the cutbacks. You see a lot of former engineers and systems analysts his age in security.

I closed the door. "I'm Lieutenant Masters. We've got a problem in this building."

"I don't know anything about it," he said automatically. The job might lack mental stimulation, but his look said he wanted to hang on to it.

"You've got a tenant called Security Concerns."

He nodded. "Real standoffish people."

"They're having a problem with a former employee."

"Yeah?" His eyebrows went up.

"They want us to find out how secure their office is. Whether it can be broken into."

"The main entrance is the only door that's unlocked after six. Everybody signs in after that. Give me a name and I'll have the night shift watch for him."

"It's not that easy. This guy's a former executive who was fired. Real smart, they say. Also very smooth."

"Fired, huh? Got a grudge, I bet."

"He didn't take it too well."

"We have supervisors who go around the buildings we contract with. I'll ask for them to come by more often to keep the guys on their toes."

"Not such a good idea. I want this kept between us."

The eyebrows went up again. "How come?"

"We think he's got people helping on the inside. Security

Concerns is trying to weed them out, but you know how that is. They're worried about lawsuits for wrongful termination."

"Lawyers," he said scornfully.

"Who's your counterpart at night?"

"We don't have lieutenants working nights. Just Sil's, which is what we call them."

"What time do they quit at Security Concerns?"

"They tell me pretty late. Midnight, one o'clock some nights. Business must be good."

"You've got a key to their door?"

"They got to give us one and we have the right to enter. It's in the lease."

"Leave it with the guy at the door. I'll come by sometime in the next few nights."

"If you say so." Macaffey was beginning to warm up to the project. "Anything else we can do?"

"I'll let you know."

"Anytime." He smiled.

"This inside help he's got might be pretty high up in the organization. The fewer people know about this, the better."

He looked doubtful. "I have to tell my boss."

"Your call. I wouldn't, though. We're dealing directly with Atlanta on this. He might think it's his duty to get clearance from this office and the whole investigation gets blown out of the water."

He nodded. "Jordine goes by rules, all right. He's ex-military. Not too smart, if you know what I mean."

"Thanks for your cooperation." We shook hands and I left.

I went back to the motel and changed out of my uniform. I walked around the block to a pay phone and dialed Mitzi at the office. "Anyone looking for me?" I asked.

"Nope."

"Mulhenny around?"

"I haven't seen him yet. You got no messages."

I wondered what color her hair was today. "There's a row of pay phones by the elevators in the Town Centre. Be standing by the third one from the left end in fifteen minutes. You can walk there in ten."

"What for?"

"Just be there." I hung up. I bought a latte from a sidewalk vendor. When it was time, I called the pay phone. It was one I used from time to time, and I had the number memorized.

"Hello?" Mitzi asked.

"It's me. I want you to look up a name."

"You couldn't tell me that when I was at the office?"

"I think the line's bugged."

She took in her breath. "Really?" Mitzi wasn't as dumb as she acted. She had a degree in philosophy from Berkeley. Unfortunately, this doesn't qualify you for much more than hanging around coffee shops in black clothing. She came to Mulhenny from a temp agency, expecting she was about to begin an exciting career. It didn't take long to discover that working for a public utility had Mulhenny beat for thrills.

"What's the name?" she asked breathlessly. At last, adventure.

"Maurice Jacobs. I want to know where he lives. The DMV is probably the best place to start." I gave her the phone number where I was and told her to call back in two hours.

Maury Jacobs had been a student radical in the 1970s, one of the movement's premier bomb-makers. He blew up a couple draft offices and a national guard armory before the feds caught him. He did eight years in prison, which cools off most political types. It didn't with Jacobs. He came out still breathing fire, more convinced than ever the government had to be overthrown so the people could rule themselves in harmony. He was a little guy with one leg two inches shorter than the other. What hair he had left was pulled back in a skimpy ponytail. You regularly saw him on TV in demonstrations against this or that. The cameras went right to him, I guess because of the steady look of rage he always had.

Mitzi called back right on schedule. The DMV had Jacobs living in an apartment in Bernal Heights, a working-class neighborhood. "He's got a lot of unpaid parking tickets."

"Anarchists don't pay parking tickets."

A shabby panhandler with one of those handwritten "Will Work for Food" signs sat against a wall near the pay phone. After I hung up, I gave him a buck.

"Thanks, man," he said. "You know, that's weird." He was looking over my shoulder.

"What is?"

"That camera up there that watches traffic."

He pointed to a closed-circuit camera on a telephone pole. The way it was turned, it couldn't monitor the intersection.

"It's looking this way," I said.

"That's what I mean. It just turned. I sit here every day, man, and I never seen it like that. It can't see cars the way it's angled now."

I crossed the street. When I got to the other side, I looked again. The camera had swiveled to keep me in view. I raised my middle finger to it. "Fuck you," I said in case it picked up sound.

They had traced Mitzi's call in the few seconds we were on the line. That was impressive. But tapping into the traffic surveillance system was more impressive. They must be able to do that with any security camera in the country. How many eyes did that give them—millions?

I moved fast. At the corner, I looked back. Every neon sign on my side of the street was on, getting so bright they hurt the eyes even in daylight. Then they all blew at once. A killing rain of glass sliced down. A woman in a pale suit fell to her knees screaming and held hands to her face where bright red blood seemed to leap from dozens of cuts. Stains appeared all over, turning her suit dark. Burglar alarms began to wail. I ran, my heart thudding as if it was going to pound a hole in my chest.

Up the street I was on now the shop signs were getting brighter. I ran to the other side and signs there started doing the same. I smelled ozone, like when lightning is near. I ducked into a laundry. A half-dozen people were reading or folding clothes. The washers and dryers kicked into a higher gear, reaching a shriek as I ran toward the back door. There was a burning smell. The door was locked. I stood back and kicked at it. Those machines were going to explode. The door gave way and I was out into a sort of courtyard. There were a series of whams behind me, like fragmentation grenades going off. I crossed the courtyard to another building and kicked that door open. I ran through a house past a surprised man eating a boiled egg at a table and came out onto a residential street. It had streetlights, but they didn't come on. Maybe they thought they had nailed me in the laundry. I wondered if there were any survivors back there.

Maurice Jacobs didn't live at the address the DMV had for him, and nobody knew him. Eleven hundred-dollar bills and a day later I found him on his hands and knees digging in a community garden.

"Are you Jacobs?" I asked.

He looked me up and down from behind the kind of round steel glasses Lenin wore. "People say you've been handing out hundreds like they were fives."

"You can find anybody if you're willing to spend enough."

"So what do you want?"

"A bomb."

He laughed scornfully. "Try the Pentagon."

"I want something smaller."

"Why can't you people stay off my back? Which fascist police agency are you with?"

"I work for myself. You want to look for a bug?"

He got up and dusted off his hands. His body search was professional.

"Careful of the family jewels," I said.

"So you're not wired," he said when he was finished. "So what?"

"So build me a bomb. I want something big enough to take out a space maybe eighty feet by a hundred feet. I want it simple. I need timers, but I don't want them electronic."

He did the calculations in his head. "You'd need two, something that size."

"Okay, build me two."

He dropped back down to the dirt and began digging again. "I don't do that shit anymore."

"I read somewhere you've got a kid at Harvard."

Anger flared behind the spectacles. "I don't care what they write about me, but they should leave my family out of it."

"Harvard's got to cost a ton."

He dug silently. "She's got a scholarship and has borrowed all she can. She works as a waitress."

"It can't be easy."

"She has to work her ass off," he admitted. "She's tired all the time. Talking about dropping out. The fucking capitalist system."

"I'll give you ten thousand dollars."

He shot a quick look at me. I knew that look.

"Cash," I said. "I want it tomorrow."

"I don't work that fast."

"Otherwise, no deal."

"What do you want to blow up? Is this some insurance job?"

"That's my business. Think of it as a blow against the system, if it makes you feel better."

"I have to think about it."

"Fine. I'll walk around the block. If you decide in that time you don't want the job, I'll find somebody else. The gold country is crawling with explosives people. I was hoping to save some time."

"Those redneck assholes don't know anything about bombs," he said with scorn. "A stick of dynamite and a fuse is their speed. They play at gold mining as an excuse to get drunk on the weekends."

I walked around the block. Jacobs was still thinking when I got back. "How come no electronics?" he asked.

"The detonator has to be manual."

"I got to fly down to L.A. I need money for that and to buy some stuff."

I gave him a thousand dollars. "The ten thousand is on top of this," he said.

"Of course," I answered. I turned to go, then looked back. "Don't get any ideas about keeping the thousand and ducking out. I can find you just as easy a second time." He didn't say anything.

As I was leaving Bernal Heights, I saw a big old Oldsmobile with gray primer spots dotting a body that had been red at one time. A sign in the back window said it was for sale for seven-fifty. I parked up the block and walked back. All sorts of people would be looking for my car by now.

"Does it run?" I asked the black guy who came to the door of the house where the car was parked.

"Runs fine," he said.

"How come you're selling?"

"I got to go to jail Monday. They just be strippin' it if I leave the muthafucker on the street."

I got him down to five hundred and he gave me the keys. "The pink slip's in the glove box. You can sign my name."

One tire was bald, the muffler was shot, and the car steered to the right, but I didn't plan to keep it long. I bought a walkie-talkie set at the Radio Shack on Geary. I sent a fax to Danforth from the stationery store next door. My hunch was the hotel fax line wasn't bugged. I wrote in longhand that he should meet me at the bus bench in front of the Clift House at eleven o'clock. "I won't make contact until I'm sure you're alone," I wrote. "I would have called, but your line is bugged."

I went into a thrift store and bought one of those long prison-look watch caps popular with lowlifes and a ratty overcoat that came down to my ankles. Then I got a long beard from a costume shop. I drove until I found an abandoned shopping cart and filled it with trash from a Jack in the Box Dumpster. I put the cart in the trunk of the Olds and tied the lid down with rope. I got to the Clift House at ten o'clock to check out the scene. There was no sign Danforth had the place watched. When you've done as many stakeouts as I have, you know what to look for. At ten-thirty I was shuffling behind the cart in beard, watch cap, and trench coat. I stopped at the trash can next to the bench and pretended to paw through the contents. I had put one of the walkie-talkies in a Burger King bag I smeared with mayo and relish. I left the bag in the trash can and sauntered off, pausing to panhandle from a man in a big Stetson and cowboy boots.

"Beat it," he said.

"Yassir," I answered and shuffled away.

I ditched the cart and took up a position near the World War II memorial. I talked aloud to myself when anybody looked like he was going to sit nearby. I had a clear view of the bus bench. At five minutes to eleven, Danforth pulled into a red zone and walked to the bench and sat down. At exactly eleven, I spoke into the walkie-talkie.

"Danforth. Over here."

He gave a little jump and looked around.

"In the trash can." He got up and walked to the trash can. "There's a walkie-talkie in one of the bags."

He hesitated and then hunted around in the trash. He found the bag and put it down to wipe his hands with a handkerchief. He took the walkie-talkie out, wiped his hands again, and threw the handkerchief into the trash can with the bag.

"This is Danforth," he said into it.

"Sorry to make you fish around in there," I said.

"No problem," he said stiffly.

"Are you alone?"

"As per your instructions."

"Grab the next bus when it comes by."

"Any bus?"

"Any bus."

"I told you I'm alone."

"And the FBI never lies, right?"

"Okay, I'll get the next bus."

"When I'm sure it's not being followed, I'll pull alongside and honk my horn. Get off at the next bus stop."

"I see one coming now."

There wasn't time to get back to the Olds. "Catch the one after."

We didn't have to wait long for the next bus. I pulled in behind and watched carefully. No cars came out of side streets and no one followed but me. I had checked the sky for helicopters before pulling away from the Clift House. After a couple of miles I pulled alongside the bus and honked. Danforth got out at the next stop.

I drew alongside him and pointed my gun at his chest. "I assume you're armed."

"I'm getting pretty sick of you aiming a gun at me."

"Take it out slowly and toss it in the backseat." He did as he was told.

"I better get it back this time."

"Come around to the driver's side and get in." He walked around the front of the car and got in as I slid over.

"Drive while we talk," I said.

He pulled into traffic. "This piece of junk drives like a tank. It pulls to the right."

We drove in silence for a while. "You're in pretty deep shit," he said.

"No kidding."

"You really nailed those guys with your shotgun. Not much of their faces left. Somebody got your license number."

"What about Madame Dulay and Alice?"

"Neighbors complained about the gas smell and firemen got there before it exploded. It wouldn't be too tough to convince a jury you killed them both."

"My prints weren't on the knife."

"You could have wiped them off. You and the princess cashed in some bonds for quite a large sum of money that afternoon. Nobody can find it."

"I got it."

"That takes care of motive."

"What's the motive with the two guys in the blue Taurus?"

"Your old pals in Homicide think it's a double cross or something like that. They think drugs could be involved."

"Did you tell them about the aliens?"

Danforth laughed sourly. "Right."

"Did you check out the other stuff?"

"That's why I'm sitting here." The hearty Danforth so sure of himself was gone. He had an unhappy look.

I waited for him to explain. He turned off the Great Highway onto a small residential street. "I don't want to drive this piece of shit anymore. It feels like a wheel is going to fall off. Mind if I park?"

"Go ahead."

He pulled in front of a neat stucco house with a lawn. Up the street, kids were throwing a football around. He turned to look at me.

"The harbormaster died. Did you know that?" I shook my head.

"They can't figure out the cause of death. All his internal organs turned into pudding. The Centers for Disease Control flew a team out to study him. They're talking like it's a new virus. It's all very hush-hush."

"He got it when the gull speared him."

"The doctors were told he was stabbed."

"By me, I suppose."

"A couple saw someone running from his office."

"So that's five deaths they pin on me."

"They haven't ID'd the perpetrator. They probably think you couldn't be everywhere, though it would simplify matters. Homicide's going crazy. Zero progress solving all those murders."

"You didn't tell them I was with the harbormaster?"

Instead of answering, Danforth said, "I went out to the yacht harbor to look around on my own. They were examining the dock. It was really smashed up. The city engineers couldn't figure it out. They said whatever landed on it had to weigh a couple of thousand pounds for that kind of damage. They were looking at some skin or hide that was scraped off. He paused uncomfortably. "There was a fisherman who came by and said it was from a shark. They were also fixing the skylight. They said vandals must have thrown a rock or something." He drummed fingers on the steering wheel for a while. "I wish I hadn't seen that dock."

"Why's that?"

"I could have gone back to Washington. I had you pegged as a psycho. People said you've been acting strange ever since your wife left. I'd be home and you would be somebody else's problem. This whole thing looks like nothing but grief."

I had figured that out a long time ago, so I waited for Danforth to continue.

"Nobody knows why that elevator failed. Those two old people died instantly. It fell less than thirty seconds after you walked out my door."

"Maybe a way can be found to blame me."

"Why didn't you get on it?"

"Something told me not to."

"Then what happened?"

"The doors slammed."

"That was it?"

"It was as if the elevator was waiting for me to show up. The people who were killed said they'd been there a long time. I show up and bingo, the elevator gets there."

"Jesus," Danforth said unhappily. "Seagulls, a shark, and an elevator. What's the connection there?"

"Aliens."

He shook his head doggedly. "I can't accept that."

"I don't blame you. I won't blame you until it is so obvious there's no other explanation and you still don't accept it."

"Those two men in the car were from West Virginia. One was in real estate in Wheeling and the other ran a little grocery store in the sticks. Didn't know each other, as far as we know. Steady, reliable types. Both vanished the same day. Left their families flat."

"When did they disappear?"

"July eighteenth."

"The day after a radio telescope got burned out in that part of the country. Also the day after psychics began getting their bad vibes. Remember? You looked for odd things that happened July seventeenth."

"What's the radio telescope got to do with anything?"

"That's for you to find out."

"How do you know my telephone is bugged?"

"How else could they lay that trap with the elevator?"

"Assuming it was a trap and not some malfunction. Why gamble the fax line wasn't bugged also? I'm not sure that was so smart."

"How else was I going to make contact? Your window is too high for me to reach throwing a pebble."

"Speaking of hotels, you never said yours burned down." Danforth acted like he had sprung something on me.

"It must have slipped my mind." I gave my forehead a slap.

"Very funny. Where were you when it happened?"

"Staying at Princess Dulay's. I gave you her phone number, remember? You thought it was funny at the time."

Danforth gave a reluctant nod. "I remember."

"Talk to the people in the fleabag across the street. They'll tell you they saw flashes in every room just before the hotel went up."

"Blue flashes. We checked it out. The fire department still doesn't know the cause."

"They never will. They're looking for one of the usual explanations."

We watched the kids throw the football for a while. They were a little older than Brady. One had a pretty fair arm.

I told Danforth about the traffic camera, the exploding neon signs, and the laundry that blew up. "A few more seconds and I wouldn't have made it."

He was silent a long time. "I suppose that will check out, too."

"A woman was cut up really bad on the street. I don't know if the people in the laundry got out in time."

"Eleven psychics or clairvoyants or whatever you call them are missing or died suddenly," Danforth said. "There might be more. We're not done."

"Have you told the police departments where the people live? It would save them shoe leather."

He shook his head. "It would leak out. Picture how the media would go nuts. The last thing we need is *National Enquirer* jackals running around with checkbooks buying up stories."

I lost my temper. "I'm trying to warn people and you want the lid kept on. Why am I wasting time with you fuckers?"

"Look, I don't know what I'm doing here. There's never been anything like this." Danforth looked hangdog.

"You think I don't know?"

"There are a lot of complications, including what Washington would think."

"What do you mean, 'would'? Do you think if you sit on this long enough it'll go away?"

"Imagine what my boss would say if I told him. He'd put me on medical leave. I need solid evidence on the table."

"The other agents working the case will back you up."

He shook his head. "I decided it would be better to play the Lone Ranger. I'm the only one who knows the big picture."

So he had been afraid to tell them, afraid of their smiles. "You'll have to come clean sooner or later."

He changed the subject. "Chief Blas's wife hasn't been seen for weeks. She usually goes to his official functions. He's been vague when asked about her. Says she's visiting family. We're checking that out very quietly. Same with the mayor. His wife is supposedly traveling in Asia. Friends of hers we feel out are surprised. She supposedly has a phobia about dirt and foreign germs. I'd be more aggressive, but your mayor has got some major connections in Washington. If I push too hard, I'd get yanked back to Washington so fast it would make your head swim."

"What about the change in the mayor's personality?"

"I don't know what you mean."

"The man's an egomaniac. He loves the limelight, can't live without it. Yet he's been almost invisible. The real mayor would be holding daily press conferences and making life miserable for the cops."

"What does that prove?" Danforth said. "Nothing."

"How about those other people who were murdered? I bet it turns out they saw something different about their spouses and had to be taken out, too."

Danforth had a faraway look. He probably wished he was teeing up at the Olympic Club. I looked at my watch.

"Hop out. You can walk down and catch a bus on the corner. I'm having lunch with Birkshire."

"Her?"

"Him."

"What about my gun?"

I got it out of the backseat and handed it to him. He stuck it in his shoulder holster. We looked at each other.

"I'm still a cop," I said.

He got out and slammed the door. "Keep in touch."

I drove to Green's and parked. I was shown to a table and sat down. I waited forty-five minutes, but Birkshire never showed.

The Hole: Did I really see that piece of paper? I can't find it anywhere. Maybe I ate it so no one would see it. If it wasn't a figment of my imagination, it raises an interesting question. Why can't Danforth walk through the doorway and tell me in person to hang in there? Why sneak me the message? Maybe someone told him it looked like I was near the end of my rope. This would mean he has friends among the guards. Or maybe he bribed one.

Surely I would have kept the paper to remind myself that I'm not crazy and forgotten. Maureen and Brady—what about them? Is Danforth looking out for them? What have they been told? Maureen will worry that the Mafia got me. Perhaps Danforth said I'm in the Witness Protection Program and we will be reunited at some point. But maybe she said, "Don't bother." I have built that kiss way out of proportion. Men kiss women on the cheek an hour after meeting them. Big deal. Even divorced couples do it. It doesn't mean more than a handshake.

It's surprising how sharp my memory is for things that happened before compared to now. I can clearly recall the bead of sweat that hung on the tip of Jacobs's nose when I saw him next. He was digging again in the communal garden under a hot sun. The battery in the Olds was weak, so I left the engine running. Jacobs turned to look at it. As he did, the bead of sweat flew off his nose. I see it clearly.

"Your car needs a new muffler," he commented.

"It needs a lot of things. Do you have what I wanted?"

"I might."

I took that to mean he wanted to see the color of my money. I showed him two stacks of hundreds with rubber bands crimping them in the middle. "Fifty in each. Count if you want." He took his time, randomly holding bills up to the light.

"You've got guts bringing this kind of money to a neighborhood like this."

"Where's the package?"

He nodded at a backpack by a wheelbarrow. "In there."

I walked over and looked. The plastique was tightly wrapped in red plastic squares with wind-up alarm clocks strapped to them with duct tape. "They're triggered by an armature striking a detonator. Pretty primitive. No way you synchronize them, if that's what you have in mind. You need digital for that." He sounded like an artist who had been forced to work in an inferior medium.

"How loud do they tick?"

"Not loud."

He looked like he was ready for a long lecture, but I didn't need to be told much about how they worked. I handled explosives in the navy.

He stuck the cash in his shirt and returned to his digging. I carried the backpack to the Olds and drove to the Redwood motel. Kids splashed in the tiny pool and ran up and down the balcony. I caught Kathy Birkshire on *The Six O'Clock News* and watched for signs of the alien within. She seemed stiff and careful, not taking part in banter with the weather guy, as the others did. But for all I knew, that was her usual manner. I had dinner and killed time at a car-chase movie. If cops drove like that in real life, they'd be brought up on departmental charges. Kathy Birkshire was the same on *The Eleven O'Clock News.* Zero spontaneity. Just the facts, with now and then a cold smile. Was that how you spotted them?

At two in the morning I arrived with the backpack at the building where Security Concerns had its office. "How ya doin'?" I called to the guard at the security desk. "San Francisco police."

He was a black guy. "Oh, yeah. Lieutenant Macaffey said you be comin' by some night. Say you had business in the building." He opened a drawer. "Here's the key."

I went to the elevator and pushed the button. The doors opened immediately, and I felt fear twist my stomach. But the guard watched, so I got on. The ride to the Security Concerns floor was uneventful. I let out a deep breath and walked to the double door that had "Security Concerns" in brass letters. I turned the key in the lock and stepped inside. There was no light, so I used my flashlight. Desk after desk with computer monitors perched at the exact same angle. All had screen-saver programs in precise phase with one another. Filing cabinets lined walls. I opened a drawer at random. Manila folders filled it. I pulled enough out to insert the bomb. The alarms were set for noon. I closed the drawer and turned the flashlight on the folders. They were accounting records from something called The Smyers Corp. in Abilene, Texas. No date was more recent than 1954. I stuck the folders in the backpack and crossed the room to the facing row of cabinets. The records in the drawer I opened there were from the Grizzly Petroleum Co. of Billings, Montana. The latest date was 1969. I put those in the backpack and the second bomb in the drawer. I let myself out and locked the doors.

I returned the key to the guard and left the building. I

drove carefully back to the motel, threading my way through back streets. The Olds was the kind of car cops stop on principle. You always find something wrong and the driver usually has warrants. I undressed and got into bed. The records were clever. If you have filing cabinets, there has to be something in them in case someone opens a drawer who isn't supposed to.

It was midmorning when I woke. The rags of a tropical storm had blown north from Mexico, and it looked like rain. I telephoned the newspaper and asked for Gilmore Ford. When I was new to the police department, he was its top investigative reporter and still was.

"Talk about voices from the past," he said. Ford spoke with a lazy drawl. He came from wealth and was in newspapers because he had a puritanical side that wanted to see sinners punished. He had put away crooked politicians, exposed extremist movements, and uncovered corruption in the police department. When I was in the chief's office, I had personally leaked stuff that needed to get out. He was older than I, late forties.

"I have a story you'll be interested in," I said.

"I'm always in the market."

"Shall we meet for lunch?"

"Sure."

"Eleven-thirty at Lefty O'Doul's?"

"Gawd, that dump? Steam tables and tourists on a budget. No, thanks. And I never eat lunch before one-thirty."

"Make an exception today."

"It better be damned interesting. But Lefty's is out. Compton Court. It's on me."

Campton Court is one of many swanky restaurants that have opened in San Francisco in recent years. When I was a rookie there was only a handful, such as the Blue Fox and Ernie's. The Blue Fox is closed, and nobody thinks Ernie's is tops anymore. At Campton Court the food arrives on the plate looking like paintings. It doesn't taste bad, either.

"How long has it been?" Ford asked.

"Fifteen years," I guessed.

Ford had the kind of lanky elegance that can make overalls look as smart as a tuxedo. He had a springy stride and leaned forward when he walked, as if in a hurry to get to where he was going.

"I'm not very hungry," he said languidly. I ordered pasta, and the waiter went away.

Ford looked me over. "I heard you went into the private-eye trade. That was years ago. You still doing that? Business okay?"

"It has its ups and downs."

"How's the family?"

He didn't know them, but it was nice to ask. "Fine," I said. "How about you?"

Ford chuckled ruefully. "I've been married three times since I last saw you."

He could tell I was doing the arithmetic. "Six. I've finally learned my lesson." He lit an unfiltered cigarette and crushed the empty package. "So what have you got?"

I looked at my watch. It was five minutes to twelve. "How does the newspaper contact you if a big story breaks?"

He patted his side. "Beeper. The invention of the devil."

"They'll beep you in a few minutes."

Ford turned his head to blow smoke over his shoulder and looked back at me. I wondered how long it would take the waiter to tell him to put it out.

"How do you know?"

"Let's call it a feeling."

"All right." He smoked some more and studied me.

"Working on anything interesting?" I asked lamely to kill time.

"The murders, what else. Goddamnedest things."

"The cops aren't getting anywhere. Are you guys having any luck?"

He sat straighter. "Is that what you wanted to talk about?"

"Does anyone wonder if they're all connected?"

"Sure. Nobody sees any."

"Let me complicate matters more. You know the harbormaster?"

Ford was surprised. "That was a straight-up robbery." His eyes narrowed. "Or so we were led to believe." He dropped his cigarette under the table and stepped on the butt.

"The autopsy should be interesting." I baited the hook. "If they let you see it."

"It's a public record."

"Where's the mayor's wife?"

"What?"

"And the police chief's wife?" Sirens started to wail far off.

"I don't follow you." His beeper went off, and Ford shot me a look. He checked the calling number. "The city desk." He got up and walked off with his springy stride. He came back a minute later.

"An explosion in the financial district." His dark eyes gave me a pat-down.

"Do you have to go?"

"They have younger legs for that. I might do rewrite later. How did you know?"

"This is the biggest story you've ever had or ever will." The waiter brought my plate. Ford was alert, the laid-back manner gone.

"You've got my attention."

"But there's no way you get this story into the paper."

"Why not?"

"Who took the publisher's place when she was murdered?"

"Her husband's running the shop." His brow furrowed. "What's that got to do with anything?"

"He won't let it be printed."

"Publishers could care less what goes in as long as the newspaper makes a buck at the end of the day. Most don't bother to read them."

"He's part of the story. So is everyone who was murdered that night. So are the two guys who got blown away in Pacific Heights and the two women killed one street over. So's the explosion just now. Knowing this means you're part of the story now and your life's in danger."

Ford held up a hand as if to stop traffic. "Hold on a minute. You're going way too fast. Let's go back to the harbormaster."

"He supposedly died of a stab wound, right?"

"That's right."

"He was killed by a virus nobody saw before. The federal government has a team investigating. They're keeping it quiet."

One of Ford's great assets was his total recall. You talked to him for an hour and he never took a note. But he would put it all down later without a mistake. It was like talking to a tape recorder. He nodded. "Go on."

I let a hammy silence pass, as if I were choosing my next words. The one thing I couldn't drop on him at that point was aliens. He would stop listening.

"Nobody's seen the mayor's wife or the police chief's wife for weeks. Check it out."

"What's to check out? I'll just call and ask."

"Make sure you have witnesses when you do."

"Why do you say that?"

That went against Ford's grain. He liked to hold a story close, only a couple of editors kept in the picture.

"Like I said, your life is now in danger."

"I don't remember you being like this."

"You mean I was levelheaded? Feet on the ground?"

"Well, yes."

"I haven't changed."

Ford was impatient. "What's the fucking story? You haven't said anything I can hang my hat on yet, for crissake."

"The details are your job. I'm just your basic deep background source."

He stared. "How did you know there was going to be an explosion?"

"Ask your television editor to start watching Kathy Birkshire. See if he notices any changes."

"What's *she* got to do with this?" Ford exploded.

"I'm going to leave you with a couple of other thoughts. Somebody's been killing psychics or making them disappear."

He took a deep breath. "Is this a gag?"

"Was the explosion a gag?"

"It was a bomb?"

I nodded.

"That's how you knew it was going to go off."

"That's right."

"And you didn't warn anybody?"

"The other thing is an FBI agent from Washington is here who knows this stuff and more I haven't told you. His name is Danforth. But don't contact him until I give you the green light."

I got up from the table.

"Wait a minute," Ford said. "That's all you're going to say?"

"That's enough for starters. Remember what I said. Be careful. Your life is on the line."

I walked out of the restaurant as a big fire truck roared past with siren and air horns blasting. I passed across Union Square and ducked into a telephone booth at the St. Francis Hotel.

"Mulhenny and Armstrong," Mitzi answered.

"It's me," I said. "Put me on hold for ten seconds and then pick up the line again."

She left the line. "Are you listening?" I said. "Recognize

the voice? Goodwin Armstrong is my name. I just blew up your office. That's just the start, motherfucker."

Mitzi came back on the line. "I'm back."

"Any messages?"

"One from a Mike Deutsch. Mr. Mulhenny wants to talk to you, only he's not here now."

"Tell him I'll call him back. Remember what I said. I'm just starting on you and I won't stop."

"Pardon?"

I checked my watch. I had been on the telephone twenty seconds. I hung up and slipped out the side entrance and walked west on Geary Street. I found a little coffee shop and sat at the counter, where I watched through the window. A waitress brought coffee.

The bomb would show the bastards we were not as stupid and helpless as they thought. Everything had gone their way up to now. It would be interesting to see how they handled adversity.

When I finished my coffee, I called Deutsch. He answered on the first ring.

"I've been waiting for your call." His voice was flat and dead.

"What's wrong?"

"You know that kid whose name I used when I was hacking for you?"

"What about him?"

"They found him dead, murdered. It's my fault."

"Don't be stupid." I heard his doorbell ring.

"There's somebody at the door."

"Don't answer it!" I yelled. But he had put the receiver down. He didn't pick it up again.

I f they diagnosed me as criminally insane, it is because of the Security Concerns bombing. My lack of
remorse would settle that. I was right about the filing cabinets. Steel fragments whirred through the
office, scything off heads and limbs. That flying metal killed
more of them than the blast itself. The carnage was so awful
that many of the emergency people needed psychological
help afterward. Forty-seven people killed outright and nineteen wounded. Seven of these died after they got to the hospital. The network anchors jetted out for stand-ups on the
sidewalk outside the building, and the story led the nightly
roundups in London, Tokyo, and Moscow. San Francisco
was stunned, and there was soul-searching. People asked why
their city had been singled out. First all those murders, and
now this. Candlelight vigils and sermons about God's un-
fathomable ways followed.

As I expected, terrorists were blamed. Telephone calls
came from half a dozen nuts who claimed they did it for
some cause. But these pop up whenever a bomb goes off, so
nobody took them seriously. People waited for the guilty

party to step forward with the justification or demand or whatever it would turn out to be.

"Did you do it?" Those were Danforth's first words on the telephone that night. He sounded afraid of what I would answer. He had called the pay phone outside a Dunkin' Donuts in Walnut Creek after I faxed the number.

"What makes you ask?"

"The blue Taurus was registered to Security Concerns."

"Those weren't humans who got blown away. They were aliens like the ones in that car."

There was silence for a long time. "So it was you." He sounded old and worn out all of a sudden.

"You're checking them out, aren't you?"

"Who?"

"The so-called victims."

"What do you mean, 'so-called'? They're dead."

"They're casualties of war, not victims. Big difference. That's what we're in, a war. I bet you find every one disappeared from normal lives, like the guys in the Taurus. They were empty shells possessed by aliens."

"Aliens," he said woodenly. He was mentally watching his career go in the toilet.

I see myself standing at the phone booth in the buttery glow of the yellow Dunkin' Donuts sign. Faded jeans, polo shirt, windbreaker, and cowboy boots (my latest thrift shop buys), the receiver hot in my ear. There are pages of private detectives in the yellow pages. Why had the Paul Revere role fallen to me?

Maybe my lack of remorse for blowing away Security Concerns is what led to the decision to isolate me like a deadly bacillus. Treatment would be useless with such a monster.

"I'm not wrong," I had told Danforth.

"I'm bailing out. Maybe I can still cover my tracks. Washington's sending a planeload of agents. Somebody else will boss the investigation while I go back to shaking hands on Capitol Hill. I let you suck me into this. I should've kept Washington in the picture from the start instead of getting in over my head."

I had half expected it. That is why I had brought Ford into the picture. The FBI doesn't take the blame when something goes wrong. It is first in line to claim credit for success, but takes a powder in a screw-up. Local cops aren't the only ones who know this. The Drug Enforcement Agency and the Bureau of Alcohol, Tobacco and Firearms can tell you.

"You've wanted to crawl back into the bureaucratic womb from the beginning," I said. "Too bad about the facts, though. You can't overlook them."

"Your idea of facts and mine are miles apart."

"What about the harbormaster and the damage to the dock? What about the elevator? What about the Ajax Arms? What about the psychics? What about all the other stuff? And I've got a couple more for you.".

Danforth was silent, not wanting to hear.

"Those two Stanford kids who were murdered?" The killings hadn't gotten much play in the news because of the bombing.

"Jesus, don't tell me they're part of this."

"One was a case of mistaken identity. The other, Mike Deutsch, was a computer whiz. I hired him to break into Security Concern's database. This is a kid who could crack anyone's code, but he couldn't get to first base with Security Concerns. First they killed the kid whose name he was using, then they got him."

"I don't want to know any more. You're somebody else's problem."

"You can't duck out now."

"Watch me."

"I told a reporter I'm working with you."

This time his silence was stunned.

"How much did you tell him?" There was an edge of panic in his voice.

"Just enough to tease him. He gets the rest if you take a hike. The first thing he will do is check with Congressman Cox. Imagine the call your boss gets when that happens."

Odd as it sounds, I felt some sympathy for Danforth. He was right about being in way over his head, just like me. He had separate investigations going hoping somebody came up with an explanation that didn't require him to utter that word he dreaded, "aliens."

I had an inspiration. "Tell Washington you think this is some weird cult deal. Say you thought that was too far out before to mention, but the bomb changed your mind. That gives you the cover to make background checks of everybody who worked for Security Concerns. People dropping everything to take up a new way of life is typical cult behavior. Have a theory about internal dissension. The faction opposed to the murders blows up the local cult front, which is Security Concerns."

"They would wonder why I didn't mention it before."

"It didn't occur to you until the bombing." With all the pressure I was under, it was my job to think up alibis for Danforth?

The Hole: "Delusions of grandeur."

Who said that? I look around. The room is empty. A hidden speaker? Not a chance. I have inspected every square inch of this room. I wait to see if there's more, but it is silent. The voice was familiar, but I can't put my finger on it right away. It was expressionless, like the guys you hear on the ground at Mission Control during a launch. Then it comes to me. I know that voice.

It's mine.

That settles it.

I'm crazy.

It is one thing to talk to yourself. It is another when you say something and think somebody else did. It shows personality is fragmenting, breaking up like a ship on the rocks.

I consider this.

Isolation would push anyone off the deep end, let alone the effects of whatever drug they have been using on me. But it doesn't mean I was insane before.

I got a room that night at Motel 6. The clerk had the TV on. "Aren't you glad you're not in San Francisco?" I said I sure was.

He was an old man with a network of creases in his forehead like dry river valleys seen from a great height. He wore a Pendelton shirt a couple of sizes too big. Mean eyes. "That place is going down the tubes. I just hope we can keep them out when it happens."

"Who?" I asked.

"The people who live there. That bunch of freaks is getting what they deserve." San Francisco hadn't been very popular with the suburbs since the hippies moved in thirty years ago.

I ditched the Olds on a quiet street in Lafayette the next morning. Somebody might have figured out by now that the bombs were Jacobs's. A bomb-maker's style is as obvious to an expert as his signature. Jacobs might describe the junker when the screws were put to him. I rode BART into the city and got off at the Montgomery Street station. I took a battered Muni bus out into the Sunset District and got a room at the Ocean View Motel, which naturally didn't have a view. I spent most of the day watching dingbats on *Sally Jessy, Oprah,* and *Ricki.* One show had a bunch of women who weighed a minimum of three hundred pounds. They had posed nude for joke greeting cards. These were held up to the camera. I switched to another channel before they could explain. The stuff on TV.

That night I took a cab to three blocks from my office. A light was on when I walked past on the opposite side of the street, hurrying as if late. I circled the block and found a fire escape in an alley that led to the roof of a rundown building whose back side looked down on the office. From the roof, I saw Mulhenny at his desk in a sweatshirt with a hood. He was just sitting there. This was unusual because normally he was a very fidgety guy, always picking things up and putting them down. I watched fifteen minutes and he didn't move.

A soft fog began to ghost in, and I zipped the windbreaker to my neck. An hour passed, then two. The fog was like a film over the light from the office window. Mulhenny still didn't move. Finally, he got up and disappeared from sight. The light went off, and a minute later he walked with his hood up to his car in the parking lot. There was something different about him. Then it hit me: He wasn't limping. He got in his Buick, started the engine, turned on the lights and drove off. I waited another fifteen minutes, but nothing else moved. I climbed down the fire escape and made my way into the mist.

An hour later, I stepped from a bus a few blocks from Mulhenny's house. He was famously boring on the subject of his lawn, which was smooth enough to play billiards on. He acted like every blade was precious to him. But tonight heavy footprints led from his car across the delicate dichondra to the front door.

A faint light was on inside. I picked the lock on the back door and slipped in. The light came from a room deeper inside. Taking care not to trip, I moved through the darkness. Emily always kept a spotless house, with everything in its place. This was quite an accomplishment, considering what a slob her husband was. Through a partially open door I saw Mulhenny in an easy chair staring straight ahead. He hadn't taken off his sweatshirt, even though the house was hot. I slipped my gun from the holster and stepped into the room.

He showed no more surprise than if I had gone to the kitchen for a glass of water a minute before and come right back.

"How did you get in?"

"The back door."

"It was locked."

"I unlocked it."

We studied one another. He was breathing without that wheezing.

"Why are you just sitting here?" I asked.

"I'm thinking."

"If you were thinking, you'd have your finger in your ear."

He should have laughed. No limp and no breathing problems. Interesting.

"Where's Emily?" I asked.

"She's not here."

"At one in the morning?"

"She's on a trip. A couple of guys from the department came by the office looking for you."

"Who were they?"

"Lodge and Fugazi. You know them?"

"I've met them."

"They want to talk to you."

"Okay. What is it you want?"

He shifted in the chair as if he meant to get up.

"Stay where you are," I said. I showed him the gun.

"What's that for?"

"Where did Emily go?"

"On a trip. Vacation."

"You always travel together."

"This time we didn't."

"How do you do it? How do you take somebody over?"

"You won't use that."

"Why won't I?"

"We've been friends too long."

"You're not Mulhenny. You look and sound like him, but you're not him." His eyes were different, too. Cold and flat, like Kathy Birkshire's. They used to say eyes were the windows of the soul. These were not Mulhenny's eyes. And why was he wearing that sweatshirt when the house was so hot?

"Where is Emily? Buried in the backyard?"

"Give me the gun. You need help." He held out his hand.

"Did you really think it would be that easy? That we wouldn't find out at some point? Or we'd just roll over and let you win? You lost a lot of—what do you call them, units?— when the bomb went off. Did it hurt? Did the rest of you feel the pain?"

His hand was still held out. "You can't run forever."

"That's what you're hoping, right? That we'll give up when everything is in place? When the president and Congress and the Pentagon are under your control. Think again, pal. We'll never give up. You think I've given you trouble? It's nothing compared to what happens when word gets out. Tell me a funny story, Mulhenny."

He dropped his hand. "Funny story?"

"You know a million. Or Mulhenny did. Tell me one and save your life. I'll give you ten seconds. I suppose other units are on the way by now."

"I can't think of a funny story."

"That's one of the ways we'll know you. No sense of humor. No wit. No repartee. No need for that when you're just one big organism, right? It would be selected out by evolution, like tails on humans. Time's up."

"I told you, I don't know any funny stories."

He started to get up and I shot him in the chest. He looked at me for two seconds with those reptile eyes, as if what I had done was very interesting. Then they filled with death and he fell back into the chair.

Even though it was an alien, it still looked like Mulhenny, a guy I had known fifteen years. It was like killing Mulhenny himself.

He had left his car keys on the table next to the chair. I grabbed them and went out the front doorway. I kept on the gravel path that bordered the dichondra. Forget the limp and the emphysema and no Emily, those brutal footprints on the lawn were all the proof I needed.

The Hole: As I lie here on the cot and consider it objectively, I see how someone could conclude I was insane. I shoot a man dead, a friend and business partner, and afterward avoid stepping on his lawn out of respect. Take aliens out of the mix and it is psychotic behavior, especially when you factor in no remorse. When I was a cop, I met a few of these types without conscience. One of them, Zeno Quantrell, was a landscape architect who killed people and butchered them. He froze the edible parts and ate them. When the last knuckle bone had made soup, he killed again. Eleven people had gone through his larder before he slipped up. I heard the tape of his interrogation. Quantrell at some level knew that killing people to eat them was wrong, but it didn't register emotionally. To him, it was like writing checks with insufficient funds. Illegal, but not the end of the world, for crying out loud. He used that phrase a lot during the interrogation, "for crying out loud."

I'm crying out loud right now. Tears pour out and slide down my cheeks into my ears as I stare at the blurry ceiling. I wipe my eyes with the back of my hand. How could I be so sure? Footprints across the dichondra and he can't come up with a joke. Who could, with a gun pointed at him? Jim Carrey? Maybe Emily *was* on vacation.

I abandoned Mulhenny's car four blocks from the Ocean View Motel and left the windows rolled down and the keys in the ignition. Whoever stole it sure would be sorry. He didn't know what trouble was.

I laid low for a couple of days, staying in my room except for meals at little cafés that catered to tourists visiting the zoo. Nobody gave me a second look, even though my picture was in the papers. Mulhenny's murder and his missing wife rated only a short article. There was no mention of me in connection with them.

I bought a Kawasaki motorcycle for cash from an ad in the paper. The seller threw in his helmet for free. Afterward, I checked into the Colonial Motel on Lombard Street and called Ford at the newspaper.

"What did you find out?" I asked.

"Everybody in the world is looking for you, that's what I found out." He talked in a low voice, and it sounded like he had a hand cupped over the mouthpiece. "You're being blamed for everything except bad breath."

"They'll find a way to pin that on me."

"You're right about the wives. They haven't been seen for weeks."

"They won't, either. They're dead."

"How do you know?"

"I just know. Did you check out the psychics?"

"I come up with seven who died suddenly or are missing. Our stringers are still nosing around."

"The FBI was up to eleven last time I checked."

"Who's knocking them off? Some religious fanatic?"

"I'll tell you later. Did you get the autopsy of the harbor-master?"

"They won't turn it loose and won't say why. Want to shed some light on that subject?"

"Later with that, too."

"I wanted to go to court to get it."

"And?"

"The publisher nixed it."

"I thought he didn't pay any attention to what goes in the paper."

"The editor and company lawyer can't believe he said no. We guess the government asked him to keep a lid on the story for fear of panic if there's a virus like you say."

"Do you notice anything unusual about him?"

"He's hanging around the city room all the time."

"How do you mean, 'hanging around'?"

"Asking a ton of questions. Who's working on what story—that sort of thing. We guess he's trying to learn the ropes now that his wife is gone. They've got a son in his thirties, but he's a fairy involved in modern dance in New York. Doesn't care about newspapers."

"Remember I said this story wouldn't get in the paper?"

"What the hell are you talking about? You talk like there's some goddamned conspiracy or something."

"Or something."

"Did you plant that bomb like the cops say?"

I decided to stay vague. "They want the world to think so."

"How about that mind reader and her companion and the two guys shotgunned to death? Was that you?"

"Same story." I gave him the same answer again when he asked about Mulhenny and his wife.

He thought for a minute. Ford assumed people in author-ity lie because it says to in their policy manual. "I checked out

Danforth with people I know in the bureau. He's not really an investigator. He's a political type who lobbies for the bureau. Did you know that?"

I said yes. "It's okay to talk to him now. He won't like it, though."

"Does he know what the hell's going on, and will he say instead of hinting around like you?"

"I count on you to put his feet to the fire."

"What's that mean?"

"He doesn't like what two and two add up to."

"You mean it *is* a conspiracy? And the government is involved? Did they make that virus in a lab and it got loose? Is that what this is all about?" He was like a hunting dog quivering on point.

"It's worse than that."

"Worse?"

"How did you explain finding out about the harbormaster?"

"I said I got a tip."

"Did they believe you?"

"Why wouldn't they?" He thought for a moment. "But the publisher gave me a kind of funny look. Fact is, he's looking at me now."

"Remember that other thing I told you? That your life is in danger?"

"I thought you were being melodramatic."

"I was never more serious in my life. Watch yourself. Your publisher is on their side."

"Whose side, for crissake?"

"Keep digging. Let me give you a couple more items to check out. Those two kids who were killed at Stanford?"

"What about them?"

"One worked for me. Deutsch was his name. He was a

code breaker. He tried to break into Security Concerns' database. That's why they killed him."

"What about the other one?"

"An innocent bystander. When Deutsch logged on, he used his name. The other thing is a radio telescope in North Carolina run by the university for the Defense Department."

"I'm trying to keep up with you. It isn't easy."

"It suffered a meltdown."

"What in the name of God is the connection here?" Ford snapped.

"Maybe Danforth knows by now. Ask him."

"Look, I gotta hang up. The publisher's coming my way." His voice got loud. "And what's more, the shirts were too small. I don't think I ought to pay for sending them back. It was your mistake. . . ."

I hung up.

D ays passed, and nothing much happened that I could see, other than Danforth was so successful selling the idea that Security Concerns was a mystery cult that it became the party line in Washington.

"The lid's on tight, so nobody's talking. But in all the cases we've checked out, the people you blew up vanished from ordinary lives," he said over the phone. "No warning, no nothing. In various parts of the country. They didn't come home from work one night. Their families can't explain why. No obvious unhappiness or unusual pressures. A dentist, a railroad brakeman, a grocery bagger, a real-estate broker, a gas station owner."

I reminded him that I had dreamed up the cult angle.

"Just because you had the idea doesn't mean it's screwball."

That sounded as if he had sold it to himself as well. People who worked at Security Concerns had lived together in an apartment building owned by the company. They traveled to and from work in passenger vans. They had no televisions, radios, telephones, or other modern distractions. They lived in Trappist-like silence, according to the neighbors.

Cults might be weird, but at least they were comfortingly familiar.

"Whatever they're up to might have to do with the millennium," Danforth said with hope. Any weirdness was still blamed on that.

It was night, and I stood at an isolated phone booth on the road to Mount Diablo. I could see headlights approach from a long distance off in both directions, the reason I had stopped here to make the call. I was changing motels every day, but I had the feeling something gained on me. I got up earlier and stayed up later. I was constipated and slept lousy. I spent a lot of time standing at windows peering through curtains, hoping I spotted whatever that something was in time to save myself.

I had left the Kawasaki with the engine running next to the phone booth. The thing about motorcycles is nobody gives it a second thought if you keep your helmet on. I bought a lot of my meals at 7-Eleven and Stop & Shop stores. Security cameras can't see through dark visors.

"If it turns out it's what you think, we'll find that out, too," Danforth said. He was humoring me.

"You want someone else out on the limb first." I pictured it. Others at a meeting would laugh when someone reluctantly came around to saying that crazy as it sounded, the evidence seemed to point to an alien invasion. Danforth would hold up a tolerant hand. Hear the man out, he'd say. It would show his mind was open to any possibility. Just for the sake of argument, Danforth would say.

Cars came into sight to the north, pearls strung together in the inky night. I guessed they were commuters still moving at freeway speed. When I was in Traffic and under pressure from the sergeant to produce tickets, I camped near freeway off-ramps. You could get writer's cramp if you didn't watch out.

"We're up to twenty-four psychics dead or missing," Danforth said.

"How do you guys explain that to each other?"

He went back to Security Concerns. "The people who didn't die in the explosion aren't being helpful, and they don't want anything to do with their families. It's like they're brainwashed. That's common cult behavior."

"Except you can deprogram them. That won't happen in this case."

There were ten or twelve cars. You would expect some to turn off. The state park began up the road, and there were no houses in that direction.

"I guess you heard about that medium named Zorwanda. He's the latest," Danforth said. Zorwanda was the psychic who spoke at the memorial service.

"What about him?"

"He was running on the freeway. A big semi squashed him flat. It happened today. I told—"

I watched the cars close the distance. I broke in, "Why did you take so long to answer the phone?"

"I picked it up on the first ring, same as you said in the fax." I had told him to wait by a lobby phone whose number I had taken down. The telephone had rung several times, and I almost hung up.

I dropped the receiver and jammed the helmet on. I jumped on the motorcycle and twisted the accelerator all the way over. The Kawasaki started to fishtail, and for a second I thought I was going to lay it over. Then it straightened, and the engine whined through the gears as the wind rushed past. It was a hot little bike, and the red needle was pushing a hundred by the time I looked in the mirror. The first car was passing the phone booth. It had switched on blue roof lights and siren and the others behind did the same.

The road curved to the left, rising up the mountain. I wasn't putting much distance between us. A sign that said "Park Entrance" a quarter mile ahead flashed past. I jammed on the brakes and went into a long skid, barely under control. I recovered to make the turn and shot up the narrow lane to the park. Coming up was the booth where they take your money. A swinging bar gate blocked the road. I slowed to a crawl and squeezed between the booth and the gate and took off again. By then, the cops were right on my butt. I thought they would stop to open the gate but the first car blew through, sacrificing its front end. It pulled over to the side, clearing the way for the others.

We left the asphalt and were on the dirt fire road. Headlights plunged wildly as the cars bottomed out on the bumps. I leaned into one curve and then another. Suddenly I was among a herd of gray deer bounding in the same direction. The whites of eyes rolled at me as we rode together like a posse. Then they divided, darting into the trees on either side of the road. A carved sign pointing to hiking trails came up on the left. I turned onto the first, and the ground got rougher. Pine needles whipped my helmet visor. A bump lifted me off the seat and I nearly lost the bike. I slowed, knowing the cars couldn't follow. Their sirens yelped at the trailhead like dogs baying for blood. I came to a wide meadow lit by a pale moon and switched off the headlight so they couldn't track me. More deer stood in clumps, staring with ears straight up. Then they wheeled and ran.

Keeping the bike in first gear, I ground through the pines. A helicopter quartered overhead, shining a dazzling light down. The cops were probably kicking themselves. They had no way of knowing I would be on a motorcycle. I knew from experience it drives you nuts to just miss a collar. You would rather the suspect left an hour before you got there. The helicopter moved off.

They would put units at all the park entrances, but no way could they control the whole perimeter. They probably hoped I was stupid or scared enough to stay hidden while they brought up horses and dogs to search.

The night would have been pleasant another time. It wasn't too cool and the moon gave just enough light, except where trees were so close together that I had to put on the headlight to see the trail. I puttered slowly, putting feet on the ground when I needed to steady the Kawasaki. A second helicopter joined the search and then a third. It looked like they were combing by sector. The park would be like a law-enforcement convention by daylight.

I got to the far side of the park at three o'clock. A barbed-wire fence marked the boundary, and I thought about cutting it so I could keep the motorcycle. But they would spot any break in the fence when it was light and know I had left the park. I would just as soon they kept searching there as long as possible. In any event, an all-points bulletin would be out for a man on a motorcycle. I buried the Kawasaki and helmet under brush and crawled under the fence. When the dove-colored dawn broke, I was heading in the open among dried cow piles down a grassy ravine. Cattle stared before lumbering off, tossing looks back over their shoulders.

A run-down farmhouse from the past century stood in trees near a two-lane road. A battered Toyota pickup truck crusted with dirt was parked at its side. I looked for keys in the ignition without much hope of finding them. I walked up slanting steps to a narrow wooden porch that creaked underfoot. The place looked like it was heaven for termites. Paint flaked in patches on the walls, and it looked like the windows were jammed shut.

I could knock and hope to be received like the Publishers Clearinghouse guy with the check. But odds were whoever came to the door would be armed and have a chip on his shoulder. The lock was a cinch and the door swung open with a sound that said please oil me. I pulled my gun and

stepped in, feeling ashamed. I had spent a lot of my life trying to collar people who did this sort of thing.

The floors were bare except for a couple of worn throw
rugs. The mismatched furniture looked like what goes last at
garage sales. Chairs with lumpy cushions and a sofa that
looked like it belonged at the Ajax Arms. But the house was
spotlessly clean. Whoever lived there was poor but not dirty. I
looked into the big kitchen, where a huge ancient stove with a
hood as big as a pup tent dominated the room. I visualized the
generations of broad-hipped women with kids at their sides
cooking for big families. Tins with a flower pattern stood on a
counter in a neat row. A cupboard had canned fruits and vegetables. The floor was worn but had a high wax polish. Photographs and schoolwork were held on the refrigerator door
by magnets. My mother, who had kept her kitchen as if Betty
Crocker was expected, would have approved.

I tiptoed down a narrow hall with doors on either side.
The first three rooms were empty, the beds neatly made and
crisp white curtains at the windows. No sign of car keys on
the bureaus. I opened the fourth door. There was enough
dawn coming through the curtains to show a large bed where
a young woman slept with a small child. Their blond hair was
spread on the pillows. The little girl lay on her side and her
mother lay on her back, a breast exposed from her night-
gown. The keys were on the nightstand. The floorboards
creaked as I stole toward them. The girl turned, and her eyes
snapped open.

"Momma, a man."

The mother's eyes opened in terror, cornflower blue like
her daughter's. "No!" she cried.

I held hands up like a man surrendering. "I won't hurt you."

They turned into each other's arms against the enemy.
"Who are you?" the mother asked. "What do you want?"

I said I needed to borrow the pickup. "Where's your husband?"

"He'll be right back," she said wildly. She realized her breast was exposed and tucked it back in with a kind of moan.

"No, he won't." The daughter turned her head to correct her mother. She was about three, the age when only the literal truth will do. "He's gone away, Momma."

"Oh, God," she said. "Don't hurt us."

There was a rocking chair near the bed, and I sank into it. "I told you I won't."

"Is he going to hurt us, Momma?" the girl faltered.

"No, he says not," her mother said pleadingly.

"No, honey," I told the toddler. "I'm a father, too. I won't hurt anyone."

"Okay," she said. She looked at me with great interest.

"How did you get in?" the woman asked.

"The front door."

I suddenly felt exhausted. "You need a better lock on that door."

"What do you want? If it's just the pickup, here, take the keys." She made a move to grab them, but I held a hand up.

"Give me a minute to think," I said. If I drove off now, they would call the sheriff's office and I'd be caught right away. I could cut the phone line, but they would throw on clothes and run to a neighbor. Stay put for an hour—I'll be watching. I could try that bluff. But I could tell from how the mother was already sizing up the situation she wouldn't fall for it. She sat up alertly, the first panic gone, and pulled the covers up to her neck. Seeing her do that, her daughter did the same.

"We have no money," she said.

"The man looks scared, Momma." From the mouths of babes.

"He has nothing to fear from us."

We listened to a helicopter approach and clatter over-head. The day shift was on the job.

"Is it looking for you?" the mother asked.

I gave her a grim nod.

"What did you do?" the girl asked.

"It's a long story."

"I like stories."

Well, why not? It was like having my own little focus group. The mother was Gwen and the daughter was Patty. While they dressed (I averted my eyes) and then as Gwen rustled up toast and cold cereal in the kitchen, I told them the whole story. I had to explain to Patty what aliens were. "People from another world who don't like us." She listened with eyes wide open. She thought it was a great story.

"Well, it sure is different," Gwen said warily when I finished.

"You don't believe it?"

"I'm not saying that exactly."

"But hard to believe?"

"Wouldn't you think so if somebody told you?" She had the kind of hillbilly looks that fade early. Dorothy Lange photographed hundreds like her during the Depression. Their men sit in the bar drinking up the week's paycheck while they wait at home with the kids.

"I would think he was insane," I said. "That's the problem in a nutshell."

"What's 'insane,' Momma?" Patty asked.

"Not right in the head, sweetheart. You remember when Rex got sick from the skunk biting him?"

"The man has rabies?"

"No, darling. Hush now and eat your cereal while the grown-ups talk." Patty spooned Cheerios, looking from her mother to me.

"Where'd your husband go?" I asked.

She turned away, her eyes filling. "He left us."

"But he'll be back someday," Patty piped up.

Gwen looked at me and shook her head.

We sat in depressed silence for a moment.

"You're not what I imagined from the TV," she said, wiping her eyes. "They make you sound like a monster. From what you say, you're kind of a hero."

"What's 'hero,' Momma?"

"A good man, darling."

"Is he a good man?"

Her mother hesitated. "We'll see."

What was I going to do? Tie them up? Kill them? If you're trying to save the world, you don't let a woman and kid stand in the way. *Save the world.* How ridiculous it sounded. Delusions of grandeur is about right.

"What happens now?" I asked.

"Shouldn't I be asking that?" Her smile was timid.

"I need to get back to San Francisco. I'm open to suggestions."

"You're afraid we'll tell if you take the pickup."

I nodded.

"I promise not to."

"I can't depend on that. You understand."

"Oh, yes, I do, I surely do." Watching me from across the table.

"They'll be looking for a man alone. Stopping cars."

"We could ride with you," she said faintly. "They'd think we're family."

I trusted her because I had no choice. They got coats on and we went out to the pickup. "You have to pump the gas to get it started," she said. We rattled out of the driveway and onto the narrow road. Patty sat in her lap.

"The truck's awful dirty. Dave said there was no point to wash it when there's so much dust. 'Course, he's lazy. Here, put this on." She passed a straw hat from the dash. "Everybody wears them for the sun. You'll look more like you belong."

We left the little road and got on a bigger one. "How's the fuel?" she asked. "I don't think there's enough to get to the city."

"I'm just going as far as the BART station in Concord."

"Look at the pretty lights, Momma."

There was a roadblock ahead with two cars stopped. A highway patrolman had his head in the window of one. I pulled behind the second. Gwen whispered to Patty.

"What are you saying?" I asked.

"I promised her a new dolly if she doesn't say anything to the policeman."

"One with yellow hair," Patty said. "And a red dress."

The first car in line drove off and the second edged forward and the patrolman stuck his head in the window. I tried the radio. "It's never worked since the first day Dave bought it from a friend. He always gets cheated."

The car ahead moved off and we crawled up to the patrolman. He had mirror sunglasses, a Smokey the Bear hat, and a sharp tan and blue uniform. He looked at the dirt on the car and decided against leaning in.

"Mornin'," he said. "How are you folks today?"

"Real good," I said. "What's the problem, officer?"

"You folks haven't been listening to the news?"

"The damn radio's busted." I hoped I wasn't overdoing the hayseed act.

"They think they got the fellow surrounded who blew up all the people in San Francisco and killed those others," he said.

"Boy, I'd like to get me a piece of him. They ought to hang him from a tree, forget the trial."

He frowned to show official disapproval. "Couldn't hardly do that, now, could we? If he's in there, they'll get him sure as you and your missus and that pretty little girl is sitting there." He was bending so he could smile at Patty. She smiled back.

"You haven't seen anything unusual, have you?" he asked me.

"Nope."

"Well, okay. We're stoppin' folks on the off chance he might have slipped out somehow or other." He waved us on. "Have a good day now."

"Same to you," I said.

We drove in silence for a while. "Thank you," I said.

I could tell she was looking at me.

"Did I do the right thing?"

"Sure, we got through, didn't we?"

"No, I mean should I have turned you in? Maybe what you told me is just a crazy lie."

"I wish it was."

We pulled into the BART parking lot in Concord. I peeled fifteen hundred-dollar bills from my poke and folded them in half. "This isn't payment, because no amount of money would be enough. But you probably could use a little help right now."

She reddened. "I can't take that."

I handed it to Patty. "Would you give this to your mother? Make sure she buys a doll with yellow hair and a red dress." She took the cash in a tiny hand. Her eyes were big.

I got out, and Gwen slid behind the wheel. I waved at Patty, and she waved back.

I joined the crowd of sleepy-looking commuters waiting for the train. When I looked back, Gwen was driving the pickup out of the lot. They were never seen again.

"Are you there?" Ford asked. I hadn't said anything for a long time after he told me they were missing.

"Yeah," I said.

"They think it was you. The husband's in the clear. He's got an alibi."

It was two days later. I had spent that whole first day and

night sleeping and still woke up feeling stale and tired. I had telephoned the newspaper from the phone near the rest rooms after breakfast at the Lyons on Geary. I left a message for Ford and he called back.

"Danforth says he wants you to contact him."

"What's happening with your publisher?"

"He's become real hands-on. He put the kibosh on a piece our TV columnist did about Kathy Birkshire. He wrote she's lost so much sparkle she's like a different person. He talked to some station executives worried about ratings. The publisher didn't give a reason for spiking the column, except to say he didn't like it." He paused. "When are you going to tell me what's behind all this?"

"When I think you're ready to hear."

"I'm ready."

"No, you're not. What did you find out about the radio telescope?"

"Another veil of secrecy. I sent a stringer to the spot with some baloney that he wanted to do a feature story, but he got turned away by federal agents. They grilled him for a couple of hours. I haven't told anyone, not even my editors. I'm being very selective who I tell."

"Assume your telephone is tapped," I said.

He laughed. "Oh, I'm about ten years ahead of you there. Taps are one of the hazards of my work. People are used to the way I move around the office using different phones. I'm in the basement in the janitor's office right now."

"Tell Danforth I'll meet him at Ayala Cove Tuesday afternoon at two. Don't use the phone. See him in private. Tell him to come alone."

"Ayala Cove on Angel Island?"

I said I didn't know any other.

The Hole: I can't blame myself for Gwen and Patty. The aliens decided they weren't worth bothering to take over, I suppose. How could a blue-collar mom and a kid advance the program? I can't say I would have done anything different even if I had known what would happen to them. They were pawns sacrificed for the greater good, the means to the end; the end being my own safety. I know how it sounds.

Thinking about them makes me even more depressed. It leads me back to Maureen and Brady. What happened when they came back from Hawaii with their suntans? Would an alien be waiting? Or an FBI agent who said I was a mass murderer and any information they might have, etc., etc. What a great welcome home. Neighbors would whisper. Friends would call, greedy for details. Brady would have to change schools. I pound fist into palm and walk. Up and down the room, up and down. I have totalled enough mileage to cross the country.

Angel Island sits in San Francisco Bay not far from its more famous neighbor, Alcatraz. It is wooded and lots bigger than the windswept prison rock. Ayala Cove on the north, formerly Hospital Cove, is named after a Spanish explorer. Only a few rangers live on the island to guard buildings dating from the Civil War and the concrete shells of barracks where Chinese immigrants were interned.

I broke into one of the small rental sailboats at Cass's Marina in Sausalito at three in the morning. I used a hacksaw to cut the lock on the cabin door. A dog barked on a nearby houseboat and then was silent. The sails and little outboard motor and gas tank were inside. I ghosted out of the slip and into Richardson Bay on just a jib and a breath of wind, then raised the mainsail when I got far enough out. When the wind died, I fired up the motor and puttered south toward the tip of Belvedere and the black mass of Angel Island beyond. A pale moon was overhead. The lights of Sausalito to the starboard looked like diamonds on velvet. I thought about the good times Maureen and I had there. Memory isn't indifferent. It either torments or comforts.

There was wind in Raccoon Strait and I turned off the motor. It was a fine evening, full of cold stars and silence. We used to think we were alone in the universe. We should be so lucky.

The water hissed under the hull, and the boat left a sparkling phosphorescent wake. Did that shark cruise beneath the dark water waiting for the go-ahead to attack? It was plenty big enough to hole the boat and pick me off the floating debris. I dropped sail and anchored in the cove close enough so I could wade to shore. You would be surprised how little water sharks need to swim in. My hair was standing on end as I came on the beach.

Small waves slopped against the sand as if it had been a long journey and now they were worn out. There were a few lights on the island but no one stirred. I climbed the paved road that winds around the island to the crest. San Francisco was laid out across the water in a brilliant grid of lights. I picked out landmarks such as Coit Tower and the dunce cap of the Transamerica Pyramid. To the right, the stagy Palace of Fine Arts was lit by floodlights. The two bridges were empty. I could see when Danforth came if he brought company by land or sea. I moved into the trees and found a place to rest against a trunk. The air was heavy with the smell of eucalyptus, the Australian import they are trying to exterminate on the island. Its curled bark, like dry skin flaked off from sunburn, crunched underfoot. I didn't want to lie on the dirt for fear of ticks, so I sat against the tree trunk. Deer and raccoons rustling around the leaves kept me awake until just before dawn. When the sun came up, I ate some cheese from my pocket and watched the pale fog slowly burn off. I felt like ground that had been fought over for a century.

The first ferry came across from Tiburon and let off a crowd of schoolkids and teachers. Danforth was the last off, conspicuous in his suit and tie. There were no other boats on the water, and the sky was empty except for a couple of big jets high up on the approach to San Francisco International. Danforth sat on a stone wall and looked back at Tiburon. He took off his coat and loosened his tie. When I got close, he heard my footsteps and turned.

"Christ," he said with disgust, "put the gun away. Someone will see you."

I stuck it in my belt. "Just being cautious."

"'Cautious' is not a word I'd use for you." He looked out of sorts. His work was glad-handing on Capitol Hill, not this sort of thing. If it was East Coast time he would be taking some politician or committee staff member to lunch. No matter who reached for the check, the taxpayer would get stuck. After a while I suppose it seems like the real world. He scratched at a rash above his collar.

"Hives. It's nerves, thanks to you." He looked around to

see if we were watched. "Your reporter friend came to see me. You didn't say anything to him about aliens."

"No, I didn't."

"It'll be interesting to see what his reaction is. He'll walk away the way I should have. What do you want? It's nice here, but I've got work to do. Half the FBI has arrived. Connory is running the investigation now. He's out of Chicago. A real son of a bitch." He spat and rubbed it into the sand with the sole of a highly polished shoe.

"What does he think?"

"Nothing yet. He's still getting his feet wet, as he keeps saying. He thinks there's a connection somewhere that ties everything into a neat little package. It's his midwestern optimism. Thanks for the cult theory, by the way. He thinks I'm a genius for coming up with it. But cults worship something or somebody, and we haven't come up with what it is. Without that, forget it." He paused. "Maybe I'll get lucky and he'll figure it out on his own."

"Figure out what?"

"You know," he said uneasily.

"You sound like you are starting to believe."

"You said that, not me."

"Can they explain the radio telescope that was zapped yet?"

"A big power surge. That's all we know at this point."

"Like the one at the Ajax Arms."

"You might say that. Look, what do you want?" He looked at his watch. "The ferry leaves in ten minutes."

"They probably fried it because they thought it was tracking them. Did you talk to Birkshire?"

"He's missing, too, like that mother and daughter who lived by the park. I suppose you don't know what happened to them? Or him, for that matter."

"They dropped me off at the BART station. That was the last I saw of them."

"The cops figure you killed them and hid the bodies. They found your fingerprints in the house. They're looking for the pickup." He gave me a critical up-and-down look. "You look pretty rough. You got leaves and stuff in your hair."

I tried to comb them out with my fingers.

"It's on your back, too. I've never seen so many bums per capita as you have in San Francisco. You look like you fit right in."

A flock of seagulls flew low over the water but kept going. "What does Kathy Birkshire say about her missing husband?"

"She's being brave. She's taken a leave of absence."

"That's smart. People were beginning to notice. Do you know yet what happened to the princess's money and credit cards?"

"Somebody broke into supersecure databases and fiddled."

"Who ended up with the money?"

"Security Concerns is at the end of a maze of holding companies and interlocking directorates, none of them real. They exist only in cyberspace. Our people are really impressed. It's the most masterful job of covering tracks anybody has ever seen. They're saying it's genius." He got up. "I have to start heading for the ferry." I walked with him.

"They nearly got you," he said.

"I got careless."

"It won't be long now."

"I'm not the only one running out of time. These things are smarter than us. Don't worry about Ford, by the way. They've got him finessed."

"Who does?"

"The publisher. He's one of them."

"How do you know that?" He was peevish.

"Behavior. He's acting different. He killed a column about

how Kathy Birkshire has changed. His wife was murdered, and now Birkshire's husband is gone because they both figured it out."

We neared the ferry. The deckhands watched us. People stay the day on Angel Island. Nobody takes the second ferry back.

"Maybe you shouldn't go any farther," Danforth said. We stopped.

"Connory won't be any different than you," I said. "He'll refuse the jump. He's got career and family to think about, too."

I took it from his silence that he agreed.

"These things might already be burrowing into the government in Washington. Maybe the FBI director's one by now," I said. "People have to know. They're being led to the slaughter by your silence."

"Bring me the evidence," he said doggedly.

"By the time there's the kind of evidence that satisfies you, it'll be too late."

Danforth didn't meet my eye. "I've got a favor to ask."

I halfway knew what was coming.

"When they nail you, keep me out of it. Nobody knows we've been talking."

"Jesus," I said. "You're unbelievable."

His face was sullen.

"Fuck your career. Nobody's going to have a career. There won't be any fucking FBI anymore."

"If you're right," he said with the same stubbornness.

"You know I'm right."

Danforth gave me a level look. "If I did for sure, it would be different."

I walked away without looking back. He could have pulled out his gun and drilled me. I wondered why he didn't.

"The suspect ignored several commands to halt." He would have been a big hero.

I waded out to the sailboat and upped anchor. The ferry-boat was halfway across Raccoon Strait by the time I raised sail. There wasn't much wind, so I yanked the pull rope on the motor and puttered east toward San Pablo Bay. An hour later, I slipped into an empty berth in San Rafael. I took a bus to the transit center and got a transfer to Larkspur Landing. I registered at the Courtyard Inn just down the road from San Quentin Prison. That is where they gas murderers when the last appeal has been turned down. Death Row was the least of my worries. I slept like one of its graduates when I got to my room. No dreams, just oblivion.

But I woke up unrefreshed, as usual. My batteries were way down. I wished I was in Hawaii with Maureen and Brady under a palm tree with a drink that had a paper umbrella. We'd throw a ball or play in the warm, blue water.

I got the afternoon paper in the lobby and read while I ate in the restaurant. "Where Is He?" the big black headline asked, meaning me. The only thing new was the mayor would have a news conference tomorrow to answer charges that he had failed to show leadership.

I walked down the road and called Ford from a pay phone in a Mexican restaurant. "Let me call you back," he said. I waited a few minutes and the phone rang.

"I didn't want to talk to you there," Ford said. "The new publisher's still hanging around. People can't quit talking about how the guy has changed. They don't know whether to be impressed or pissed off. The editors don't dare go home while he's in the building for fear he thinks they're slacking off. I'm across the street." His voice faded. "A gin and tonic. Make it a double."

He came back. "What have you got for me?"

"Forget the FBI. They're going to stonewall."

"Stonewall what?"

"What they know."

Ford spoke with elaborate patience. "And what is that, exactly? You said this was the biggest story I would ever work on, but I'm still waiting to find out what."

"Why is the mayor coming out from hiding?"

"He couldn't hole up any longer. People were beginning to talk."

"What kind of talk?"

"Insider political garbage. Lack of leadership. Not there when the city needs him. Who cares? That's a minor sideshow."

"Did you ever ask where his wife is?"

"I will at the press conference."

"Where is it going to be?"

"City hall. It'll be a zoo. There are news organizations from all over the world in town."

"Do me a favor."

"What is it?"

"Ask about the missing psychics. The FBI is taking its sweet time sharing that with the rest of the world."

"What does the mayor know if the bureau's not talking?"

"He knows, believe me."

"Any other questions you want answered?" he asked sarcastically.

"This whole thing is about to blow. You'll be way ahead of the pack." That cheered him up.

The next morning I went to a uniform supply house in San Francisco and bought a blue jumpsuit like technicians wear. I got a tool belt at a hardware store and enough tools to fill it. "Looks like you're starting from scratch," the clerk said.

"Mine were stolen."

We agreed there was a lot of that going around. I bought a stack of work order forms at a stationery store. I changed in a restaurant rest room near city hall. A homeless guy so dirty he looked like he had been digging coal was riding an expensive mountain bike, obviously stolen. I stopped him and offered a hundred bucks for it.

"Sure, okay," he said eagerly. He was already thinking how drunk he could get.

"And another hundred if you have it at the steps of city hall at one o'clock. I'll give you the money then."

"Yeah, sure." Even more eager.

He wanted a down payment but I said no. "Be at city hall." I showed him two hundred-dollar bills, and his eyes got wide. I put them back in my pocket.

I hung around the park across the street until I saw the news vans start to pull up. Out-of-town crews arrived by cab. Inside, a line of reporters and cameramen waited to go through the metal detector. Security is usually a joke, with guards lazily waving you through. But they were showing off, combing through the trunks the TV crews pack their gear in. TV people don't think the rules apply to them because of the public's right know or something. They were loudly beefing about the searches.

"I've got a work order!" I yelled over the bitching. "Air conditioning." I held it out to a guard trying to communicate with a Japanese newsman. "The poor bastards are cooking up there."

He ran his eyes over the work order and motioned me through. The tools on the belt set off the metal detector, but it was ignored. That's how I got my gun through.

Nobody was checking names in the mayor's office. There must have been sixty newspeople and technicians already setting up. The press conference was to be televised live. I walked in and squatted at an electrical outlet and pretended to work on it with a screwdriver. A few minutes later there was a stir as Mayor Mario Fortunato walked into the room. I stood and watched while sound guys did their voice levels and fiddled with the mikes. Bald and immaculately tailored as usual, the mayor stood without expression. He should have been trading insults and jokes with the newsies. That was his trademark. Instead, he was still and cold. When somebody said they were ready to roll, Mayor Fortunato woodenly read a statement. He promised that the person or persons responsible for the bombing would be found and prosecuted to the fullest extent of the law.

"Mr. Mayor," Ford's voice boomed when he was finished, "no one has seen your wife for several weeks. Where is she?"

"Jesus Christ," a British reporter near me muttered. "Can't we save the small town gossip for later?"

"And psychics are disappearing all over the Bay Area," Ford continued. "What's your explanation?"

Mayor Fortunato would not have turned a hair. He would have filled the air with verbal uppercuts if he didn't want to answer. He would have said something in Latin or quoted Mark Twain to gain time. He was famous for his ability to duck and weave. Instead, he just looked at Ford.

"I don't know what you are talking about," he said finally. I had no doubt he was one of them.

"Do you expect arrests anytime soon?" somebody yelled. Screw the mayor's wife and the psychics, they were in town for the bombing story.

"What about cults?" a woman cried. "*Action News* has learned exclusively that cult involvement is suspected."

"The investigation is proceeding and I am confident we will locate the individual or individuals responsible," Mayor Fortunato said. His expression didn't change.

"Where's the police chief's wife?" Ford bellowed. "She's missing, too."

"What's with this guy?" the Brit complained to his sound man.

"I don't know what you are talking about," the mayor said.

I had the tool belt off. I stooped to lay it on the floor and pulled my gun from inside my shirt. Everyone's attention was on the mayor. They didn't know what was going on between him and Ford, but they suddenly smelled story.

The mayor's press secretary was the only one who saw me. He started to raise his hand in warning.

I shot the mayor in the chest.

I turned and ran like a deer.

Screams and yells behind me as I tore down the corridor. I took the steps three or four at a time down the grand marble staircase. People scrambled out of my way. Instinct takes over when a man with a gun who looks nuts is coming at you. I burst through the entrance and spotted the bum with the bike. He threw it down and took off running when he saw me coming. I stuck the gun in my belt and straddled the bike. A couple of quick-witted cameramen got to a window upstairs and got footage of me pedaling away. As news producers say, the press conference produced great visuals.

I rode the two blocks to Market Street and bumped down the escalator to the Muni Metro station. A train bound for West Portal was about to leave. I jumped off the bike and just make it before the doors closed. I sat down blowing, my heart hammering in a scary way. If stress shortens your life, I was lopping months off with every hour that passed. I had armpits down to my waist and kept wiping sweat off my face.

By the time we got to West Portal, my breathing was seminormal. I went into a neighborhood men's store and bought a change of clothes, light colors because the police would be looking for dark. I had the salesman take the tags off and I wore the outfit out the door, with the blue uniform in a bag. There were a lot of black-and-white units on the streets as I walked back to the West Portal station for a train back downtown.

When the train went through the Civic Center station, there was a mob of detectives standing around the bike. They jawed as they waited for the fingerprint people. I stood like the others and pretended to gape until the train pulled out for the Powell Street station. I walked from there to the downtown transit center and boarded a Golden Gate bus back to Marin. The street in front of city hall was closed off and filled with police cars when the bus made the turn on Van Ness Avenue.

"What now?" a woman a few seats from me wondered aloud.

"There's always something," a man answered.

"The mayor's been shot," the driver said over his shoulder. "We heard it from dispatch." The passengers gasped.

"Oh, my God," said the woman who had asked what now.

"This place is a shithole," the driver said.

I already had the next move figured out. When the bus got to San Rafael, I walked to the cable television building where people go to appear on the public access channel. The sun was warm on my shoulders. You would think it was a wonderful day unless you knew better.

"Are you here for the taping?" an elderly secretary asked when I walked in. Good. I didn't have to round up the technical people.

"Sorry I'm late."

"They haven't started yet." She pointed at a door. "Right in there."

A man and a woman sat at a table on either side of a moderator. A man behind a camera faced them. All four looked at me as I walked into the studio. I locked the door and pulled out my gun.

"Nobody gets hurt if you do what I say."

"This is the debate on the neighborhood arts program," the moderator said. He was a small man in an ugly plaid jacket. It doesn't matter what you look like on public access TV.

"Lie down on the floor with your hands straight out. Not you," I told the cameraman.

"What's this all about?" the moderator asked in a shaky voice. I motioned with the gun and he got down. The neighborhood arts debaters followed.

"You ready to roll?" I asked the cameraman. He swallowed and nodded.

I sat in one of the chairs on the set. I nodded at the camera. "Start taping." A red light appeared.

"I'm Goodwin Armstrong," I said. "I just shot the mayor of San Francisco" (the woman on the floor gave out a muffled sob) "and I put the bomb in Security Concerns. I want to explain why."

I wasn't the least bit nervous in front of the camera. It was like talking to a stranger who was too polite to interrupt. I took twenty-seven minutes to tell it all. "I know what I have said sounds crazy and many of you will think I am, too. But think about what I said. Too many things have happened to be explained away. Maybe, like the missing and dead psychics, some of you have also felt the presence of the aliens. You don't have to be a psychic to have extrasensory perception. Many have it to some degree. What is important is we have to put pressure on the government to do something; otherwise we're all finished. Call your member of Congress and senator. Call the president. Now. Before it's too late." I nodded to the cameraman, and the red light went off.

"The goddamdest thing I ever heard," he said. "Is it true?"

"How long to make ten copies of that cassette?"

"Not long."

"Get going," I said.

While he started, I told the people they could get up from

the floor. "Sorry I had to do that. I needed to concentrate on what I was saying."

They brushed themselves off. I told them to take a seat. I had a funny urge to ask how I had done, but I doubted they would be honest if they thought I stank. When the cameraman gave me the cassettes, I took their car keys and herded everybody into a closet. I said I would be right outside.

"All done?" the secretary asked when I came out of the studio.

"A technical foul-up. They have to start all over again. I can't stay, unfortunately." I was aware of a blur of movement on the wall to my left.

A security camera had jerked around aggressively to stare. I hadn't noticed it when I came in.

I hoped saying there had been a problem kept the secretary from ducking her head in to see what was taking so long. They would kick the closet door open as soon as they realized I was gone. I gave it ten minutes. I picked a brown Honda in the parking lot and left the other keys on the roof of the car next to it. Four counts of kidnapping (I forced them from one room to another), unlawful imprisonment, and grand theft auto. The list of criminal offenses was getting longer.

I had already got the addresses from Ford, so I drove to the Federal Express office and mailed the tapes to the major newspapers and the networks in New York and to their local affiliates. In case they were too high-minded to use them, I also sent tapes to the tabloid newspapers and TV shows.

Being hunted sharpens the senses. You hear better and notice more. I knew I was being followed as I drove north on Highway 101 in the brown Honda. Traffic was moderately heavy, as was usual that time of afternoon. What I felt was like the small change in air pressure when somebody stands behind you. You can't see him, but you know he is there. I took the Black Point cutoff and headed east. A couple of miles ahead was a vast dirt parking lot where windshields winked in the sun. It was the Renaissance Pleasure Faire, where thousands paid to watch hundreds in period costumes act as if the Middle Ages had made a comeback. Maureen loved the pageantry. She dressed Brady in velvet like a page and did herself up as a lady-in-waiting. I was always too busy to go.

In the rearview mirror I saw five Tauruses behind me peel off the freeway when I did. Only one was blue. They must have leased a fleet of them, or maybe they took over a Ford franchise.

I drove into the dirt parking lot past a tank trunk spraying water to keep dust down. Each Taurus that followed carried two or three men. They had me now.

A parking attendant made hand signals to direct me toward the far reaches of the parking lot. I ignored him and gunned for the close-up VIP parking. He held a hand up and started to step in the way but thought better of it. He yelled as I went past, then his eyes went to the cars behind me. He stepped in front of the first Taurus and stopped it. I left the Honda blocking an aisle with the engine running and ran to the entrance. I pushed twenty bucks at the cashier and didn't wait for change. I ran past knights in armor jousting on horses. Buxom women nearly burst from low-cut gowns, and men were in smocks and tunics. Maureen and Brady always came back dusty and happy and full of stories about their day at the faire. What work of mine had been so important at the time? Insurance fraud? Somebody's divorce? Some snotty rich kid who tried to find himself by getting lost?

I burrowed into the faire, which meandered a mile or more into an old oak forest. It was warm, and dust rose from shuffling feet and hung in the sunlight coming through trees. A single person would attract more attention, so I latched on to groups that kept forming and breaking apart.

A couple of times I saw big men moving with purpose through the crowds, looking hard into faces. Had the aliens possessed an entire teamsters local for the muscle? They were ahead as well as behind now. I thought of sneaking off into the woods but decided I was safer with people around. They would take me over on the spot if they got me. My soul or personality or whatever would be sucked out just like that, leaving only the husk. What came next was obvious. When the tapes were shown on TV, they would have me turn myself in and act so crazy the public would shrug me off as just another nut case. Maureen and Brady would have to be hunted down and killed. The thing that formerly was me would tell the aliens where to look.

It was about then that I realized my gun was gone. I had

taken it out of my belt and put it on the passenger seat. When I jumped out, I left it behind. I raged at myself. It wasn't much, but it was still better than nothing. Like an animal worn out by the chase, I looked for a place to hole up. I saw two men dressed in Elizabethan finery stroll from a hut. I ducked inside after a look around to see if anyone was watching.

It was a changing room with a curtain at the rear. A man sat on a rough bench. He played a rustic, judging from his costume. He wrapped his legs with rags.

"Good day to ye, sir," he said. Maureen told me the costumed characters always stayed in character.

"Bless you," I faltered, "and . . . and . . . a fine one it is, sure."

"It is the evening you're working?"

"Aye." I wondered if I should risk a "blimey."

He finished winding the rags and stood. "And how do I look to ye, good sire?"

"Very well indeed." We traded bows and he left.

Costumes hung from pegs. I looked behind the curtain and saw three cots with blankets and pillows. Voices approached, so I got on one and pulled the covers over my head. The door opened and a voice said, "Powerful hot, wouldn't 'e say, good sire?"

"Verily like the hinges of hell," said a second voice. I heard footsteps on the plank floor. "Shush," the first voice said. "I see someone's entwined in the arms of Morpheus."

"Eh?"

"Asleep."

"Oh."

They drew up chairs and whispered for a while, then left. If I hid long enough, maybe the things chasing me would give up. This was as good a place to hide as I was likely to find, so I stayed on the cot with the covers pulled up. Cast members came and went, peeking behind the curtain from habit to see if someone was sacked out. A couple of hours passed. The door opened and closed. Two new voices spoke.

"A strange thing with Leslie-Marie. Freaked out, she did."

"You can't say 'freaked out,' good friend. It is a modernism."

"I misspoke. I crave your pardon."

"Freely given, sire. What about the fair lady you mentioned?"

"She is a fortune-teller."

"That I knew."

"Supposedly, she has genuine psychic powers."

"The ability to foretell, you mean."

The pause was testy. "Do ye want to hear the tale told or not?"

"Hold forth."

"Everyone has an aura, by her accounting. She is able to perceive them."

"Pray continue."

"They are of different colors and signify many things, including health."

"Such is my limited understanding of auras."

"They have been photographed."

"You mean likenesses made."

"I crave your pardon again."

"Freely given."

"She told others she began to notice there were many men in the crowd who had no auras."

"And?"

"By her reckoning, this is an impossibility."

"If the absence of aura is an impossibility, how did she explain this curious circumstance?"

"Alas, there was no explanation to be had."

"And why is that, pray?"

"She became greatly agitated. She cried aloud that there were strange critters among us."

"Faith and surely the right expression would be 'creeturs.'"

"Whatever." This in an impatient voice. "In the event, she ran off, screaming."

"Screaming?"

"Literally screaming. Saying they were after her."

"Who was?"

"Those things without auras."

"What happened then?"

"She ran into the trees and hasn't yet returned. There is no one to tell fortunes until Rachael comes."

There was a thoughtful silence, then their talk drifted to all the terrible things that had happened in San Francisco. They wondered if the person who had committed all those unspeakable crimes would ever be caught. And didn't it make more sense that there was a conspiracy involving many? One man surely could not accomplish so much evil. When their break was over, they left.

I couldn't stay any longer. People were bound to notice the same shape occupied the cot. They would ask if I was sick and needed help. I got up and poked around the costumes on the pegs. The one closest to fitting was a soldier's getup. Boots, gloves, green tights, a tunic with chain mail, and a helmet with a visor that opened and shut, with a slit to see through. A two-handed sword in a scabbard hung with it. I put the costume on and checked out the blade. It was hand-forged and had a keen edge. I crammed my clothes into a gunnysack with a drawstring.

It was dark outside, and lights hung in the trees cast a cozy glow on the faire. I blended in with the crowd. Now and then a lady dropped a curtsy or a courtier bowed. I ducked my head in reply and kept moving. When someone mentioned the French threat or, the Lord preserve us, had I heard of the scandalous behavior of the duke of Northumberland, I pretended I didn't hear. In fact, it was almost as hard to hear with the visor down as to see. The crowd showed the effects of the ale and wine shops. Grinning men slurred words, and women laughed shrilly. I was a quarter of a mile from the entrance when the lights dimmed and then went out. There was a surprised silence and then an uproar.

"Did you forget to pay the bill?" a wit yelled.

I lifted the visor to see better. The only light was from torches and campfires burning for atmosphere. The flames showed the Elizabethans peering with worried looks. Thunder muttered.

"I warned you rain was forecast," said a voice in the darkness.

"They have to give our money back," another answered.

Someone with a bullhorn said not to panic. "We'll get this fixed in a minute."

The crowd was too mellow for panic, even when the lights didn't come back on. Flashlights appeared, and monitors directed people toward the parking lot. I lowered the visor and joined a guild of weavers who sat watching the shadows shuffle past. A campfire lit their faces.

"Welcome, good sire," a woman in a bonnet said. "A most strange occurrence."

"Verily." My voice boomed in the helmet. Someone in the darkness invited me to take my ease. I said thankee and moved to a bench where shadows were deepest. The weavers went back to studying the crowd.

This was a planned blackout. Maybe the aliens decided the search was taking too long and wanted to force the pace. They would scrutinize the crowd as it funneled out the exit. When it was gone, they would wait for the faire players to change from their costumes and leave. They would spot me sooner or later.

The first drops of rain hissed in the fire. "Christ," said a man at a loom. "That's all we need."

I slipped into the dark forest behind the weaver encampment and climbed the hill. The rain pattered harder on the leaf-covered ground, and a thick, earthy smell rose. Lightning flashed suddenly, scalding the trees with lurid white light. A thunderclap came at once. It was a passing autumn shower, and the raindrops were fat and warm. They made a bonking sound on the helmet.

If I continued through the forest over the hill, I would hit the highway, where I could change into street clothes and hitch a ride. I reached a clearing at the crest of the hill and started across. Two men stepped from the shadows on the left and right when I was halfway across.

They had outsmarted me. They guessed I would run for it rather than follow the crowd. They moved toward me. A far-off stab of lightning glinted on something in their hands. Suddenly, adrenaline lit a red-flamed rage in me. Fuck them. I wasn't going down without a fight. I yanked the sword from the scabbard and ran straight at the man on the left. I brought the two-handed sword around like Babe Ruth swinging for the fences. He raised an arm, but the blade flashed underneath and caught him in the rib cage.

"Die, sucker!" I yelled.

He grunted as sword bit into bone. I didn't have time to give him another lick. I spun, and the other man was nearly on me. My long backhand connected with a sound like a ripe melon hitting the floor. No words from him, either, just oomph as the breath left him. He stood as if pondering his next move, and I ran him through. He fell to his knees and then forward, his weight yanking the sword from my hands. The other man held himself where he had been slashed. I kicked him in the stomach, and he went down. I swept up the bag with my clothes and ran. I left the sword behind. I didn't have the stomach to pull it out.

They had known I would make for the highway, so it was a safe bet more were in that direction. I moved east along the ridgeline instead. I kept stumbling over low brush and into tree trunks, but the rain covered the sound. Then it began to let up. Far off toward Black Point, I heard music and headed for it. I came to a deer fence and climbed over. Through the trees I saw bright lights. A party was going on outside the rear of a big house. A swimming pool sparkled like a sapphire. Musicians in a gazebo decorated with balloons played a rhumba. A well-dressed older crowd was just coming out from under the shelter of beach umbrellas and beginning to dance again. The smell of meat being barbecued made my guts twist from hunger.

Nobody noticed as I stepped from the trees. I pulled the visor down and walked onto the lawn that sloped to where they danced. A couple in their sixties at a table under an umbrella looked up.

"I got the dates messed up," I told them. "The costume party is next week."

"That blood sure looks real," the man said.

I looked down. The armor and tights were covered with it. "They give it to you at the rental place," I answered. "It's the stuff Hollywood uses."

"It's too realistic," the woman said. She turned her face away.

I kept moving, heading toward a rectangle of light in the back of the house that was a doorway. People gave way with amused smiles. They thought I was the surprise entertainment.

I played to it. "It won't be long now. You will be amazed and delighted."

I went through several rooms with this line. A hum of conversation followed me. The men looked like top-echelon business executives, and a lot of the wives had tight faces from plastic surgery. I came to a study with books filling the walls. A television was on and men smoking cigars watched my driver's license photograph on the screen.

"The search goes on for Goodwin Armstrong. . . ."

I kept going until I spotted the front door. Outside, a young valet parker in a long white coat leaned against a porch column. He straightened up when he saw me. He had a red crew cut and freckles and looked like the kids who steal pies from windows in Norman Rockwell paintings.

He grinned. "Yes, sir, which car?"

"The BMW." I could just as easily have said Mercedes or Lexus. It was that kind of crowd.

"Blue or red?"

"Blue."

He trotted off and a minute later wheeled up the blue BMW. "Great outfit," he said as I slid behind the wheel.

"Thanks." I took off the helmet so I could see to drive.

"You ought to wear it at the faire."

"There's an idea." I pulled away with a wave.

It must have been just moments later that everyone at that party was killed, including the kid. Chuck Dean, age nineteen, was listed in the paper as one of the victims. Had to be him. Nobody else was under sixty. The aliens had tracked me to the house. They must have hoped I was hiding in a closet or under a bed. When the search came up empty, they didn't want witnesses. The fire burned with amazing speed. The only case the experts could compare it with was the Ajax Arms fire.

I drove up the road until I found a place to pull off and change clothes. Then I continued on to Sacramento. I slept in the car overnight and drove to a small airfield. I was waiting at the door when the air charter outfit opened in the morning. I hired a pilot and a twin-engine private plane to fly me to Portland. I counted what was left of the princess's money as we flew. I still had sixteen thousand dollars and change. I caught a Delta flight to Atlanta via Dallas. The papers in each of those cities had big stories about the hunt for me.

I think about those poor people at the party. One minute they are fox-trotting to some old number popular when they were young, and the next, strangers with blank faces filter down from the trees and push them inside. I know from talking to victims that they never believe the bad stuff is really happening. The screams must have been awful when the house was zapped and began to burn.

Every war has innocent victims. Military people call this collateral damage so they don't have to think about the people who die. I think of that freckle-faced kid who was parking cars.

t was like a war scare or a presidential assassination. People gathered around television sets or bent to radios. News specials showed crowds standing in front of store windows watching TV, in offices, even at sports bars where bulletins interrupted the games. When they came back on, the play-by-play guys and color commentators talked about my tape. It got saturation air play. "What do you think?" the sports guys asked each other dryly or uneasily. Nobody knew what line to take. Were we talking hoax here, or should people be scared? There were shots of players in dugouts watching on portable TV sets or listening with radios held to their ears.

Flipping through the channels, I saw myself at the start of the tape, halfway through, and then at the close, when I asked people to demand action. "Before it's too late," I said. I have to say it was an inspired line. It was put in quotes in newspaper headlines and was the sound bite used most.

The cameraman must have sensed I was coming to the end, because he had me in a tight close-up when I said "Before it's too late." That close-up was shown over and over. Strain was in my face, and fatigue. Desperation, if you looked closely enough. But I appeared sane. Various experts interviewed agreed on that. "But often," a bearded psychiatrist cautioned on *Nightline*, "the people who look sanest can be the most delusional."

I walked down the hallway of the motel I checked into near the Atlanta airport. I felt like I had been living in motels forever. I carried a bag of fried chicken from a fast food place. I passed a group of Mexican housekeepers watching a Spanish-language station as an announcer translated my words. They glanced at me and turned back to the television. Two had rosary beads out. Maureen believed in total isolation on vacation. No television, no radio, no telephone, just stacks of books and CDs. So there was a good chance she and Brady didn't know yet. Maybe there was a village in Asia or Africa that hadn't heard either.

I locked the door and turned on the TV. Grease from the chicken had soaked through the bag. "The man is a murderer," the president's press secretary was saying. "Why should the administration have a comment? This is a matter for the police and the courts."

A quick cut to Congressman Cox. "I am as revolted by the crimes as everyone else. They occurred in my district, and very dear friends were among the victims. But in light of the great concern being expressed at the grassroots level, there should be hearings to explore the man's allegations. I would expect that if the administration has nothing to hide—and I want to be clear at this point that I'm not saying that it does—it will cooperate fully. The American people deserve no less."

The radio talk shows couldn't begin to handle all the calls. Half the listeners who got through said it was an outrage that so much air time was given to a mass murderer shooting off his crazy mouth. The others said the government knew aliens had landed but was hiding it. Otherwise, how did Washington explain the destroyed radio telescope? And how about the dead and missing psychics? I wasn't a murderer to these callers, but a hero. Many suspected the United Nations was mixed up with this somehow.

My lawyer, Hal Trump, held a press conference to call on me to turn myself in. A legal defense fund had been established. He held up an 800 number for contributions as he worked up a sad smile. "We stand behind you, Goodwin." There was a little catch in his voice. You had to give him credit. This kind of opportunity doesn't come in a hundred lawyer lifetimes. It was clear the story would put even O. J. Simpson in the shade. Trump wanted to make sure he was in on the ground floor.

I'm trying to remember what I was feeling. Relief for sure. The word was finally out. Blowing up Security Concerns and shooting down the mayor ensured that the video would be aired for days. I was both news and entertainment, a media commodity, a global celebrity who made ratings and circulation jump. Everybody makes money in these cases except the poor bastard in the spotlight. I bet movie deals were already being pitched.

If most people believed I was nuts, fine. Enough would think I was telling the truth that the government would have the burden of proof. Good luck trying to explain everything that had happened. I wondered how our visitors were riding out the storm. After months of silent tunneling nobody but psychics had noticed, the anthill had been kicked over. I said on the tape to watch for big personality changes, particularly in leaders.

"They don't need ordinary people," I said. "We're nothing." That was a nice touch. Piss off people enough and they forget to be afraid.

I hoped being found out made the aliens pack up and leave for some other place to colonize. But Princess Dulay had made a point of the big emotional surge when they found Earth. They knew just how vast and empty space was. So the odds were they would tough it out. Their weapons had to be way beyond ours, but maybe they couldn't use them without damaging ecological systems as vital to them as to us. So they had a big problem.

So did I. I was bone tired. A week in bed and a diet to flush out the junk-food toxins and I might get back to normal. But I wasn't going to ease up. I couldn't. God or fate had called me to defend the human race.

Security Concerns's head office in downtown Atlanta was under surveillance, not only by government agents but by the news media. Their cars and vans lined the street, ignoring the no-parking signs. Uniformed cops were at the entrance to the tall office building, questioning everyone. If you couldn't prove you had business inside, you didn't get in.

I wore overalls, a blue work shirt, and battered lace-up boots. I had on a straw hat, dark glasses, and a big wad of chewing gum bulging in one cheek like a chaw of tobacco. The look I hoped for was a peckerwood in by a mule from the piney woods. People would see that and not the face that overnight was as familiar as the pope's.

"Is this it?" I whined to a woman waiting in line to enter the building. "Is them aliens up in that there building, like they say?"

She gave me a look of dislike. "I couldn't tell you."

A man in a business suit in front of her turned. "You don't really believe that aliens crap?"

"Wal, ain't that what the TV says?" I lifted the hat to scratch my head. He laughed with scorn. Another man told him, "What makes you so sure? Did you see *Final Edition* last night? They said Armstrong could be on to something. It can't all be coincidence."

"Final Edition—don't make me laugh. That's yellow journalism."

Others put in their two cents' worth. The whole thing was a crock, some said. The aliens really had arrived and something should be done, others argued. A few said there wasn't enough evidence one way or the other to know. I shifted my cud to the other side of my mouth and drifted away. I overheard somebody say the Security Concerns people came and went in two vans with a police escort because of telephone threats. When I saw how thoroughly officers checked out IDs and questioned people who wanted in the building, I decided against trying.

I got a newspaper for the classifieds. Waiting for inspiration to tell me what to do next, I looked for a used car. Then I saw an ad for a gun show. I bought an old Plymouth with bald tires for cash from a redneck and drove it to the gun show. It was hot, and the humidity had to be near 100 percent. There were dozens of booths at the show—gun manufacturers, private dealers, and people who sold specialty stuff. I made two circuits of the hall before I zeroed in on the dealer who had a Confederate flag and stacks of militia literature on a table. He sold heavy-duty military equipment, including surplus tanks and personnel carriers. Photographs of his inventory were pinned to corkboards.

Tanner was his name. A skinny guy with a prominent Adam's apple, he had burning dark eyes and Elvis sideburns under a fatigue cap. "I guess it wouldn't be hard to switch this Chinese assault rifle to fully automatic," I told him.

"I wouldn't know."

"I wouldn't either."

We both smiled knowingly.

"Where do you keep your big stuff?"

"Out on my farm. You see anything you're interested in? I

got maps show how to get there. If financin' is a problem, I can carry the paper myself."

"My garage ain't big enough."

"You got a backyard, don't you?"

"Nope. Apartment."

"Come on out and look anyhow. Whenever you want. Just phone ahead. I'm kind of a tourist attraction. Fact is, I'm thinkin' of chargin' admission, that's how many folks come by."

"I'm kinda worried guns might not be enough these days," I said.

"You mean the aliens?"

I nodded.

"I'm ready for 'em."

"I bet you are."

"If they can take what I can throw at them, there ain't no point in further resistance." But he seriously doubted that. He didn't care who they were or where they came from, they were dead meat if they stepped foot on his property without his okay.

We talked about the government and the U.N. and how they were pretty much two aspects of the same problem. Then we went back to the aliens.

"I'm looking to buy extra protection," I said.

"Extra like what?"

"Oh, I dunno. Something shoulder-held. Something that can penetrate a soft target like a car. Feller on TV says they're driving around in cars."

"Not much of that ordnance around, it bein' somewhat illegal." He gave me a careful look as he reset his cap on his head. "What there is is mighty expensive."

"I got the money," I said. "Cash."

He looked off into the crowd. "I might know somebody

who knows somebody could help you. I hear he wants four thousand. Likes used bills. No hundreds."

"That sounds reasonable."

"This man or woman, I'm not sayin' which, could probably get it to you as soon as tonight, if you want it that quick."

"This afternoon would be better."

He looked back to me. "You're in a real hurry, ain't you."

"My momma always said there weren't no flies on me. If these aliens are up to somethin', might as well be ready."

I drove out to his farm that afternoon. An employee in bib overalls who looked like he had an IQ well into the double digits checked to see if I was wired, while another went over the Plymouth with a fine-tooth comb. When they were satisfied, Tanner had me drive to a lonely swamp and leave the money under a bridge. There was a map taped to the spot where I put it. It directed me to a culvert twenty miles away, where a missile launcher was wrapped in plastic. It was a Blowpipe, made by the British. I had fired it a couple times during a NATO exercise when I was in the navy. It's aim-and-fire and hold the sensor on the target until it locks in. Simplicity itself.

I watched the building where Security Concerns's home office was for a couple of days. The vans that carried its employees never arrived or left at the same time, probably on advice of the FBI. Being guarded against possible harm must have confirmed the aliens in their belief we were stupid. Maybe there wasn't much doubt lingering when they realized I was a fugitive for having put up the only resistance to date.

Perhaps they wrote off my troublemaking as a fluke, a quirk not likely to be repeated. Even at that, matters hadn't turned out as badly as they feared. The people who counted still could not believe another species had landed. It didn't take digging to find this out. All they had to do was watch TV and read the papers.

The vans took different routes to and from Security Concerns. They went through red lights with their police escorts. Motorcycle cops waved you off if you followed too closely. But the vans had to use the same street to reach the office building. A crowd always waited to jeer and yell threats. There was an empty lot where winos hung out that the vans passed. At dawn the third day, I pulled up at the lot with a dozen bottles of 150-proof Puerto Rican rum in shopping bags. A dozen derelicts lying in the weeds were just beginning to wake up and wonder where the next drink was coming from. Santa himself would not have been more welcome. A couple of hours later, eight had passed out, and the others weren't far behind. The rum compared to the fortified wine they were used to was the difference between heavy artillery and firecrackers. The sober citizenry avoided that side of the street so they didn't get panhandled, meaning now I had it to myself. The morning commute was just beginning. A plainclothes cop car stopped a half block from me.

I set up the Blowpipe and waited. The police escort always used sirens, so I had plenty of warning. I crouched on one knee between cars at the curb. The motorcycle cops flashed past, then a couple of black-and-whites. I timed the shot and pulled the trigger. The rocket slammed into the side of the first van. The gas tank exploded, and my face was scorched by the heat. The second van hit the first, veered to the left, and rolled, throwing passengers out into burning wreckage. I didn't wait to see more. I dropped the launcher and ran for the fence at the rear of the vacant lot. The winos were sitting up in terror.

"Is Judgment Day come?" one cried as I ran past.

When I got back to the motel, I called Ford at home from the pay phone in front. His telephone rang several times before his sleepy voice answered.

"It's me," I said.

"This line is not secure," he warned, fully awake now.

"I got the aliens in Atlanta. I used a Blowpipe."

"You used poison darts?"

"A missile launcher."

The receiver was getting warm in my hand. "I don't want people to think it was anyone else but me."

I hung up and ducked behind a wall that separated the motel from the sidewalk. The telephone box blew up, scattering metal and hard plastic shrapnel in a fan-shaped arc. As I ran past the motel office, its security camera jerked in my direction and panned to follow me.

he Hole: Popping sounds. It is gunfire unless it's Chinese New Year and the celebration has started. Now the whack-whack of rotors. A helicopter. Shouting. The popping is closer.

The door swings open.

Danforth.

He is all in black. Black bulletproof vest. Face streaked with black. A black 9-millimeter pistol in his black-gloved hand.

"Let's go," he says.

We run down a corridor past closed doors. Body on the floor. Hop over it. Other figures in black running ahead of Danforth, boots drumming on the floor. More shots pop. Somebody holds a door open. We run through, down steps.

We're outside. Jesus, fresh air. It is night, with a starry sky overhead. Cold. It was summer when they brought me here.

Danforth and I run for the chopper. Whack-whack, the noise is deafening, beautiful. Up steps through the cabin door. Somebody behind me. "Go!" he yells.

The inside is dim and red-lit. We lift off, and the chopper reels drunkenly to the left. I'm thrown against someone, then slammed into a bucket seat. A safety belt is yanked tight. We are a couple of hundred feet high already. Streetlights lay out the grid of the city below with exact precision. Eight men in black jumpsuits and boots sit in facing rows. Two jam new magazines into their assault rifles. Nobody says anything. I can't tell which is Danforth. After this long isolation my senses are swamped, and I can't process it all. It's like the circuits are overloaded. I look around stupidly. A navigator behind the pilot and copilot talks into the mike on his helmet. I can't hear what he is saying, but it looks like he is relaying data from a computer. What I see of his face is bathed in a faint green light from the screen.

The helicopter rises and falls and tilts left and right like a carnival ride. If I had anything in my stomach, it wouldn't stay long. I guess we are hugging the ground to fool radar.

Questions fill my mind. I want to ask where are we going and what was that place and why did they keep me so long? There are hundreds of others I could ask. What about the aliens? and why are we running? top the list. I would have to yell for them to hear.

But there is something about these men that discourages talk. The minutes pass. There is a long last finger of streetlights that probes the darkness, then only blackness beneath. Our flight is level now, with no sudden course changes. After another half hour or so, the helicopter descends. We land and the door is yanked open and we exit into the blackness, the others going before me. They are swallowed by the dark. A hand is at my elbow. A jet engine whines somewhere nearby. A flashlight winks and we head for it at a dog trot. Asphalt beneath my bare feet and a pebble now and then make me hop in pain. The flashlight beam shows steps up into a Gulfstream and we climb aboard. Dim interior lights reveal six seats.

"Sit wherever you want," Danforth says.

Klunk. The door shuts and the whine increases in pitch:

eeeeEEEEEEEE. We're moving down a runway. The jet's running lights come on as we gather speed. The asphalt races past. Then we're airborne and climbing steeply. Danforth labors uphill to the cockpit and closes the door behind him. The cabin has a spartan interior. A little plaque on the bulkhead says Department of Transportation.

Danforth returns. "Put 'er there," he says. We shake hands and he sits down across the tiny aisle. The light is so dim I can barely make out his face. The cabin is warm. "You hungry? I've got sandwiches."

"No, thanks." I don't think I'll ever eat another sandwich. "Where are we going?"

"Camp David. The president wants to meet you."

"Huh?"

"You're getting the Medal of Freedom."

"I don't have any shoes." It's all I can think of to say.

"We'll fix you up. Get you a shower. Maybe you want to shave that beard off. Change of clothes. Whatever you need. It's a private ceremony."

"What's this all about?"

"He can't give you public recognition. A lot of people think you should be hanged. The president can't go against that kind of public opinion."

My thoughts whirl like confetti.

"Who were they back there?"

"Contract people. No government agency wanted their hands dirty, so they outsourced it."

"Outsourced what?"

"Those were the people who were going to get rid of you. Hired killers."

"Were?"

"When the decision came down."

"*What* decision?"

"What to do with you. There's been a big internal fight in

the administration. One side wanted to bring you to trial. Another said put him away and maybe the whole problem goes away. Some argued you should be honored for saving everybody's ass. Shades of opinion in all three camps, which is why the debate went on so long. When it looked like the people who wanted you silenced for good were going to prevail, we put together the escape."

The Medal of Freedom or a bullet in the back of the head. Quite a range in the options category.

"Maureen and Brady?" I ask.

"They're fine. You'll see them soon."

I start to unwind a little, but my body feels as kinked as old rope. "I was surprised it was night."

"Come again?"

"I would have bet it was day."

"Time gets screwed up in solitary." Danforth looks out the window.

"What about the aliens?"

"Gone. Out there somewhere. Some dairymen up early to milk in the Ozarks saw them burn through the stratosphere when they left."

The Gulfstream tunnels through the night. Every now and then I see points of light on the ground.

"Where are we?" I ask.

"Idaho."

A long silence passes. "Why kill me?"

"There were billions riding on it. Hundreds of billions, I suppose."

"I don't follow."

"The government had to take the position the alien thing was a hoax. Otherwise the hysteria would have been uncontrollable. They did polling that confirmed it. The public would want the administration to spend whatever it took to defend the country from a threat that was already gone. They wanted us prepared in case the aliens ever came back. No politician who wanted to keep his job would dream of bucking those numbers. Military spending would suck up every penny. Everything else would be zeroed out. No domestic programs would be left. The experts said we would become an impoverished garrison state. Stacked against that, one man's life doesn't count for much."

"How do they explain everything that happened? The psychics who were killed? The people abducted and possessed?"

"It will be like the Kennedy assassination. Hearings, studies, and reports. Theories contradicting each other. Nothing ever settled. Your police chief, the television woman, the newspaper publisher, and a couple of others we have identified are in custody until we decide what to do with them. My guess is they'll be quietly killed and buried."

"What happens to me?"

"You get the medal."

"I mean afterward. What good is a medal if part of the government wants me dead?"

"The president didn't know you were being held. When he found out people in his own administration meant to have you silenced for good, he green-lighted the rescue. He'll see that the hounds are called off."

"What happens to the people who want me dead?"

"Nothing. They meant well."

"What's the public opinion on me?"

"You haven't been heard from since Atlanta. The aliens left a couple of days later. As far as people know, you're still on the run. Congratulations on the Blowpipe stunt, by the way. We had to wipe a lot of egg off our face. A deputy director of the FBI was forced to take early retirement, and a lot of reprimands went into personnel files. Want to catch up on the news?"

"Sure." I turn the little overhead valve to let in a jet of cool air.

Danforth aims a remote at a small screen next to the cockpit door. When it comes on, a moon-faced man with blond hair is talking. At least his lips are moving. Danforth fools with the remote, and the sound comes on. A flat midwestern accent. ". . . an inch of rain should help the winter wheat, analysts say. More than that could damage crop yields. Marcy?"

A woman with another broad, wholesome face appears. She recounts the problems of the day. Drought in the sub-Sahara and hundreds of thousands are starving. The trade balance has worsened again, and the Japanese blame us for not being more competitive in their markets. The Russians had a new minister. The French and Canadians are in a fishing dispute.

"What made you come around finally?" I ask Danforth.

"Down deep I believed you almost from the start. They finally got around to brain scans on the survivors of the office you blew up. The deep brain structures were different. The reptilian part was enlarged. They're still trying to figure out how it was done."

"How do they keep that quiet?"

"They've set up something like the Manhattan Project, except more secret. The whole research team and all the survivors are out in the Mohave Desert. You can't get near the place even if you are secretary of defense."

We look back at the screen. Marcy has a playful look that says it is time for the lighter side. "On the subject of topics nobody talks about anymore—remember the so-called alien scare of last summer?—here is our Eric Konig with a retrospective on something else that doesn't get much mention these days—the Hula Hoop." Vintage film with most of the color washed out shows people spinning hoops on their hips. "As crazes go," Eric Konig's voice-over says, "the Hula Hoop was as big as they get. It swept the nation back in the 1950s, the same as the twist, a dance made famous by a singer with the name Chubby Checker."

It is a five-minute piece. Chuckling, Marcy and the moon-faced guy come on to say good night. Danforth clicks the program off. "The news doesn't change much. Makes you wonder why they call it news."

"You still haven't said what happens after I get the medal."

He glances at me, his face unreadable in the dim light. "That's because I don't know."

"Maybe they give me the medal and then shoot me. Everybody's happy that way, except the ones who want a trial."

"A trial would never work anyhow. Your lawyer would subpoena records. He would try to prove the survivors were aliens. The talk would start all over. Despite what she said"—he nodded at the screen—"a lot of people think something happened. They talk about you all the time on the Internet. One chat group is named after that kid at Stanford who was killed, the one who worked for you."

"Mike Deutsch."

"Yeah, him. Look, you don't take somebody to Camp David to be executed. If you were going to be killed it would be a lot easier to let those guys back there do it."

Of course he is right. Too much has happened too fast for me to think straight. "I've got a suspicious nature. It's what keeps me breathing."

He looks at his watch. "It's three more hours if you want to grab some sleep." He settles deeper into his seat and crosses arms across his stomach. His chin drops to his chest. I can't tell if he is sleeping or thinking deeply.

The lights of cities glow on the horizon and then pass beneath like bright patterns branded on the Earth. So many people, yet so much room. No wonder the aliens had been so cautious. They didn't want to blow a prize so rich. And yet they had. A fat woman hired me, and that was the difference.

I have to laugh. I'm a hero and I'm going to get a piece of metal on a ribbon around my neck as proof. But instead of a ticker-tape parade, there will be a secret ceremony at Camp David. Not that I care. Being famous is greatly overrated. I am going to arrange my life from here on out so I'm never in the spotlight again. We can take new names and start life fresh. There might be a problem collecting my pension, but I'll cross that bridge when I come to it.

When the sun comes up, Danforth wakes and looks out the window. He puts on dark shades. "Boy, that sun is bright at this altitude. They've got a coffeemaker on board. Want some?"

"I forgot what it tastes like."

We land at a small airfield in the Virginia countryside. Three Broncos with tinted windows are parked on the apron. When we roll to a stop, they drive in single file to the Gulfstream.

"Put this towel over your head so nobody gets a look at you," Danforth says. I feel like a boxer entering the ring as I follow Danforth down the steps. The cold has a bite, and the ground is as hard as iron under my bare feet. We get in the rear doors of the first Bronco. The two men up front don't even look back. The driver steps on it and we go through a gate and pull onto a service road that leads to a four-lane highway.

"We're going to the Rustic Inn. You can clean up and change," Danforth says.

When we arrive, the other Broncos park on either side, but the men inside stay put. Danforth leads me a few steps to a door and opens it with a key. Clothes are neatly laid on the bed, and a pair of shoes are parked underneath.

"There's shaving stuff in the bathroom," Danforth says, picking up the telephone and walking with it to the window.

When you have been trying to keep clean with sponge baths, a hot shower is heaven. I scissor off my prophet's beard—lots more gray than I remember—and use the razor on the rest of it. My brand of shampoo and shaving cream. Same with the cologne. The jeans and polo shirt are a perfect fit, as are the shoes.

A little warning bell goes off in my head. How did they know? Even Maureen guesses wrong sometimes.

"Everything okay?" Danforth asks. He pushes the shades higher on his nose.

"Everything's fine."

"I'm waiting for a call authorizing us for Camp David."

"They don't know we're coming?"

"You know what bureaucracy's like."

I push the TV on button.

"It's busted. I told the manager. He said he'd get us another before tonight."

"We're going to be here tonight?"

"That's the plan."

The phone rang. "Danforth," he says. He listens to someone talk. "Armstrong's right here." Hands the receiver to me.

"Hello," I say.

"Is this Goodwin Armstrong?"

"Yes."

"We're going to do a voice analysis. Do you know the Lord's Prayer?"

"Yeah."

He has me recite it. "Okay, hang on," he says afterward. I hand the receiver to Danforth. "He says to hang on."

A few minutes pass. "Roger that," Danforth says. He hangs up. "Let's go."

Our little motorcade returns to the airfield. One of the men in the second Bronco runs to the gate leading to the grassy runway apron and unlocks it. The three cars pull through and the gate is swung shut and the padlock put back on.

"They're sending a Marine Corps helicopter," Danforth says.

"How long will it take?"

"Not long."

"Maybe I'll stretch my legs."

"Not a good idea," Danforth says. "You might be recognized."

We sit in silence until a dot appears on the horizon. It rapidly grows into a big helicopter bearing Marine Corps insignia. We get out and so do the men in the other cars. They look capable and fit. Broad shoulders and thick necks. All wear sunglasses and bulky jackets. The warning bell goes off again.

When the helicopter lands, the prop wash is so strong it flattens the grass in a big circle. A door opens and a captain in a smart green uniform comes down the steps and approaches with a man in a suit. He snaps a salute.

"Agent Danforth?" the suit asks.

Danforth steps forward. "That's me."

"Darrell Potter, Secret Service. I need to see your identification."

Danforth hands him his ID wallet, and Potter studies it like a jeweler making an appraisal. He hands it back. Gives me a look. "I recognize Mr. Armstrong. I need to see the IDs of these other agents."

They line up, and Potter gives their identification the same careful scrutiny. When he is satisfied, he waves them onto the helicopter. A couple of marines in combat fatigues stand with automatic weapons on either side of the ladder.

"You don't trust the FBI?" I ask Potter.

"I don't trust anybody. I'd ask to see my own mother's ID."

ox-hunting country gave way to suburban sprawl and then Washington, D.C., was below. I peered through the window at the famous monuments and buildings and spotted Cabin John Bridge, which carries the Beltway across the Potomac. Office buildings were replaced by plowed fields crisscrossed by two-lane highways. We followed Interstate 70 north toward the Catoctin Mountains.

Marine One shuttled important visitors, which explained the plush seats set in rows like a theater. There were headsets with three channels of music. After months of hearing only the sound of my own voice, angels singing wouldn't sound better. I switched from channel to channel. Danforth had earphones on and tapped fingers and nodded his head to a beat. But his nods and fingers were not in synch to the music. Not to the Bach on Channel 1, the country and western on Channel 2, or the easy listening on Channel 3.

I had not seen his eyes. He and the other FBI agents still had shades on. So did Potter, for that matter. It looked like a convention of blind men. Windows of the soul. You spotted an alien by his eyes and his wooden manner. They were like actors who didn't have the role down yet.

Yet Danforth had been convincing. "Put 'er there," he had said. But after all these months of study, they were bound to improve. The time would come when they had it down pat. They would even learn how to follow a beat. But they couldn't do anything about the eyes. There was no hiding that cold soullessness.

There was a pad of notepaper and a row of pencils in a pocket of the seat. The letterhead said OFFICE OF THE PRESIDENT. "Aliens on board," I wrote. I tore off the note and waited to catch Potter's eye. I silently prayed it was a human eye behind those shades.

At last he looked over. He was a fair-haired man expensively tailored. When the president travels you can tell his bodyguards from the local gendarmes. The bodyguards dress better. I beckoned, and he unstrapped himself from the seat and came over. Danforth stopped nodding and drumming his fingers. The other FBI agents were still and watchful.

"I just have one question," I boomed as I pumped his hand. "What do I call the president?"

"Call him 'Mr. President.' " He withdrew his hand with the folded note. Good man. He didn't look at it.

"Thanks. I've been worrying."

"Don't. He puts everyone at ease."

Potter returned to his seat. He didn't read the note right away. He picked up a magazine and flipped through it. Put it down. Looked out the window a long time. Then he gave the note a quick look. He showed no reaction.

A wooded slope rose to meet us, and then Camp David came into sight among the bare dogwoods and pine trees. We landed on a pad near a softball diamond. Marines were dug in behind sandbags, and a party waited for us with weapons ready.

"Gentlemen," Potter said when we landed, "there is a brief arrival ceremony for Mr. Armstrong as the president's guest.

Please remain on board until it is completed." He looked at me. "After you."

"I owe Danforth a lot. Mind if he joins us?"

If Danforth was surprised or relieved, he didn't show it. I wanted the people at Camp David to see those eyes.

"Not at all," Potter said. The marines were first off. I was next, then Danforth. Potter was followed by the pilot and copilot. At a nod from Potter, the copilot shut the door.

Three sixtyish men in casual clothes separated themselves from the waiting marines and approached.

"Mr. Armstrong," one said, "come with us." He seemed tense and jittery. "I'm Ralph Keegan, the president's chief of staff. This is Mr. Morgan, his appointments secretary, and Mr. Rheingold, the White House counsel." The two jerked nods at me.

Potter was at my side. "Which ones?" he asked in a quiet voice.

"All of them."

"Danforth?"

"He's one."

"You sure?"

"Reasonably."

Keegan and the others were impatient. They were important men not used to waiting.

"He's carrying a weapon," Potter said.

"He's outgunned, even counting the ones in the helicopter. It looks like you've got a brigade here."

"Mr. Armstrong?" The White House counsel looked at his watch.

"I'm afraid I can't let him any closer to the president," Potter said in the same quiet voice.

"Keep him here for now. Tell him the first part of the ceremony is private or something."

I joined Keegan and the others. We got on a golf cart and

hummed along a path through the trees. We passed rustic
bungalows with names like Poplar and Hickory. A sign said
the speed limit was fifteen miles an hour. There were fire hy-
drants with orange tops, a chapel, tennis courts, a three-hole
golf course. It was quiet and peaceful. A lot of history had
been made there.

"In all candor, Mr. Armstrong," Rheingold said suddenly,
"I must tell you the president's advisers were unanimous in
urging him not to meet with you. He could not be persuaded.
When word leaks that he received a fugitive from justice, the
consequences will not be favorable."

"Were you guys in favor of putting me away?"

There was an uncomfortable silence. "The administration
was not aware you were being held, much less did it partici-
pate in any dialogue concerning the disposition of the case,"
Rheingold said. He had a red face and silvery hair and wore
a polo shirt that said Bohemian Grove over the pocket.

"'Disposition of the case.' That's one way to put it. Was it
going to be a bullet or lethal injection?"

"We're still asking questions," Keegan said in a clipped
voice. "We don't like the answers we're getting. We were
kept in the dark. It was a rogue operation."

A man stood on the steps of Aspen Lodge. He was tall and
raw-boned in a sweater, jeans, and moccasins. There was no
mistaking President Kent Woodbridge. That long youthful
face and grin disarmed the most hostile questioners at his
press conferences. A shock of red hair and pale blue eyes. I
had seen him so often on TV I felt I knew him better than my
old neighbors in the Sunset district. I might see them once a
month getting in or out of their cars. You saw Woodbridge
every day if you watched C-Span. I had watched a lot of C-
Span in motel rooms when I was on the run.

The first Texan elected president since Lyndon Johnson,
he was as popular as LBJ was disliked. "Welcome to Camp

David," he said, coming down the steps to shake my hand. I said I was honored. He gave the aides an amused look. "You guys been sucking lemons?" He winked at me. "They didn't want me to see you. Come on in."

We trooped up the stairs. The place looked like a lodge at a middle-class resort. Beamed ceilings, paneled walls, and a big picture window that looked out onto a broad valley. A fire in the fireplace.

"Would you like something to drink?" he asked. "A Coke? Iced tea?"

"You wouldn't have a scotch, would you?"

"Glenlivit all right?"

"If you don't have anything better."

A steward appeared, and Woodbridge gave the order.

"I'll show you around later if you want," the president said. "Eleven presidents before me go back to FDR. He was the first." He sighed unhappily. "But nobody's spent more time here than me."

Two people, a man and a woman who I guessed were Secret Service, stood against opposite walls. Woodbridge led us to a sofa and easy chairs and we sat.

"You look like you've been through the mill," Woodbridge said.

"You could say that."

They looked at me expectantly. When I didn't say anything, Keegan cleared his throat. "You told the FBI you have vital information."

"I thought I was here to get the Medal of Freedom."

They looked at each other with surprise. Woodbridge laughed. "I'm not so sure you don't deserve one, but who said so?"

"Danforth. Or what used to be him."

"Who is he?"

"An alien in human form. I didn't realize it at first. He

came in on the helicopter with more of them. The marines aren't letting them off."

The crackle of automatic weapons reached us. The Secret Service agents sprang to the president's side with guns drawn. They hustled him through a doorway.

"What the hell is going on?" Rheingold asked. He went to the window.

"Firefight by the sound of it," Keegan said. "A nasty one."

"What do we do?" Morgan asked. He was thin and precise, the kind of man who looks old when he's young and then doesn't change for decades.

"If the U.S. Marines can't protect us, nothing can," Keegan said.

We walked outside in time for an explosion at the helicopter pad that shook the ground. A thick cloud of dirty smoke rose beyond the roofs of the lodges. A minute later, Potter trotted up the path, breathing hard.

"They busted out of the chopper and started shooting," he told me. "The marines returned fire. It was suicidal. We got them all except Danforth. He's in custody."

The president joined us, trailed by his bodyguards. "What was all that shooting?" he demanded.

"They were trying to get to you," I said. "I was the bait."

He nodded. "Damned smart of them. I can't think of anybody else I would agree to see."

"I don't understand," I said. "Danforth and the others busted me out of that prison I was in, which is why I trusted him. They wanted to use me to penetrate your security screen. What I don't get is why you would want to see me."

A company of marines double-timed to the lodge and took up positions around it. "Shall we go back inside?" Woodbridge said. We returned to our seats. The president was on one side of a wheat-colored sofa and I was on the other. Our shoes almost touched. His keen eyes seemed to bore through me.

"We couldn't say so publicly," Woodbridge said, "but I felt from the beginning there was something believable in what you said on that video of yours. Nobody could explain to me the missing psychics and how those people in San Francisco and Atlanta left their families and never looked back. Some with small kids they doted on. That's unnatural. And that TV spot you did. I wouldn't have gotten as far as I have if I wasn't a good judge of people. I watched your tape three or four times, studying it. The more I watched, the more I was certain you weren't a psycho. What happened later convinced me."

Potter was right. Woodbridge put people at ease. Maybe it was the grin or the way he leaned forward to listen. He made it seem like it was just you and him.

"What happened later?" I asked. "I heard traffic reports for a while, but lately I've been blacked out."

He frowned. "We'll get to the bottom of your imprisonment. I wouldn't be surprised if there are indictments if things ever calm down. You've got grounds for a good lawsuit." He shook his head. "It was the little things at first. Unauthorized troop movements. Whole divisions put on the road without the Pentagon knowing. Not that they did anything bad. They just rambled around the countryside. Their convoys screwed up local traffic. That's how we found out, in fact. People complained to their congressmen. Then systems failed on air force planes and came back on. They were taken apart, but nobody could figure out why they quit any more than they could find out how orders were issued that put the soldiers on the march. Navy ships went dead in the water all of a sudden. Missile systems were taken off line. This has been going on for a month now."

"Has it been reported in the media?"

"How could you keep it out? People are scared, and it's not

just us. Religious revivals are sweeping the world. Self-appointed prophets are yelling that the end of the world is at hand. I have to get back to Washington. The public was already starting to think I'm hiding out here because I'm afraid. This attack will throw the country into a blind panic."

I realized that newscast I saw on the airplane had been a fake to keep me in the dark a little while longer.

"We thought it was computer glitches," Rheingold said. "Viruses."

The president said he for one hadn't bought it. "It never felt right here." He patted his stomach. "So when we got word you wanted to see me, I hoped you would shed more light on the mystery."

"There's no mystery. Aliens are trying to take over. Simple as that."

Morgan turned to the president. "Although no one argued harder against moving here than I, I thank God for your instincts."

"Something told me it wasn't safe in the White House," Woodbridge explained to me. "I guess it was my intuition again."

"If it wasn't for the sixth sense some people have, we'd all be in the crapper by now," I answered.

"But what about the line of succession?" Keegan said. "There is still a government if you die. The vice president . . ." He stopped with a strange look.

"I told you there was something different about Burgess," Woodbridge said in a quiet voice. "I've felt it the last few times we've spoken."

"How well do you know him?" I asked.

"We go back a long way."

"And he seems different?"

"Yes."

"Jesus," Keegan whispered.

"Right. With me out of the way, Burgess calls the shots."

There was a knock at the door, and Potter stuck his head in. "Do you want to see this guy before we lock him up?" he asked me.

"We all do," Woodbridge said, rising.

Danforth was handcuffed between two burly marines. He stood submissively. I took off his sunglasses. A knot of fear twisted in my guts.

They were normal.

Then there was a glint of—what? Not amusement at my shock but something close to it. Mockery. *Did you think we didn't know?*

The president pushed in front of me. "What do you want?" he demanded. "Where are you from?"

"We want what you have," Danforth said simply. "You could not begin to understand where we are from."

"We won't let you have what's ours," the president said. His face had reddened.

"You can't stop us."

"You're wrong, pal," the president said with a snarl. "We may be primitive compared to you, but we know how to defend ourselves."

Danforth shrugged as if the conversation no longer interested him.

"Take him to the brig," Potter told the marines. He left with them.

The room was silent as the four of them came to terms with the horror. I bet each thought about his family. Rheingold seemed to be having trouble breathing.

"You knew this man from before?" Morgan said at last.

"When he was human, yes. He was the agent Washington sent out when this whole thing started."

"It's clear the bureau is infiltrated," the president said. "And who knows what else."

"Danforth said something about changes in the deep brain structure," I said. If they had found a way to make their eyes normal, this was the only way to identify them. Unless he had been feeding me a line.

"There are changes," Keegan said. "They found them in the survivors of the San Francisco bombing. Your bombing."

"So at least there's a way to tell them apart," I said.

"Do you know how long a brain scan takes? The Secret Service made each of us go through one."

"That was my idea," Woodbridge admitted.

"You're in the hospital the better part of a day," Keegan continued. "There aren't enough machines to check out the people we need to. Or time."

The president rose and took a turn around the room. "What do these things look like?"

"Like humans," I said. "Like Danforth."

"No, I mean in their own form."

I shrugged. "The only people who could say are possessed or dead."

"You mean they might be—what?—spores or germs or something like that? Worms that crawl into the brain through the ear? What are we looking for here?"

"Your guess is as good as mine. Princess Dulay said they traveled all joined together as something that looked like a bowling ball."

"A bowling ball?" Keegan said with disbelief.

"Who is Princess Dulay?" the president asked.

It seemed years ago that she had hired me. "A client," I answered. "She was a psychic, one of the ones who sensed they had arrived."

"If they traveled from wherever they came from in this ball, maybe that's the command post." Keegan said. "If we can destroy it we can beat the bastards."

"It would be easier finding a needle in a haystack," Morgan said.

"You can narrow it down," I put in. "All this began in northern California. That's where they started to figure us out."

"What about Atlanta?" the president asked.

"I bet it was just a sideshow. It was supposedly the home office, but I think that was just to throw us off the track if we began to look for them."

"All right, northern California," Woodbridge said. "That simplifies it a little. But how do we find them?"

"Maybe your scientific people can help."

There was a sharp double knock at the door, and a marine colonel entered. "Sir, we don't think Camp David is secure anymore. We advise immediate departure on foot through the woods."

"Through the woods?" Rheingold cried.

"Yes, sir. We're worried about ground-to-air missiles if we fly out." The colonel looked at the president. "Can you leave in five minutes?"

The marines set a good pace coming down the mountain, and we ended up on a two-lane highway just before dark. Rheingold twisted his ankle and was left with a couple of riflemen as escorts. He looked frightened as we left him behind. Woodbridge was grim but determined as we walked. "Those boys don't know what we're like when we're cornered. They'll find out rats ain't in it by comparison."

In addition to the leathernecks, a dozen civilians were attached to the presidential party. "We've kept staff real bare bones at Camp David," Woodbridge explained as we hiked down.

He had a long, loping stride, like a frontiersman. He gave me a sidelong look. "You have a wife and kid, I recall. Know where they are?"

"Hawaii, last I heard. I told her the Mafia was after me."

"Maybe we could help find them if they are . . ." He stopped.

I finished the sentence. "Still alive."

Maureen was smart. She would figure out it wasn't Sicilians I was trying to protect them against. But was she smart enough? Cunning was needed, a quality I didn't think she had. Yet she had hired a private detective to document my infidelity without letting me know she even suspected. Wasn't that cunning?

"I'm sure they're just fine," Woodbridge said too heartily. "I'll put the word out to find them." I told him where I would look. He wrote it down.

I said no telephone or electronic communication could be trusted. He grinned. "I guess we'll just have to go back to carrier pigeons."

Everyone else was in a state of shock or plunged in gloom, but the president seemed cocky, as if nothing suited him better than the prospect of a good fight.

We reached the road and stood around until three big buses rolled up and stopped with hissing air brakes. They were purple and had silver letters on the side that spelled out "The Country Cousins."

"The Oval Office on wheels," Woodbridge said proudly. "Looks like a band on tour, right? My idea. They were forest green before and just about shouted government-issued. My idea was paint them to look like a country-western band. Nobody would ever think the president of the United States was on board one of these, would they?"

"They'd fool me."

"Exactly. A purple-and-silver shit-kicker bus. Nobody ever heard of the Country Cousins, so there's no problem with pesky fans. Conspicuous yet unsuspicious. Hop on. I want you close at hand. Nobody's fought these characters up to now but you. I figured you for a cool head when I read the citation you got for your medal. I had it dug up so I could see what kind of person you were. A whole company of Cubans surrendered to you on Grenada. That took guts."

"They were engineers working on the airfield. They didn't want to die for nothing."

The buses were divided into tiny offices and sleeping quarters and crammed with communication gear that unfortunately would give away our location if used. We drove day and night, stopping only for food and gas and to pick up and drop off couriers. These carried videos the president taped in a minuscule studio on the second bus. It had a backdrop that made it look like he was in an office with a view. He issued commands in the videos to cabinet secretaries and others in his administration. Or they were typed out on old manual typewriters, as even laptops were considered risky.

Once somebody had the idea of calling in Woodbridge's orders from telephone booths an hour after the buses had left so the aliens didn't get a fix on where we were. A presidential aide was electrocuted on the second day. His brains were fried and his hand was fused to the telephone when they found him.

"I could have predicted that," I said when I heard.

After that, I sat in on nearly every meeting the president had. Or rather stood. Most were in a cramped compartment whose door had a paper taped on it that said Oval Office. My status as unofficial presidential adviser gave me clout. That meant I got a pretty good bunk. People worked shifts around the clock. When I wasn't sacked out there, the chairman of the joint chiefs of staff was.

Television was full of the attack on Camp David, and we saw big headlines in newspaper racks that asked, "Where Is the President?" The country was in pandemonium.

"It's not only us," Woodbridge said gloomily as he stared

out a tinted window at the passing countryside. Cars with marines in civilian dress with weapons hidden were ahead and behind. "The whole world is falling apart."

He was right. TV was full of pictures of Hindus and Muslims slaughtering each other in India, and other old scores were being settled all over the map. At home, there were riots in cities and huge wildland fires burning unchecked in a dozen states. We started to see families on the roads fleeing the cities in cars crammed with household goods.

Rondell Ames joined us one dark afternoon. He was a lanky guy bald to the crown with a big nose. When I found out he was the president's science adviser, I sat down next to him. The buses were rolling through Virginia horse country. He was listening to music on a CD player and writing on a yellow pad. He pulled off the headset when I sat down. We introduced ourselves and he said he just might be the only person in the country who had not seen my video.

"The president doesn't need me very often, so I spend most of the time in my lab at MIT. I only come out of my cave to eat. My wife says she's a widow." He laughed and then looked despondent.

I asked how aliens could have traveled those vast distances through space.

He looked around to see if anyone was listening and dropped his voice. "I'm kind of an atheist on this subject. No offense to you, but I have to ask where's the hard evidence? I don't see any so far. That attack on Camp David—why drag in aliens to explain it? Isn't human conspiracy far more likely? But the president and his people take it seriously, so I suppose I must. As to your question, who knows? The nearest planet where life is theoretically possible is so far away it would take an impossibly long time to get there."

I remembered that Princess Dulay said they had been on the road when humans still walked on knuckles. It had been so long they had given up hope of ever finding another home.

"But as you're asking me to speculate about this 'bowling ball' and how our visitors supposedly combine into a single unit and separate into individuals, I am reminded of the experiment in quantum physics a few years back that confirmed a prediction of Albert Einstein. Do you know about it?"

"I guess I must have missed it."

"When you suspend a ball of gas in intersecting laser beams and magnetic fields and cool it enough, its atoms come nearly to a standstill. They lose their individual identity and merge. It's called the Bose-Einstein condensate. Einstein said this could only happen at temperatures so absurdly low they could exist only in the mind of God."

"So he was wrong?"

"Yes, he was wrong. But there was some speculation that you could form beams of these superchilled atoms and achieve a practical result."

"Like travel in space?"

He shrugged. "It's not a field I work in."

A kind of garrison mentality set in on the buses. We didn't know who could be trusted in the capital. People could get brain scans in the morning, but that didn't mean they couldn't be taken over by afternoon.

The National Security Agency was an obvious target for infiltration, so Woodbridge had experts from the Department of Agriculture crop forecasting service secretly study satellite images of northern California. At the end of the first week, we stopped at a lonely intersection in the country where a man in a raincoat waited in a gray drizzle. He climbed aboard the bus when we stopped. Potter inspected a paper that said his brain had been scanned.

He was ushered to the presidential cubicle. "Everything

you see and hear is in the deepest confidence," Potter warned. "The nation's fate is riding on it."

"Yes, sir." He was a deputy secretary named Horace Borden, an ordinary-looking man who looked like he put on a funny apron and barbecued when the weather was good. I stood as usual. Borden opened a manila folder. "We didn't know exactly what we were looking for, but we compared pictures on and around July seventeenth of last year." He took photos from the envelope. "This is about all we came up with."

He took them from the envelope and passed them to the president. "See that line? They look like burned trees. A hundred yards of them in a straight line, maybe more. A week later they are back to normal, or seem like it. This one is more recent, an infrared imaging. The same place. See the spot there? It's a heat source."

"A campfire?" Woodbridge asked, passing them to me.

"It's not hot enough and seems constant."

"What do you think it is?"

"An anomaly. That's all we were told to look for. Nobody in my shop can guess what it is."

"It's just a pinpoint," Woodbridge complained. Borden looked apologetic.

"What we're looking for is not big," I pointed out.

"True. Give this to General Hodges," he told a young aide. Like the rest of us, the president was unshaven and his clothes were wrinkled.

The bus stopped to let off Borden. The drizzle had become rain. He gave a sad little wave as we drove away. I wondered if he would ever have another chance to grill burgers on his Weber. A minute later, General Hodges, the man I split bunk time with, came into the office. He was as brisk as a terrier.

"Funny you should give me this," he told the president.

"Well, General, tell me why you think so. I sure could use a smile right about now."

"Another of those troop movements nobody approved. A National Guard unit started to stop all traffic into that area two days ago. Deadly force authorized, apparently. Shoot-to-kill orders. We're trying to get them back where they belong, but they aren't responding."

"Bingo," Keegan said.

The marines seized the Merchant's Inn as if it was high ground instead of a cheesy motel for traveling salesmen. As ex-military myself, I was impressed. They secured all the approaches, laid down fields of fire, and then sent parties through the motel to root out guests and employees. The civilians were taken to a holding area out of sight and told it was a national emergency.

Only when they were gone did the Country Cousins entourage roll into the parking lot, and everybody piled out after the president. He led them into a banquet room with a low ceiling. We all joined in moving tables around as men and women began to arrive by car. They weren't limousines and official cars that would be a tip-off. Instead, the top people in the Woodbridge administration, the political opposition, and Pentagon brass hats drove up in everything from sports cars to pickups with camper shells. One woman came on a motorcycle. They were dressed as if on a weekend outing. A few shot me looks, as if trying to remember where they had seen me before. I heard somebody whisper I looked enough like the man who had killed all those people to be his twin.

When the room was full, the president stood. "I just

wanted you to see that, despite all the rumors you may have heard, I'm alive and well." They started to clap, but he cut them short. "The world faces the worst crisis in the history of the human race. The hour is late and perhaps we won't prevail, but we owe it to all who came before us to go down fighting." An astounded silence fell.

I would compare what he said to the Gettysburg Address and other great speeches, and I hope it was recorded or somebody copied it down. Talking without notes, Woodbridge explained what had happened so far. He said every difference must be set aside in the fight against the common enemy. I could tell from faces, many of them recognizable from the Sunday interview shows, that no one had suspected aliens. It was obvious something was terribly wrong—a raging computer virus or something weird like that had screwed up things, and nobody had a handle on it yet. There were the fires and the breakdown in public order. But most people still thought that the media showed gross irresponsibility in passing on these rumors about aliens, even if only to make fun of them.

"We can't be certain of the command and control of our military at any level," General Hodges said when the president asked him to speak. "Seemingly authentic orders come from unknown and unauthorized sources and are obeyed at levels from corps down to company. Real orders are altered in transmission or are not received in the field. In any event, they are mainly ignored. There has been an epidemic of equipment breakdown that we cannot explain."

A tall, silver-haired man in jeans and a windbreaker stood. I recognized him as Jarrod Michaelson, the leader of the other party. He had been mentioned as a presidential candidate in the next election, and Maureen liked him. "You make it sound like the country is defenseless," he complained.

I could see people hoped Hodges would laugh and say no,

things weren't nearly that bad. "Effectively, yes, it is." Gasps and cries.

"What do they look like?" a handsome woman in a blue jumpsuit asked. Her face was ashen.

The president looked over at me with a nod. "Like us," I told her. "They take over our bodies. In the beginning you could tell by the eyes. They were that different. But I'm not sure you can anymore. They also act like they're always cold."

"The brain scan I was given," Michaelson asked Woodbridge. "That was the reason?"

The president nodded. "All of you had it. It's the only way we can tell."

Michaelson sat down. He looked like he had been kicked in the stomach. A babble of voices began. Who were they? Where did they come from? How did we know they were hostile? Had anyone tried to communicate with them? What could be done? It died down when the president raised his hand.

"They are technologically far superior. They probably think of us the same way we do about Stone Age people." They might be smarter, he continued, but they didn't know what fighters we were. We would never give up. Not ever. *Not ever.* His eyes flashed.

Somebody asked if there was room for negotiation. Live and let live.

"Not as far as I can see," the president replied. "They invaded our world. I'm not sure I'd want to coexist on the same planet with them. They're hostile and aggressive. They immediately started killing and taking over human beings."

The meeting went on for hours. I slipped outside for fresh air. The trees were bare, and a cold wind blew. A Secret Service agent warned against going beyond the perimeter the marines had set up. "We can't let you back in if you do." I nodded and retraced my steps.

The motel had a lounge attached and I went inside. There was no Glenlivit, but I found a satisfactory substitute. Keegan came in a few minutes later. "What a grand idea," he said. He went behind the bar and mixed himself a drink. He brought it to where I sat at a table.

"What's happening in there?" I asked.

"They're talking about declaring a national emergency. The president would rule by decree. Woodbridge doesn't think it's such a hot idea."

"Why not?"

"He says if we're going to beat these characters, it will be from the bottom up, not the top down. He sees a people's war starting when the balloon goes up. Ruling by decree would create the wrong mind-set."

"I think he's right. The aliens will find him sooner or later. Kill him or take him over. The marines can't protect him forever."

"That's what the president thinks." He smiled. "He's going to pack the six-shooter his grandpa the sheriff had. He'll take a few with him when he goes."

We sat in silence until we heard the meeting breaking up. Keegan finished his drink and left. I heard car doors slam outside and engines start. A frowsy young aide poked his head into the lounge. "The buses are leaving soon."

I was invited into the president's cubicle when the convoy was back on the road. He sat with his feet up. He wore a pearl-handled .45 in a holster with a gunbelt. He patted the six-shooter. "My grandpappy's." He gave me a long look. "How'd you think it went?"

I shrugged. "Good, I suppose. I wasn't there the whole time."

"Wrong. You saw their faces. They're sick with fear. You

could smell it." He looked out the window. It was starting to drizzle again. "I wouldn't be surprised if that turned to snow." He looked back at me. "I want you out there."

"Where?"

"California. I'm sending Hodges, too. Maybe the chairman of the joint chiefs of staff can tell those boys from the National Guard to stop guarding the enemy so we can get at them."

"Not if they've been possessed."

"As they're not answering the phone, the only way to find out is to eyeball them in person." His jaw tightened. "I want to nuke the bastards."

"What's stopping you?"

"We can't get an airplane over them. A couple we sent in for reconnaissance this morning went down in fireballs. The pilots didn't eject, so we don't know what happened. Same result with Tomahawks we fired at them."

"What do you want me to do?"

"Be eyes and ears for me. I want the straight dope, and I'm not sure I'll get it from official channels, screwed up as they are." He smoothed a topographic map on his desk. "Look at this."

The map was of the empty country east of Roundville, three hours or so north of San Francisco. It was the Yolla Bolla Wilderness Area. "That's where they are. Down there in that valley." His finger pointed.

All I knew about the area was lots of marijuana was grown in hidden plots guarded by bearded men with guns. Every now and then you read about an innocent hiker mauled by dogs or shot for trespassing.

"Railroad tracks go right by it," I said. The scale of the map said the tracks passed within an eighth of a mile of the heat source.

Woodbridge shook his head. "It's an abandoned line loggers used way back when. The Geological Survey people say it hasn't been used for years."

"If you can't bomb them, what are you going to do?"

"We have a Ranger division on the way. They'll cut through those National Guard people like butter."

"Unless they're taken over, too."

"You proved they're not invincible."

"I sneaked up on them. They learned their lesson. That's why they've got troops around them."

"If the Rangers go over to them, the game is over." His voice was bleak.

I didn't answer.

General Hodges and I flew to California on a Federal Express cargo plane to throw off suspicion. The Country Cousins bus let us off at a lonely country crossroads where a car was parked with the keys in it. We drove to an airfield in Pennsylvania where the plane waited. We bedded down in the canvas sacks of mail.

Hodges was thin and wiry, one of those small Napoleonic types with the will to command. He looked like he had zero doubts about his ability to climb higher and faster than anyone else. "We'll kick their butts. You showed it can be done."

I didn't say they had learned a lot since then. He struck me as the kind who didn't care to hear negative thoughts.

"You a family man?" he asked.

"Yes."

"Where are they? My kids are scattered all over creation. I sent Maggie to our farm in South Dakota for the duration."

"I'm not sure where my family is."

He was quiet for a moment. "That's hard."

He didn't want to dwell on it and neither did I. "We'd be up shit creek if it wasn't for you," he said.

The hero stuff was starting to wear thin. Winners write history and decide who the heroes are. The losers may have as many so-called heroes, but you never hear about them. When people call you a hero, you begin to understand how arbitrary the whole process is.

"What makes you think we're not up the creek?"

He barked a laugh. Self-doubt wasn't in his nature. "Once we get everything together, we'll wipe the floor with these suckers." He had gray eyebrows and thick, dark hair cut so short you could see pink scalp.

The pilot came back a couple of hours into the flight with a worried look. "Half the air control centers in the country are down. It happened just like that." He snapped his fingers. "Just before they went down there were orders for altitude and course changes. There have been a lot of midair collisions. We're flying on visual flight rules now. Would you gentlemen mind coming forward and help us look for traffic?"

I thought about all those airplanes dropping to the ground in pieces. The smaller objects would be luggage and bodies strapped in seats. They would dig small craters in the vastness of America.

How would the aliens deal with us? Perhaps our bodies were like space suits to them, necessary for survival. In that case, enough of us—or our physical shells—would need to survive to give them shelter. A breeding program would be necessary for new shells when old ones wore out. But they were smart bastards. Maybe they could delay mortal decay enough to get centuries of use out of us.

The FedEx jet landed at San Francisco International just at sunset and we were met by four generals and a clutch of colonels. "Glad you made it despite all the air traffic foul-ups," one of the generals said. "A hundred and three flights didn't make it where they were going."

"The first of the Rangers are arriving at Travis," another said.

"I thought that was closed in the cutbacks a few years

back," Hodges said. He didn't have time to think about civilian disasters. We were walking toward an army helicopter.

"The runway's still there. The local media wonder why all the activity."

"Keep them in the dark as long as possible."

We boarded the helicopter, and it rose into the sky. "Traffic is at a standstill both directions on the Bayshore," one of the colonels said. "It's like a parking lot. This panic has got everyone on the move." I looked down at the freeway. Headlights in one direction, taillights in the other. None of them moving. There were big fires burning in San Francisco.

"It's like a social meltdown," a colonel said hopelessly.

Hodges bristled, terrierlike. "Knock that off," he snapped. "The next man I hear sounding defeatist will be charged with cowardice in the face of the enemy." The generals and colonels were silent.

Hodges bent over a map. "With respect, General Vaughn, I don't think your people will be able to keep out the Rangers for long."

General Vaughn's shoulder patch said he was a National Guard. "Of course not," he said humbly.

"How many of your people are in there?"

"We think about five hundred."

"What have the Rangers been told about this operation?" Hodges asked.

"That some demented militia is holed up defying the federal government," another general answered. "We'll give them the straight dope just before they go in."

The helicopter took us northeast over the Bay Bridge and the Berkeley Hills. The bridge and the freeways we passed over also were jammed, and fires burned in Oakland. Travis was full of lights and bustle. Big transports roared in every three minutes and off-loaded men and equipment. Mobile field kitchens prepared the evening meal.

Before General Hodges got caught up in staff meetings, he signed a pass that let me come and go. I watched the activity. If you couldn't get the marines, the Rangers would do nicely. They looked fit and eager. While a squad double-timed past, a staff car drew up to where General Hodges and the other brass were meeting. Four officers got out and hurried inside. I sauntered casually to the car. After a quick look around to see if anyone watched, I leaned through the window and took the keys from the ignition.

I bummed a mess kit and meal at a field kitchen and strolled to a knot of soldiers who watched a playoff football game on a portable TV on the back of a truck. It had been early in the preseason when Brady and I saw that 49er game, and now it was almost time for the Super Bowl. The 49ers led the Lions, 27 to 10. A beer commercial was interrupted by the picture of an official seal. A voice said, "We interrupt this program for an announcement by the vice president of the United States." The face of Byron Burgess filled the screen. He was in the Oval Office.

"My fellow Americans, I come to you today sore of heart. It is my sad duty to report that President Woodbridge was tragically killed an hour ago in a traffic accident in a rural part of Pennsylvania."

"Jesus Christ!" one soldier said.

"Did you hear that?"

"Woodbridge is dead."

"Man, we're going down the tubes fast."

"You think them aliens did it?"

Others were shouting for silence, but it took some time before we could hear the TV again. By that time a network anchorman was repeating in a breaking voice what Vice President Burgess had said. "He offered no details about the tragedy, leaving it open to conjecture whether the president's death is connected in some way to the still unexplained attack on Camp David. More details as they become available."

Someone started to switch from channel to channel to see if other networks had more. I got in the staff car and drove through running soldiers to the gate, where I showed my pass to get out. The car was a bare-bones model without a radio, so I couldn't listen to the developing story as I got on the freeway to Sacramento. People were crying in their cars. I felt cold and empty.

It was clear the country was worse off than just without a leader. An alien intelligence had seized power at the top. Their only worry now was the attack by the Rangers, and Burgess would halt that right off the bat. Meanwhile, in a few days chaos would be total. The aliens could sit back and watch human society disintegrate. Pick up what pieces they wanted afterward. The rest of the world could only watch and wring their hands, knowing they were next.

There wasn't a room to be had in Sacramento, so I slept in the backseat. Sort of slept is more like it. I climbed out stiff and cold at dawn and drank coffee at a café until I thawed out. The waitress had red eyes from crying and kept blowing her nose. Newspapers proclaimed the president's death in big black headlines. The stories complained about the lack of detail and the strange secrecy that had surrounded the White House for weeks. "No wonder people say it's the aliens," an editorial said. Congress promised an investigation. Vice President Burgess's whereabouts could not be revealed for security reasons, a spokesman said.

I walked through the grounds of the state capitol to kill time. The day was as gray as pewter. Squirrels skittered from me on the frosty grass. At ten o'clock I was at the door of the state Railroad Museum when an old man in an engineer's striped overalls and cap and a red scarf around his neck arrived to open up.

"Didn't think anybody'd show up today, times what they are," he said. "Didn't have much business yesterday and I thought none today. Two presidents killed in my lifetime and three others shot at. Then there was Bobby Kennedy." I paid the admission and he gave me change.

"I want information about a spur line near Roundville," I said.

His face brightened. "You've come to the right place." He led me to a map room and picked a large volume from a shelf and blew dust off it.

"There's a Western Pacific line goes through that area, but you wouldn't be talking about that, I reckon."

"These tracks are supposed to be abandoned."

"Off the top of my head," he said with furrowed brow, "I'm going to say you are talking about the old Norris Lumber Company line. It was used to bring timber from Shasta County, oh, forty years ago."

He opened the book and paged through the maps. "Yes, sir, I was right. The last time they had a train over those tracks was ten years ago. A special excursion for railroad clubs. I was supposed to go but had to back out at the last minute. Always regretted it. Beautiful country, they say. The track has deteriorated since and you're not supposed to run a train across it anymore. The insurance they make you buy is way too high. I have some hot coffee in the office. Come on back and I'll bring the book."

The museum featured steam and diesel locomotives so polished they gleamed. The office was modeled after those in podunk stations a century ago. It had a teller's cage, a pot-bellied stove, a rolltop desk, and a little telegraph machine. Old photographs of legendary locomotives hung on the walls. He motioned me to a chair and poured coffee from a tin pot.

"You can't get a train over those tracks any longer?"

"I didn't say that. I said the insurance is too high. Nobody can afford it. Why're you interested, if you don't mind me asking?"

"Do steam locomotives need electrical systems to operate?"

His face changed. He had thought I was a fellow hobbyist. The question showed I was a layman and dumber than most. He hesitated in passing the cup he had poured, as if not sure whether I still had it coming.

"Stupid question, right?" I took it before he could change his mind.

"I've heard worse." His tone made me doubt it.

"Are there any steam locomotives in running order around?"

"One or two."

"Where could I find one, and how soon could it reach Roundville?"

"Depends on a lot of things."

"I need it there by tomorrow."

His eyes twinkled. Then he chuckled. This became loud laughter. The laughter turned into wheezes and by then his face was very red. "You might be able to pull that off if you were the federal government."

"Just for the heck of it, assume I am."

"So happens the *Flying Cloud* is up in Eureka. They had a convention of trainmen a couple of weeks ago and she's still there."

"What is the *Flying Cloud*?"

"Built by Baldwin back in 1925. By then it was part of the Standard Steel Works run by Mr. Samuel M. Vaulcain, president. She pulled the *Orange Blossom Special* for many years, if you ever heard of that. That was the run between Hermitage and Raleigh." He looked toward the ceiling. "She had a boiler pressure of two hundred pounds, a maximum tractive force of forty-eight thousand, two hundred pounds, which may sound like a lot to you. But the biggest in that day went a hundred and forty thousand pounds. Driving boxes on the first axle, flange oilers—"

"I can get the details later. All I care is whether it runs."

"Like a Swiss watch. Those train people in Pennsylvania know their business. She burns coal. Nine pounds of coal per car per hour, which is real efficient. Some of them—"

"Is there someone in Eureka who knows how to operate it?"

He took off his engineer's cap and scratched his gray head. "Well, I dunno about that. She's supposed to stay there six months before going back home to Pittsburgh."

"Could you run it?"

"Why, sure." He put his cap back on. "My daddy was a railroad engineer. He taught me the ropes." A wistful look crossed his face. "I was going to follow in his footsteps. Diesels were the engines by then. But by the time I got old enough, you could see the end of trains was coming and I didn't want to risk it as my career. I sold insurance instead. Made a good living, but it wasn't where my heart was."

"Why couldn't it be in Roundville by tomorrow?"

"There are working trains on that track," he said indignantly. "You can't just snap your fingers and tell them to pull off on sidings to make room for a fossil. There would be ten kinds of hell raised."

"Can I use your telephone?"

"Is it long distance?"

"Travis."

"That's a toll call."

I reached for my pocket.

"That's all right," he said grudgingly. "It's on the museum. I can't leave the office for you to call, though. There's important stuff in here."

"Not a problem."

I telephoned Travis. After some searching, General Hodges was located. "I wondered where you disappeared to."

"Have you heard from Burgess?" I asked. I sensed the old man sit up alertly.

"He told me to discontinue this military operation."

"He's one of them."

"I know. The president told me."

"What did you tell Burgess?"

"I lied and said I would. The men are already in the air. They'll parachute in short of where the fighters were knocked down and engage the enemy on the ground."

"Those nuclear land mines that were supposed to keep the Russians from overrunning Europe?"

"What about them?"

"Are they still there?"

"In Europe? Lord, no."

"Where's the nearest one?"

He put his hand over the receiver and I heard him asking questions. He came back on the line. "There are a few at Lawrence Livermore Laboratory. They test them for readiness. That's not far from here. Why do you want to know?"

"The president told me he wanted to nuke the aliens."

"He told me the same thing."

"No missile or bomber can get inside their defenses."

"The Rangers will take care of that."

"But if they don't?"

"They will."

"I've got the perfect delivery system."

"What is it?"

"A steam locomotive."

"A choo-choo train?" Hodges was not a playful man. He wanted to make sure we were talking about the same thing.

"A choo-choo train."

"I can give you about a minute to explain."

"There are no electrical systems to jam. The map says the aliens are in a valley. We climb the train out of Roundville with the mine and let gravity pull her down into the middle of them. They get vaporized."

"What about the Rangers?"

"Pull them back out of range just before—that is, if they haven't already accomplished their mission."

He was silent for a time. "I thought the steam locomotives were all gone."

"There's one up in Eureka. It can be brought down in a few hours. I'm sitting next to a man who can run it. I need transport up there and a mine brought to Roundville. I also need the tracks cleared between Eureka and Roundville."

"Technically, I have no authority over the railroads in the absence of a war or declaration of national emergency."

keep thinking this is a dream and I'll wake up any minute!" the old man shouted.

We were highballing south through forests an hour from Roundville. The tracks were clear before us, and the *Flying Cloud* pumped out a long plume of white smoke that bucked and flattened in the slipstream. The black locomotive pulled a coal tender and a gondola car. Every now and then we passed trains pulled off on sidings. Their crews cheered. They didn't know what was going on, but they were collecting overtime.

The old man's name was Calvin Stone, and he was having a ball. He hung on the steam whistle as we hurtled through tiny towns and rail crossings where lights flashed on barricades and bells ding-donged. Kids came running, and adults watched in astonishment. We were a sight not seen since their grandparents were little. Judging from the looks on faces, some figured we were another entry for the strange-portents file.

Woooooooo, the whistle cried. *Woooooo.*

I watched Stone run the engine. It was surprisingly simple for something as big and powerful as the *Flying Cloud*.

You pushed a lever to go faster and pulled to slow. The mechanical brakes worked the same way. I was glad for the coal feeder. I had been afraid I would have to shovel coal in hellish heat. Stone peered at the gauges as we rocked back and forth. He wore heavy engineer's gloves that came halfway up his forearms. The trees flashed past. We were doing seventy miles an hour.

"Unbelievable speed for that time!" Stone yelled.

He had told me a little about himself when we flew north from Sacramento in the small military jet. His wife had died two years before. Three grown children in other states. If it weren't for the railroad museum, he reckoned he would die of loneliness. "Society doesn't have much use for old men." He started to say he had got some bad news about his health but then clammed up.

Clickety-clack, clickety-clack. The sound of the wheels would be exhilarating under other circumstances. Now they seemed to count off the time mankind had left. When we chugged into Roundville, the streets were jammed with military vehicles, much of it self-propelled artillery. They waited for room on the congested two-lane road that led up to where the aliens were. I saw only soldiers, so I guessed the townfolk had been evacuated. It was one of those hamlets with a few shops, a gas station, and a hardware store. It did a big business during deer season but otherwise was dead. An officer swung onto the ladder to the cab as we were stopping.

"Mr. Armstrong?" he asked.

"That's him," Stone said, jerking a thumb. He looked out with amazement on the teeming military scene.

"General Hodges would like to see you, sir."

"I'll be here when you come back," Stone said. The *Flying Cloud* slowly chuffed, as if panting.

Hodges had set up headquarters at city hall. It was filled

with officers talking into telephones or rushing back and forth. Hodges sat alone in the city manager's office. "I've been relieved of command. The new president gave a verbal order over the telephone, and the secretary of defense is flying in to see it is obeyed. I suppose he's one of those bastards, too."

"What happens now?"

"Unless the secretary stops off first in San Diego and brings the First Marines with him, he won't get anywhere near this place." He flashed a wolfish smile. "You could say I'm in a state of insubordination." He walked to the window. "See all that artillery? I sent for it when the Rangers were repulsed. You wouldn't think it possible. Five hundred National Guard troops holding off a crack division. But none of our communication gear works up there, so it's like war in the eighteenth century. You send messengers back and forth. Hell, we've been signaling with mirrors. It screws things up unbelievably. And the strangest damn thing. Our guys up there say they're being attacked by wildlife."

"I guess I forgot to mention that."

He didn't hear me or ignored it. "So they're dug in deep and nobody's giving up, like the Japs in World War II. I'm not much of one for ordering suicide charges. A pounding at long range will pucker assholes and change minds. Without someone to protect them, we'll see just how tough these guys are."

"How long will that take?"

"A couple days, maybe three."

"Do we have that much time? Burgess could appeal over your head to these men. I seem to remember you sign a pledge to obey the commander in chief."

Hodges turned from the window. He walked over to me and whispered in my ear. "Burgess is not the president. Woodbridge is still alive." He stepped back to see the effect of this bombshell. He must have been satisfied, because he smiled.

"Keep that under your hat."

"How do you know?"

"A messenger brought a video."

"Are you sure it's legitimate?"

"The president held up a newspaper with headlines about his death. Made a joke about it. The others with him, Keegan and the rest, didn't seem to find it as funny. It's authentic, no doubt about it. As he ordered, I destroyed the video, otherwise I'd show you."

I would think about that later.

"I brought the train. Where's the mine?"

"On the way. The people at Lawrence said it took a while to encase it in lead and put the steel shell on top of that."

"If the lead doesn't protect the detonating charge, the game's over." I looked at him. "I wouldn't bet money your artillery shells will work."

"They won't have time to mess with all of them. It's going to be like a World War I barrage. Dozens of shells dropping at the same time."

"Don't underestimate them."

The first shadow of doubt crossed the general's face. "If that doesn't work, your land mine has to."

"At least it lacks sophistication. Gravity delivers it." I wondered how long it would have taken the generals to come up with the idea. Probably weeks.

The military traffic continued to inch up the road most of the rest of the day. Toward nightfall, a large helicopter arrived with a land mine once planted in the path of a historic invasion route into Germany. It was designed to destroy Russian armor as NATO regrouped. I watched while technicians welded the outer steel shield to the floor of the gondola car. I expected the timer would have a red button, but it was black.

Later, Hodges and I stood at the city hall window. The general looked at his watch as we waited for the bombardment to commence. "Right about . . . now." The sky to the east flashed, and he had a look of triumph. A rumble like thunder reached us.

Then nothing more.

The triumph left his face. "Only one round? What's holding them up? They should be firing nonstop." A half hour later, his telephone rang.

"What happened?" he barked. He listened for a minute and then hung up, pale. "Air bursts. Our people took a lot of casualties on the ground." He sat down. "Eighty-nine howitzer shells arcing in at different angles at the same time. How could they all explode prematurely?"

"Artillery is still a good idea."

The general looked at me like I was crazy. "I've got hundreds of casualties up there." He had been so sure before, but now all the confidence was gone. I could see him going into a funk.

"Look, pull everyone back. When the train drops down into the valley, fire more rounds. The National Guard will keep its head down and won't be shooting at the train."

He looked around blindly without answering. "I'm not doing any good here. I'm going up with my boys." He put on his helmet and walked out. I'll take physical suffering over mental anytime.

I walked back to the engine. Stone opened the door of the cab when he heard my feet on the steel ladder. "Did you see that big flash a while ago?"

"Yes."

"What was it?" He was eager.

"A military disaster."

"God." He pulled at his nose. "Many of our fellas hurt?"

"It seems so."

A couple of officers came by to work out the details of the barrage. A short time later, the choppers and trucks began to arrive with the wounded. Stone watched, appalled. "Is there anybody up there who isn't dead or hurt?"

"A division has a lot of people."

He shook his head, tears suddenly in his eyes. It had been a boyhood fantasy up to now. Trains and aliens, what a double bill. But those maimed young bodies changed it for him.

"You never told me what you have planned for the *Flying Cloud*, but I hope it's something good."

"We're going to deliver a nuclear punch."

"I figured as much. They ran me off so I couldn't see what they did back there in the gondola car, but I suspected." He hesitated. "The *Flying Cloud* won't be coming back?"

"I'm afraid not."

"The last of her kind."

"The people who built her would be glad she cashed out like this."

"Oh, yes. They were very patriotic in those days."

He shot me a shy look. "Us either? We won't be coming back?"

"I've watched you run this train. I can ride it down where they are. I'll let you off at the top."

He nodded.

It was cold, and clouds kept hiding the remote quarter moon. A stubby noncom came by with helmets and bullet-proof vests for us.

"Were you up there today?" Stone asked.

The soldier nodded.

"Pretty rough?"

"Never saw anything like it. The shrapnel came down like

rain. We heard the guys on the other side cheering and taunting afterward."

"My friend here says they're aliens now."

I wondered why they didn't just move someplace else. It would be days or weeks before we found them again, and everything would be all over by then. Did they need to be tethered to the planet like a nursing infant? Or maybe they felt invulnerable. Just sitting there taking everything we threw at them would demoralize us all the sooner.

"Time to start up the mountain," I said.

"I'll get up boiler pressure."

I walked to the brightly lit city hall. Officers stood in clumps talking in low voices or sat glassy-eyed, trying to take in the catastrophe. General Hodges was meeting with officers in combat gear. They looked up as I opened the door.

"We're leaving now."

"See a Captain Meredith at the top. He'll liaison the artillery. We already started pulling our personnel back."

I didn't move and he looked impatient.

"Anything else?"

I don't know what I expected. "Good luck" would have been nice. But that was Hodges, all business. I went back to the *Flying Cloud* and swung aboard. We slowly chuffed out of Roundville. Chopper traffic out of the city was still heavy, and their lights stabbed the night. Stone gave a soft little "*woo-woo*" with the whistle as we left the town behind.

Captain Meredith was young and scared-looking in the pale dawn. He stepped from a group of soldiers alongside the track and climbed aboard. He saluted and gave me a hand radio. "They're jamming our radios. You'll lose your signal once you get beyond that point of land." He pointed at a bluff. "Just before you get there, give the word and we'll count down to the shelling."

Stone and I calculated it would take ten minutes for the train to make it down to where the tracks came closest to the aliens. I would activate the timer just before starting down the grade. There were a couple of places where a touch of the brakes would be needed if the engine wasn't to go off the rails. That was my job.

I felt a dry clarity. I was sorry to have to die. Like everyone, I expected death would be postponed until I was full of years. Brady would be proud of his dad when he found out. But he would trade the honor to have me around to throw the ball back and forth. I was pretty sure Maureen would miss me, too. After everything that had happened, I thought we had a decent shot at getting back together.

"Thanks for all your help," I told Stone.

"Is that it?"

"That's it."

"There's curves up ahead. Let her go too fast and she'll go off the rails."

"I know."

Stone looked worried. "The brake's been dragging on the back end of the gondola. Left side. It'll just take a minor adjustment. You don't want anything going wrong now. If it's sticking, it'll just take a couple of minutes to fix."

"What am I looking for?"

"Sparks." He was still scornful of my layman's ignorance. "Look for sparks."

I climbed over the coal tender into the gondola. I hit the black button to start the timer and climbed down to the ground. The train jerked and started to move. Stone was leaning out the cab and looking back at the wheel. Great billows of white smoke pumped out the stack. As the *Flying Cloud* accelerated, I trotted alongside. I saw no sparks and waved to Stone. He waved back.

Maybe I could have climbed on board the moving train.

But it was moving pretty fast by then and maybe I would have miscalculated and fallen under the wheels. Maybe I didn't want to climb on board.

Captain Meredith ran up. "I thought you were going to ride her down."

We ran for his Humvee and tore down the road toward Roundville. First came the thunderous artillery barrage, then a quick stab of blinding light overhead. A few seconds later, the ground leaped underfoot and we nearly overturned. The mountain was between us, so we didn't get the full effect. But we got the sound. Even with fingers in my ears, it was head-splitting.

I bet Stone hung on the whistle right up to the last millisecond. *Wooooo. Wooooo.*

Spring in the capital, the cherry trees ablaze with color. Maureen hangs us up deciding among three outfits before finally picking an apricot-colored suit. "Do these shoes match?" she asks as we hurry out the door.

"Mom!" Brady cries. He doesn't have my patience in these matters.

"An inspired choice," I say.

The White House car waits at the curb, and we get in. I'm to get that medal after all, in a ceremony in the Rose Garden. "No funny faces when we're in front of the cameras," I tell Brady.

"Gee, Dad, why would I do that?" All innocence.

Maureen and I got back together during our week at Big Sur. A lot of couples all over the country have been doing that. It seems like people have a better handle on what's important and what isn't after the late unpleasantness. You see it everywhere. People are nicer to one another. Everybody is talking about it.

There is such a big business in the renewal of marriage

vows that we were lucky to get a place to stay in Big Sur. Maureen joked that she came back because I was going to be so rich from the lawsuit against the government for false imprisonment. I'll show you how changed everyone is. I offered to shake hands with Gloria Rodell-Heifitz. Instead, she fell into my arms, crying. She doesn't seem so bad anymore.

There is so much rebuilding of the big cities going on that the economy is humming. It's like living in boom times. The rest of the world is sending us foreign aid to help us get back on our feet. They feel grateful to us for taking it on the chin for everyone.

A Global Defense Force is being formed in case the aliens come back, but the psychics say they don't pick up any sign this is going to happen. You could almost make the case that the world is a better place because of the invasion, strange as it sounds.

"They got too cocky," President Woodbridge is saying. "Overconfidence loses as many wars as stupidity." We're in the Oval Office waiting for the ceremony to start.

He came out of all the craziness a big hero, and the pundits say a second term is a gimme. People admire how he faked his own death to keep fighting on and love how he buckled on the six-shooter and was ready to go down with guns blazing. The leader of the Free World and his staff holed up in the Amish country in a barn after the phony bus crash. They wore disguises and pitchforked manure and milked cows by hand in case anybody came snooping.

"First honest work the White House staff has done in years," the president joked.

Stone is the biggest hero, of course. Four biographies are in the works and a couple of movies. His birthplace and the house where he lived in Sacramento have become shrines. Dozens of bouquets and written tributes from ordinary people are left at both places every day. The public has a tremendous appetite for the smallest detail about his life. I didn't know much about him, but I've told what little I did.

You see *Flying Cloud* T-shirts everywhere. They show Stone waving from the cab window, a big grin on his face. He's yanking on that whistle. *Woooooo. Wooooo.*

Jerry Jay Carroll

"A captivating romp."—*Entertainment Weekly*

"If Kafka and Tolkien shared an office on Wall Street, this is the novel they might have written."—*San Francisco Chronicle*

Top Dog

One day, William "Bogey" Ingersol sat in an office high above Wall Street conducting corporate takeovers.

The next day, he was a big dog, surviving by instinct alone in a strange new world.

Same difference.   ☐0-441-00513-6/$5.99

Dog Eat Dog

Bogey's back.

An evil being has set his sights not on Wall Street, but Pennsylvania Avenue. And Bogie's going to have to get mean. Mad dog mean.   ☐0-441-00597-7/$12.00

An Ace Trade Paperback

Prices slightly higher in Canada

Payable in U.S. funds only. No cash/COD accepted. Postage & handling: U.S./CAN. $2.75 for one book, $1.00 for each additional, not to exceed $6.75; Int'l $5.00 for one book, $1.00 each additional. We accept Visa, Amex, MC ($10.00 min.), checks ($15.00 fee for returned checks) and money orders. Call 800-788-6262 or 201-933-9292, fax 201-896-8569; refer to ad # 824 (12/98)

Penguin Putnam Inc.
P.O. Box 12289, Dept. B
Newark, NJ 07101-5289
Please allow 4-6 weeks for delivery.
Foreign and Canadian delivery 6-8 weeks.

Bill my: ☐Visa ☐MasterCard ☐Amex _____(expires)
Card#_____
Signature_____

Bill to:
Name_____
Address_____City_____
State/ZIP_____
Daytime Phone #_____

Ship to:
Name_____Book Total $_____
Address_____Applicable Sales Tax $_____
City_____Postage & Handling $_____
State/ZIP_____Total Amount Due $_____

This offer subject to change without notice.